DRAGON BONES

THE DRAGONWALKER BOOK 1

D.K. HOLMBERG

ASH
PUBLISHING

If you want to be notified when D.K. Holmberg's next novel is released and get free stories and occasional other promotions, please sign up for his mailing list by going here. Your email address will never be shared and you can unsubscribe at any time.

www.dkholmberg.com

2 | D. K. HOLMBERG

PROLOGUE

I rritation bubbled within Fes, and he crept forward through the alley carefully, trying to make as little sound as possible. In all the time that he'd been living in the slums, he had grown especially skilled at moving quietly.

The alleyway was narrow, and the smooth walls of the neighboring buildings rose up on either side of him. They were damp, unpleasantly so, especially considering the last rain had been over a week ago. An awful stench filled the air, that of rot or something worse, and he fought the urge to look down and make sure he wasn't stepping into something nasty.

He glanced back to see Alison trailing him. He wished that she wouldn't have come after him, especially as she knew that he preferred to work alone, and she knew that he didn't like having her follow him, but even if he objected to her presence, he doubted she'd listen to his arguments.

He spun, pushing his back up against the neighboring building, and made a motion toward Alison. He was far enough into the depths of the shadows that it was unlikely she could even see him, but he was determined to try to get her attention.

Skies of Fire, but she needed to leave him to this assignment. If he failed, Horus would be angry, and Fes couldn't risk angering the man again. Another mistake and Horus would likely send Fes away, and it was hard enough finding jobs in the slums as it was. Most of them were run by men like Horus, men who coordinated all the activity within the area they controlled.

When he reached the end of the alley, he glanced back to see if Alison still followed him. It was difficult to tell if she did as her dark hair and her black cloak seemed to blend into the shadows, making her practically invisible. Fes didn't have the same dark hair. His brown hair was dark enough, and no one could see his blue eyes glimmering in the darkness. And he wasn't foolish enough to wear brightly colored clothing. He kept the deep brown cloak covering his face, trying to conceal himself in the shadows.

There was a door here, and Fes unsheathed one of his daggers, slipping the tip into the lock. He wasn't nearly as skilled as Alison at picking locks, but then again, he didn't need to be. With these daggers, dragonglass that was nearly indestructible, he was able to get past almost any lock. There probably wasn't a single one within the city he couldn't get past by jamming his dagger into it.

The lock snapped with a loud crack.

That was the only downside to the way that he forced his way into doors. Others could make it much more quietly, but quiet had never really been Fes's strong suit. He did his best, and he tried to remain as silent as possible, but there were too many times when he didn't manage to do so as effectively as he thought he should.

The other side of the room was dimly lit. There was a lantern somewhere that cast enough light for him to see a hazy outline of everything in front of him, but not much more than that. Fes had good eyesight, but even the best eyesight couldn't pierce through this darkness. The air was warm enough that a fire had to be burning nearby, drying out the air.

He crept forward, moving slowly through the hallway. His footsteps were the only sound here, a soft thudding along the wooden floor. Fes tried to keep his breathing silent, but it still sounded loud in his ears.

If Horus was right, then the item he was after—his prize—would be in here, at the end of a hallway and inside a large room behind a cabinet. A jewel of value. And all Fes had to do was grab it. It should be easy, especially now that he was inside, and it would give him a chance to prove himself to Horus.

There was sound at the door he'd come through, and Fes glanced back to see the door swinging open. He jumped back against the edge of the wall, holding onto his dagger, prepared for the possibility that he might need to use it. If he did, he needed to maintain control of himself. It was too easy for him to lose control, and when he lost control... well, things started to go badly. He couldn't afford to have things go that way, not in a place like this, and not on the job for Horus.

Alison stepped forward, separating from the shadows.

"What are you doing?" he hissed.

"What do you think I'm doing? I'm helping you with this job."

"I don't need help."

"Someone seems to think you do."

Had Horus sent her after him? He wouldn't put it past the man. Horus had a soft spot for Alison, though it was more of a fatherly thing than anything more. And since the two of them had gotten close, Horus had tolerated Fes a whole lot more than he ever had before. Then again, he preferred to use Fes for the violent side Fes tried to keep hidden.

Could that have been why Horus sent him on this job?

He shook that thought away. Horus knew that Fes had a temper, but it was only a temper that he had when someone tried to hurt those he cared about. Fes made a point of trying not to care for anyone, especially after what had happened with his brother. It was bad enough that he'd gotten close to Alison. Other than her, the only other person he cared about had managed to get out of the slums and was no longer in danger.

"You have to let me do this job. He needs to know I can do this."

"I think he knows," she said.

"If he knows, then why did he send you?"

Alison shook her head, stepping toward him. She smelled nice, clean, and with a hint of lilac. How did she ever manage to find such fragrances in the slums?

"Listen, Fezarn—"

Fes raised his hand, quieting her. "Don't use that name."

"I don't know why you don't like it. I think it's nice."

Fes squeezed his eyes closed. "You know why I don't like it."

"I know that your parents choose to use it. That should be reason enough for you to want others to."

"Hearing it only makes me think of them. And it's still hard."

She took his hand and squeezed. He smiled over at her, wishing that things in Anuhr were easier than they were, but they were in the slums, a part of the capital of the Arashn Empire that made the emperor prefer to look the other way, a place where even his fire mages rarely came. It was left to men like Horus to keep the slums running smoothly. If not for Horus, Fes would've starved to death long ago.

"I'm sorry. I won't use it again. I still think it's nice."

"It reminds me of my mother."

Her gaze flicked down to his dagger before looking up at his face. She was the only person who knew that his daggers were the last memory he had of his parents. They had belonged to both his mother and father and when they had died—been killed, really—Fes had recovered them. They were precious to him.

"Go and finish this job. Return the prize to Horus and get the credit."

"Just like that?"

"I don't need the credit. Horus…" She shook her head, looking up at Fes. "It doesn't matter. Just go and do what you need to in order to keep him happy. But make sure you get the right thing."

Fes nodded. "Did he give you any idea how?" If what he'd heard about this place was right, there would be several items of value, but he was only supposed to grab one. He stared at the door at the end of the hallway. It was hard to completely make out, but that *had* to be where he was supposed to go.

She planted one hand on her hip and stared at him. "Now you want my help?"

"I don't want your help, I just... Fine. I want your help."

Her face clouded. "I was only supposed to keep track of you, and if you got in trouble, I was to—"

"Supposed to what?"

"To make sure the prize got back to him."

"Just the prize? Not me?"

"I don't think Horus worries so much about you. You've proven that there's no reason to do so."

That was true, and Fes hated that it was true. He had proven himself, thanks to that part of himself that he wished he didn't depend on, but when it came to fighting, it wasn't so much that he was good at it, it was more that it seemed to come naturally.

"We shouldn't spend any more time in here," Fes said, looking around the hall. He could see barely nothing, just the hazy outline, but with the faint lantern light in the distance, he had to believe he was heading in the right direction. What else would be down there?

They crept along the hallway, and Fes moved slowly but not nearly as silently as Alison. In that way, she was a much more skilled thief than him. It was why Horus usually preferred her. It made Alison safe in a way that Fes was not. Few people could ever really claim safety, at least not in the slums. And he felt particularly unsettled. Horus favored him now, but that was because he was tied to Alison. What happened if their relationship failed?

Alison looked over at him, almost as if knowing his thoughts. Fes forced a smile, hating that those thoughts rolled through him but unable to get rid of them entirely. He was no different than anyone else in the slum and wanted out, a way to a better life. For most, that meant working for one of the crime lords, using that as a way to leverage themselves to safety. Considering Fes's reputation, he wasn't sure that he would always be able to find safety.

As he made his way along the hallway, something pulled on him, drawing him toward one of the doorways. He paused in front of it, running his hands along the surface.

Why should he be drawn here? It was ahead of him that mattered, not behind the door. But there was no questioning that he felt something here.

As he stood there, his hand just above the surface of the door, he traced the heat on the other side. It was faint, but definitely there.

"Fes? What are you doing?"

Fes nodded at the door. "I don't know. It's just…" How could he explain it to Alison? It was almost as if he were meant to open the door, and that whatever he wanted to find would be behind here, but that wasn't what Horus had sent him after. Horus had sent them after a prize, and it would be worth nearly two coppers. That was enough money to feed Fes for a week, especially if he stretched it.

"It's down at the end of the hall."

"Are you sure?"

"Fes, I know what we're after."

"I know what we're after too, but if it's so valuable, why do we bring it to Horus?"

"Because if we don't, we're dead. Besides, anything of value needs to be sold, and neither of us knows how to do that."

Fes rested his hand on the door handle. It was locked. "I'm just going see what's behind here."

Alison glared at him. "Don't be stupid. We've already been here too long."

"Why don't you go down the hall and I'll meet you."

"If I take care of this job and Horus learns of it—"

"How will Horus learn of it unless you tell him?"

Alison stared at him.

"You'd tell him?"

"Why wouldn't I? He needs to know that I can take care of my assignments, too."

"Even if that means that I fail?"

"Then don't fail," she said. "Don't get distracted, Fes."

He stared at the door. He couldn't shake the sense that there was something behind there that he needed to know and he unsheathed his dagger, shoving it into the lock. With a sharp twist, the lock snapped, and he shoved the door open.

Alison stared at him a moment before hurrying down the hallway.

What was he thinking? This was the reason that people like Horus didn't trust him with jobs. He failed to follow instructions, and when he got into buildings like this, merchant buildings outside the edge of the slums Horus controlled, buildings that he should know better than to enter, he went off on his own even when he knew that he shouldn't.

And now?

He was in a strange storage room. There was a table at the center of the room, and shelves lined the walls. On the shelves were various odd sculptures. Fes approached the nearest shelf, and his jaw dropped open.

Not sculptures. Bones.

He could think of only one reason that there would be a place full of bones like this.

They were dragon bones.

Bones like this were valuable to the fire mages.

Could this be a fire mage's warehouse?

That wasn't where he was supposed to go. It was a merchant home, nothing more than that, and it wasn't supposed to be guarded.

Horus wouldn't have sent them into a place where they'd risk the fire mages. Not with Alison after him.

No. Something like that would be foolish and would

be bound to draw attention to them, the kind of attention that even Horus was loath to attract.

Fes picked up one of the bones. It was long and slender and had a strange weight to it. The entire thing was cold, and the surface of it was smooth. Everything he'd heard about dragon bones said they were supposed to be warm unless one of the fire mages had already used them. There was power stored within the bones, and the fire mages used that power to perform their spells, magic that rivaled that of even the dragons they came from.

Fes set down the bone he was holding and replaced it on the shelf. If it was a real dragon bone—and forgeries were far too common—it had already been used. The used dragon bone might have some value, but not enough to risk angering a fire mage if that's what this place was.

Fes continued to make his way around the room, staring at the shelves. Alison was right: He was taking far too much time here. He knew better than to linger. If he were caught here, the punishment would be severe. He would be outside of the slums, and because of that, Horus's reach would be limited, if he even cared enough to try to help Fes.

Fes would be subject to the whims of the Dragon Guard. They were dangerous, soldiers who trained from a young age to become frighteningly skilled, the defenders of the empire. They were different than the commissioned army, though Fes would never serve in the army to know. At sixteen, he was of the right age, but he refused to submit himself to the empire. If they couldn't take care of orphans like him, why should he bother fighting on behalf of them?

On the far side of the room, something seemed to shimmer.

Fes frowned as he approached it. Like the other items in this room, it was a bone, but it looked different than the others. There were striations of color to it, and when he lifted it, he found it warm.

Could this be an actual dragon bone? Could it still be active?

If he brought this to Horus, he would be rewarded. He would have to be.

Fes stuffed the bone into his pocket.

He hurried back out of the room and found Alison waiting for him in the hallway. He pulled the door closed.

"I don't understand what you were doing."

"You wouldn't guess what I saw in there."

Alison pulled a necklace from her pocket, holding it up. A blue jewel at the center reflected the light. The rest of the necklace was cast in gold, and it seemed to glow. "This is the prize. This is what Horus wanted us to come for."

Fes patted his pocket, feeling the warmth from the bone. "We should—"

Footsteps thudded from the far end of the hallway,

and Fes glanced over at Alison. She shook her head and swore under her breath, grabbing his arm and dragging him behind her. "See? We've taken too long. If we get caught, we have to worry about more than the Dragon Guard."

They reached the door leading to the alley, and as they pushed it open, Fes thought he felt a strange stirring of warmth, and he glanced over his shoulder. He caught sight of a flash of crimson, followed by a blast of heat that dried his mouth. Before he had a chance to think about it, Alison shoved him forward into the alley. They raced ahead, reaching the street, where she dragged him all the way back through the slums and to Horus's home.

"I can't believe you, Fes," Alison said as they went.

"Why can't you believe me?"

"After everything that you've gone through, you let me get this first?"

"Maybe I wanted you to be rewarded. Maybe I didn't want to be the one to claim the prize."

"Don't be stupid," she said.

"Why is that stupid? How long have we known each other?"

"It's been a year, Fes, but you can't keep doing this." She glanced over at him before entering Horus's home. It was much nicer than others within the slums. He had a thick carpet across the floor, something that Fes had never seen anywhere else. The table and chairs resting near the hearth both matched, and from somewhere in the back came the smell of baking bread, a savory scent that made Fes's mouth water. He doubted Horus would allow him to have any, especially now that he wasn't the one to have completed the job.

Horus emerged from a back room, dressed almost regally in a chocolate-colored jacket and pants, smiling warmly at Alison before turning to Fes. "Did you get it?" he asked. He had a deep voice and flat gray eyes. He had to be in his fifties, but he was still fit, and he was still intimidating.

"We got it," Alison said.

"The two of you?" Horus asked.

Alison pulled the necklace from her pocket and handed it over to Horus. "We got it."

Fes glanced over at her guiltily. She was giving him too much credit. Seeing the way that Horus's eyes lit up when he saw the necklace, Fes didn't know if it was because of the gold or whether it was the jewel at the center. Either way, the necklace was far more valuable than the few coppers that Horus had offered for it.

Reaching into his pocket, he felt for the bone. It was warm, and it pressed against his thigh. How much would Horus offer for something like this?

Probably not nearly what it was worth.

"I'll be honest. I didn't think Fezarn was going to be successful," Horus said.

"Well, we were," Alison said.

She was far better than him. Would he have included her if the situation was reversed? He knew that he would. Alison might be the only person he protected.

Horus reached into his pocket and handed Fes a pair of copper coins. He squeezed them tightly. They would feed him for the week, and in that time, he had to hope that Horus would come up with another job. And then another. As long as the jobs kept coming, and as long as Fes managed to succeed with them, he would be able to keep eating.

The coins he handed Alison seemed shinier than the ones Fes held.

He glanced over at Alison. Fes had taken the job for a few coppers, but how much did Alison get paid? They didn't talk about it, but he wouldn't put it past her to be paid twice as much as him.

"Go," Horus said.

Fes looked around the room a moment before getting dragged away by Alison. There was wealth here, the kind of wealth that Fes would never know. He would never reach the luxury that Horus knew, and if his jobs failed to deliver, there might come a time when he starved.

When they reached the street, he looked over at Alison. "How much did he pay you?"

"Fes—"

Fes shook his head. "How much were you paid? We were offered the same job, more or less."

"You were offered a job, and mine was to ensure it succeeded."

"Then I should have been paid more."

"Except I was the one who completed the job. Were it not for me, you would have wandered off like you did and we never would have managed to get the prize."

"How much?"

"It doesn't matter."

"Then tell me. You know how much I got paid."

She stared at him for a moment. "Two silvers, okay?"

Fes blinked. Silvers? He couldn't imagine being offered two silvers. Even a single silver would be enough for him to eat for more than a month. Two would let him sleep in his own room, albeit not all that nice of a room.

"Why are you getting paid so much?"

"Keep working for him, and you will get rewarded. Maybe find a prize that you don't need someone's help for."

Fes thought of the dragon bone, and he glanced toward the door, wondering if maybe he shouldn't go and tell Horus about it, before deciding not to. If he did, there would be no point. What would Horus even do if he brought him a dragon bone? Maybe he'd offer him two coppers, but maybe he would offer less. And if it was less, what was the point of it?

"Where are you going?" Alison asked as he turned away.

Fes looked over at her, shaking his head. "I'm just going away for a little bit. I might go visit Tracen." At least if he visited his friend, he would be out of the slums, if only for a little while. Tracen was one of the few people he knew who had managed to escape, finding an apprenticeship that offered him a life beyond this part of the city. While Fes missed him, he didn't begrudge Tracen the opportunity to live a life where he wouldn't be forced into stealing. Tracen was better than that. He deserved better than that.

"Come on, Fes. You know that we need to take what we can, especially here."

He nodded. The message was clear. Life wasn't fair in the slums, and he knew that, but that didn't change the fact that he wished that things were different. Had his parents not been lost—or his brother—maybe things would've been different for him.

As he made his way down the street, he stayed in the shadows, keeping off to the side so that others didn't bump into him. He rounded a corner, barely paying attention, and came face-to-face with a tall man dressed in a crimson-colored robe.

"I'm sorry," he said, turning off to the side.

"Sorry. Yes. Perhaps you *are* sorry." He leaned toward Fes, and he ran his hand along Fes's jacket until it was just outside of the pocket containing the dragon bone. A smile drifted across the man's face. Warmth radiated from him, reminding Fes of the sensation he'd had before leaving with the necklace. He jumped back, trying to get away, but the man smiled at him. "Interesting."

Somehow, he had known that Fes had the dragon bone.

This couldn't be the same person he'd caught a glimpse of during the job, could it? How would he have followed?

"Listen, I'm just going to be—"

The man started to laugh, cutting Fes off. "You're just going to be what?"

"I'm just going to be going," Fes said.

"Oh no. Not quite yet."

He started to turn, but the man grabbed his sleeve, keeping him from turning. "You can have it. I—" Fes started.

The man jerked him around, and Fes came face-to-face with him again. "How did you find it?"

"It was in a room."

"Yes. I know that it was in a room. How did you find this one?"

Fes shook his head. "I don't know."

The man cocked his head to the side, seeming to study Fes. The crimson cloak was the color of the empire, and there was something about this man that made Fes nervous in a way that even the Dragon Guard might not.

"What's your name?"

"Nobody."

The man took another step forward. "What's your name?"

There was a command within it, and he felt almost as if he were compelled to answer. "Fes."

The man smiled slightly. "Fes? That's quite the unusual name."

Fes only shrugged. "What do you want with me?"

"It's not so much what I want with you, it's what I can offer you."

"And what can you offer me?"

The man smiled widely, but it never seemed to reach his hazel-colored eyes. "A job."

CHAPTER ONE

F es knew better than to take so long completing the most recent job to acquire a dragon bone. In the year since accepting Azithan's offer, he'd learned the fire mage was patient, but there were limits to that patience. He needed to acquire the bone, and when he did, he would get paid. Three gold coins, enough to keep him fed for the next month given the lifestyle he now kept. It was much more than he'd once been paid for similar jobs, but then again, Azithan appreciated Fes and his work.

There was movement along the street and a flash of red hair. Fes swore under his breath.

Carter.

If she managed to get to this before him, he'd miss out on his payment. Fes prided himself on completing Azithan's jobs, ensuring that he did everything that he asked, not wanting to fail him. He rarely failed Azithan, something that made both of them happy. It certainly allowed Fes to remain out of the slums and stay in nicer parts of the city. The jobs Azithan asked of him required him to sneak around, but for the most part, Azithan wanted him for his ability to find Dragon relics, something Fes seemed particularly skilled at. For some reason, he was drawn to them.

Fes raced forward, chasing after Carter. The street was busy, but not so busy that he couldn't navigate through it, and he bumped past a few people as he made his way through. Storefronts lined the street on either side, but he didn't pause to look at any of them, not wanting the distraction. He hadn't been through this section in the city for a while, and even if he had, he wasn't sure that he would recognize any of the stores. This was a better section, a place where merchants sold their wares and would expect to be paid what they were worth, nothing like the slums Fes had come from.

Carter turned a corner, and he chased after her. She was a thief, but she was more than that. She was violent in a way that Fes never was—at least not anymore—and when she got involved, people ended up hurt. It wasn't that Fes minded violence, certainly not if he was the one inflicting it, but he didn't like the idea of Carter getting involved in a job he was after.

There had been enough interaction between the two

of them over the years, going back to when he had worked for Horus, hat he knew better than to take her lightly. She often chased the same dragon relics as Fes, and she had an ability to sniff them out that rivaled his, something that he suspected annoyed Azithan.

Fes turned a corner, and there she was. She stalked toward a child standing near the merchant he'd been following, a knife in hand.

His mind flashed back to what had happened to his brother. He'd been lost in the city, killed by someone too much like Carter.

Fes lunged, grabbing her and pulling her focus away from the boy.

Carter spun around with a growl that faded to a smile when she saw him. "And what are you after today, Fes?" she asked, leaning toward him. She shifted her hips, swaying them as she took a step toward him, almost as if trying to seduce him. She was an attractive woman, but far too deadly to be of any interest to him.

"Stay back, Carter. This is my job."

"And what does your master have you doing today?"

"The same thing that your master has you doing."

She grinned. "Oh, that."

"And who is your master?"

Carter stepped up to him, leaning toward him. She was about a head shorter, but incredibly strong. He'd seen her fight with the two swords she had buckled at her waist and knew better than to tangle with her. All Fes carried were his daggers, and he hesitated to use them in any way that would draw attention. All it took was one wrong move, an attack on someone who mattered within the city, and he would attract the attention of the Dragon Guard, something Azithan warned him against. Azithan protected him, but there were limits to his protection, and Fes had no interest in testing them, not wanting to jeopardize his position with the fire mage.

"I'm sure you would like to know," she said.

He *would* like to know, and that was entirely the point. As far as he knew, she served someone much like he served Azithan, but he still had not been able to figure out who that was. Carter took higher-end jobs, and as far as he could tell, she was even better off than him, and Azithan paid well.

"So, it's like that?"

Carter smiled, leaning toward him with a slight shake of her hips.

Fes danced back, grabbing for his dagger almost too late. She grinned as her sword slipped free from her sheath.

"So jumpy," she said.

"Stay back from me," he said.

"Are you worried I might hurt you?"

Fes stared at her. "I know well enough to be concerned."

"Good."

"Are you sure that you really want to get involved with what I'm after? If you know anything about me, you know that the person I work for has no tolerance for those who get in his way." Since Azithan served the emperor, it gave Fes a little more cache, but with Carter, it was hard to know if that mattered.

She took a step back and slipped her sword back into her sheath.

At least she still gave him the treatment that he thought that he deserved, a certain level of respect that should exist between them. They were competitors, but they weren't all that different, other than the fact that she was willing to maim and kill to accomplish her goals, and Fes was the more cautious of the two. It was different than what he had experienced when he still had worked in the slums. When he was there, there had been no honor between thieves. It had been everyone for themselves, which was part of the reason that he had struggled as much as he had.

"Yes, about that. I am certain your master has no tolerance for such things, but at the same time, neither does my employer."

There was a flicker of movement behind her. Fes glanced past and saw the merchant he had been trailing. He needed to get past Carter, or it was entirely possible that he would miss out on this job.

"Carter, I'm sorry that I don't have any more time to chat with you, but I really do need to be going."

Carter glared at him. "What are you after?"

She didn't know. And if she didn't know, then maybe he could mislead her.

"There was something taken from the palace, and I was asked to retrieve it." She already knew that he worked for Azithan, so he wasn't revealing anything too far from the truth. What did it matter that it was a dragon relic rather than some jewel?

"Something was stolen from the palace, and you were the one sent? Not the Dragon Guard?"

"There are certain things that they don't necessarily want revealed. This happens to be one of them," Fes said with a shrug.

She eyed him for a long moment. By telling her that he was after something taken from the palace, it hopefully would delay her, if not prevent her outright from trying to go after it herself. More than that, he wanted her to believe that it was something other than a dragon relic. There was a market for many things within the palace, but the dragon relics were valuable enough that Azithan paid well for them.

"I'll be watching you," she said.

"I'm not interested," Fes said.

She stepped off to the side, pressing her back up

against the wall as she watched him. "We both know that's not true."

"I'm not interested."

"You know, I'm sure I could find a role for you within my organization," she said.

"Is that right?"

"I'm sure that she would pay more than your current compensation."

"I already have an employer."

"For how long?" She smiled at him, and there was a hint of menace within it. "Eventually, he'll grow tired of you. That's the story with him, or haven't you heard?"

"If he does, he'll have paid me well in the meantime."

"Perhaps, but I wonder if it's quite as well as you could be paid? Do you not realize what you're worth?"

Fes snorted. "Now you're resorting to compliments. Interesting."

"It's better than the alternative."

"And what's the alternative?"

"You know what the alternative is, Fes. Don't cross me. I'm not the kind of person you want as an enemy."

"Is that what we've become?"

She flashed a smile, and there was something both beautiful and dangerous about it. "This? No. We're competitors, nothing more. For now. I'm happy to chase items throughout the city and beat you to them."

"You haven't beat me to all that many," Fes said.

"Enough that it's valuable to me," she said. "But even I have limits. There are certain things that I won't tolerate you challenging me on."

"And those are?"

"You'll know them when you see it," she said.

Fes slipped past her, not wanting to stay too close. She unsettled him, and he wasn't afraid to admit that. He would have to let Azithan know about this, especially as he knew that Carter went around collecting items throughout the city that he was interested in. Neither of them knew quite who she worked for, but Fes had a sense that Azithan was a little more aware of what it might be than he let on. That was fine with him. He didn't necessarily care to know; all that mattered was that he was paid for his jobs, and Azithan had never failed to pay.

As he disappeared along the street, blending into the crowd, he caught sight of the merchant once again. He hazarded a glance over his shoulder but didn't see any sign of Carter. She was easy to make out in a crowd with her red hair, but somehow, she did manage to sneak up on him far too often.

Fes crept behind the merchant, watching as he meandered through the crowded market. He really shouldn't be dressed in such bright clothing. The stripes of red and gold made it easy for Fes to find him—and to follow. Hopefully, Azithan was right with what he knew and that this man and had what Azithan sought. Fes couldn't detect anything, but his knack for finding real relics wasn't what Azithan wanted from him right now.

A cart nearly crashed into him, and Fes barely managed to duck out of the way. What was that doing here anyway? With the market crowd as thick as it was, there shouldn't be any carts moving through here. It was set at the edge of the city, in an open field designed for the migratory tents from merchants who would come to the city to trade. Wagons were hidden from view, most of them parked on the other side of the market, tied off so that the animals didn't get in the way. Why was this idiot driving through here?

The man ducked into a tent, and Fes swore under his breath. The tents would be much harder to follow him into, and much harder to separate the man from the dragon bone.

Fes reached the tent door and parted the fabrics, glancing inside. Most of the tents were colorful, and this was no exception. Striped canvas in nearly a dozen different colors assaulted his eyes. The smell on the inside was pungent, the food eaten by the people from the plains permeating everything. Fes nearly jerked his head back, wanting nothing more than to get away, but the merchant was inside.

So were a dozen other people, who wandered the tables inside. They were shopping, picking up items off the tables that created rows upon rows within the tent, though most were intending to purchase, not trade, not the same way as the priest likely intended. Each tent catered to a different market, and this one seemed to sell dragon relics—or replicas of them.

Fes lowered the hood of his cloak. It would do no good coming in here looking like a thief. He was careful with his dress not to draw attention, and in a place like this, he would have to be especially cautious.

Where was the dragon blasted man?

There wasn't any other way out of the tent other than the way they had come in, and Fes made certain to keep his eyes on the entrance. If nothing else, he wasn't about to have the man slip away, not now that he finally had him cornered. Azithan wanted the dragon bone this man supposedly had, and Fes had been sent to acquire it. That was his assignment.

He moved behind a pair of people murmuring excitedly about a hunk of stone, still keeping an eye on the entrance. He overheard the merchant they were speaking to telling them how it had been burned by dragon flame, which gave it a particular shape. Fes glanced over their shoulders and saw nothing other than rock. There wasn't anything particularly impressive about the shape that would make it likely that it was genuinely dragon-shaped. Fes had heard stories of places where the earth had been scorched by dragon flame. Stone had melted, leaving it dripping in sheets. All of that stone had been harvested, brought to places like the emperor's palace, and saved. A single fistful of true dragon-burned stone would actually be worth twenty gold. It was why he prized his daggers.

Fes moved on to another table. This one featured carvings of stone, and many of them bore scratches, with a placard in front proclaiming them to be dragon etched. Fes shook his head. The people of the plains were far too gullible. They believed everything was dragon touched. Considering the creatures were exterminated almost a thousand years ago, anything that really was dragon touched had long ago been scavenged by the dragonwalkers for the empire or destroyed.

"Are you interested in something dragon blessed?"

Fes considered the merchant who was speaking to him. He had a deeply tanned face and eyes that were so brown as to be nearly black. Much like the tent, his clothing was striped in multiple colors. How could he stand wearing something like that?

Now that Fes thought about it, the man he'd followed had been similarly dressed.

Could he be a merchant in this tent?

His gaze darted around, looking for the man but seeing nothing. "I don't know. Do you have anything worth looking at?" Where had the man gone? He couldn't have disappeared, and there was nothing on the other side of this tent.

Maybe there was another way out. He didn't like the idea of disappointing Azithan. The fire mage had been kind to him, but there was no reason he needed Fes. All it would take for him to move on was a failure.

"We have many items that are dragon blessed. Look at this stone. You can see these markings. These were made by talons from the great creature as it pierced the stone."

"How do I know it's not a fake?" Fes didn't want to get into a conversation with this man, but if he didn't, there would be no reason for him to stay within the tent. He had to look as if he intended to purchase. He shifted his cloak, pulling it around to conceal the long daggers he had sheathed on either hip.

"A fake? The Bayars do not carry fakes. All of these items are dragon blessed."

Fes blinked. He'd heard that name before. The Bayars were one of the oldest families from the plains. They lived in the far north, practically at the base of the Sapiar Mountains before the start of the dragon fields. Maybe there *was* something more to these items. "What else do you have?"

What he really needed was that bone. Get that, return it to Azithan, and collect the bounty. That was all Fes cared about.

The merchant swept his hands wide, motioning toward the table. "What else do we have? You have come to the Bayars tent at the Great Market! Everything we have is incredibly rare."

Fes looked along the table. He doubted that. More likely, everything here was incredibly forged. Fakes were valuable to those gullible enough to believe anyone other than the fire mages would be able to acquire true dragon relics.

"What about that one," he said motioning toward what appeared to be a necklace.

It was at the far end of the table, and he was surprised to see a jewel mixed in with all of the other stonework. Most fools who promised dragon blessed goods brought out stone, thinking to pass off nothing more than rock as something truly touched by the ancient dragons. Given how long it had been since the dragons roamed, it was an easy claim to make, and it was incredibly difficult to disprove. His own daggers were supposedly made from dragonglass, and considering how hard the blades were, he believed it.

"That? Ah, you have quite the eye, sir."

The merchant tottered down to the end of the table. He had a slight limp that gave him a bit of a wobble, and when he returned, he held the necklace in the palm of his hand. Fes thought that it had been stone work, but seeing it up close, it was nothing more than a smooth black sphere.

As the merchant twisted his hands, streaks of blue

rolled across the surface. "Do you see how the light catches it? A dragon pearl this is. Incredibly rare, and possibly the most valuable item we have."

"I thought dragon pearls were larger," Fes said.

"Anything larger would be held by the fire mages. What we have is inert, but still quite lovely."

"And you're willing to sell it, knowing what it is?" Fes asked.

"Ah, it is but a small pearl, and as it is inert, no power remains in it. Unfortunately, that makes it not quite as valuable as it once would have been."

Fes squeezed his hand around the pearl. "How much?"

The merchant beamed at him. "You like it?"

Fes shrugged. If he failed to recover the bone, at least he could bring Azithan something. He wanted all the dragon relics Fes could find. "I can see the appeal."

"I would part with it for twenty gold shil."

Fes blinked. "Twenty?" He handed the necklace back. There was no way that it was worth twenty gold, even were it a dragon pearl. It could be resold for maybe half that if he were lucky, and he doubted that Azithan cared enough about an inert pearl to spend even a quarter of that.

"As I said, these are incredibly rare, and the opportunity to acquire them does not come along that often. If you would only..."

Fes shook his head. "I don't have twenty gold."

"How much do you have?"

"Not twenty gold," Fes said, smiling.

Out of the corner of his eye, he saw movement near the back of the tent.

Glancing back and seeing stripes of red on the hat, he concluded it had to be the man he'd followed here. Fes tipped his head, nodding to the merchant. "I think I'm going to have to pass."

"If this does not interest you, I'm sure I could come up with something that would. I have many items, as I have said. And all of them are dragon blessed. If you would tell me what you would be willing to spend, I think I could find you something that would fit your needs."

Fes shook his head. "Only fire mages need something dragon blessed. For the rest of us, it's nothing more than decoration."

The merchant took a step back, suddenly eyeing Fes warily. He had made a mistake. He shouldn't have dismissed the merchant so quickly. He knew better than to reveal his feelings, especially in a place like this, with the fools so tied to believing in the dragon artifacts.

Fes nodded, trying to be polite, and slipped around the table, catching a glimpse of the man he'd followed. With his thick beard and balding head, he was distinctive enough.

Maybe he could wait, and the man would sell the bone. If he did, then Fes could buy it back from the merchants—or steal it, if it were necessary. He wasn't above stealing, especially for an assignment like this, with the payout being what it was.

As he continued to make his way around the outside edge of the tent, he realized that the merchant that he'd been talking to trailed him. Did he know what Fes intended? He wasn't necessarily a thief, but he wouldn't know that Fes served the emperor, if indirectly.

He continued to let his gaze drift down to the table, making it seem as if he were interested in the items there. If he lingered too long in one spot, he ran the risk of another merchant approaching, or even the first re-engaging him. After the conversation they had, he didn't think the first merchant would be too kind.

It had been a mistake to even bother pausing and looking at the items on the table. His focus was on acquiring that bone.

The man stood near the back of the tent, wearing the brightly colored clothing that had marked him as Fes's target. He was locked in conversation with another man. Fes studied the man he'd followed, realizing that he wore a necklace with what appeared to be another dragon pearl, this one larger than what he had seen on the table. Fes suspected it was inert, even if it were real. Should he grab that along with the bone?

The other man was dressed more simply. Red embroidered along the sleeves of his gray cloak marked him as a priest. They were found throughout the Arashn Empire, though rarely spent much time in the city. Priests were tolerated in Anuhr, but not as respected as they were in places outside the city, places that still believed the empire was wrong for destroying the dragons.

Fes edged closer. He *would* get that bone.

"You understand what this means," the priest was saying.

Fes looked down at the table, shifting his feet. He needed to be able to listen, yet at the same time, he didn't want to draw the attention of one of the merchants. He moved back, positioning himself so that he could listen. Standing behind an older couple who were murmuring as they handled different pieces made for excellent cover.

"We need to confirm that it is real," the man was saying.

"Which is why you came to me?"

"If anyone would be able to determine its authenticity, it would be a Priest of the Flame."

The priest bowed his head a moment before looking around. "Your faith is appreciated." His gaze drifted toward Fes.

Did he know that Fes had followed the other to the tent? It had been difficult to find the man in the first place, especially when the only thing Azithan had given him had been word that he'd been in the market.

Fes shifted, wrapping his cloak around himself again,

twisting so that he stayed out of view. He was of half a mind to pull up the hood of his cloak, but doing that would only draw more attention, not less.

"How long before you would be able to make the journey?" the merchant asked.

"I will need time to prepare. What you ask will take time and might require alliances that aren't fully formed."

"I'm not certain how much time we have," the other man said, his voice a tight whisper. Had this all been a setup to a meeting? "We already fear that others will learn of this. We have been doing what we can to protect it, but if those with the right kind of power come after us..."

"I will do what I can," the priest said.

"If it's what we think, then we are one step closer to returning them."

Fes stiffened. Was that what this was about? The priests often preached that the dragons would return and that by bringing the bones together, they could resurrect them, though they never shared *how* that might be possible.

If that was what they believed, then they really were simple.

Fes sidled a step closer to them.

"I will need something to convince the others," the priest said.

"I understand. Take this as a demonstration of what

we've discovered." The man pulled a long length of bone out of his pocket, surprising Fes.

Now was his chance. If he didn't act now, the priest would get it, and it would be harder taking the bone from a priest.

Fes darted forward and grabbed it before the priest could. When he turned, the way was blocked. Two merchants watched him. One was the same man who had given him the eye after he had made the mistake of revealing his feelings about the dragon artifacts. Turning the other way put him in the path of the priest and the merchant.

That left through the tent.

Fes slipped the length of bone into the pouch hidden beneath his cloak. He grabbed his daggers and reached the tent wall. He stabbed through it, cutting the fabric. One benefit of dragonglass was that it could cut through nearly anything.

Out on the street, crowds pushed around him. Fes slipped into the crowds, needing to disappear as quickly as possible. He pulled the hood of his cloak up over his head and ducked down, better to disguise his height. He kept one of his daggers unsheathed but slipped the other back into the sheath, not needing to accidentally stab someone as he made his way through the streets. He rubbed his finger along the hilt as he often did, feeling a soothing relief from it. There was something to the comfort of having these daggers, the only thing that he still had from his father.

He needed to get out of the market.

There was too much of a crowd here, and it made it difficult to move quickly.

He glanced over his shoulder. Three merchants raced toward him, shouldering people out of the way and approaching more quickly than he could escape.

Fes ducked between a pair of tents. He was still in the middle of the market, the place far too enormous to easily escape. And now he'd stolen an item from one of the merchants.

He *wasn't* a thief, not that he hadn't stolen on behalf of Azithan before. A better term would be a tracker, a collector of items of value for Azithan. And now he'd revealed himself. Maybe that was a mistake, especially with how many people jammed in around him, and even for what Azithan would pay.

Someone grabbed his sleeve, and Fes spun, jerking his arm free.

Carter smiled at him. "What do you have, Fes?"

How had she kept pace with him? "It's nothing. Now get out of the way."

Fes danced around, spinning out of the way, and crashed back into the crowd in the street. It was better to push people out of the way than to run the risk of one of the merchants reaching him.

Someone shoved him, and Fes went stumbling, staggering forward until he managed to catch himself. Someone kicked him, and he grunted, rolling out of the way, and slashed with the dagger.

As he got to his feet expecting Carter to continue her attack, he faced an average-sized man. Could he be with Carter—or the priest? He didn't really want to cut down anyone in the market. It wasn't that he couldn't use the daggers—after an upbringing like his, he was more than competent with them—but he had no interest in hurting someone unnecessarily. Azithan offered a certain sort of protection in the city, but there were limits.

The man grabbed his arm and Fes tried to jerk free, but the man had a firm grip. One of Carter's men, probably. The priest wouldn't have employed anyone to attack.

"Not a good idea," he said. He stabbed with the dagger, just deep enough into the flesh of the man's arm that he would let go.

The man cried out, and Fes darted off, slipping back into the crowd.

Fes wiped the dagger on his pants before sheathing it. Blood didn't go well with blades, and he didn't like contaminating his sheath with it. It was easier to clean his pants than to clean out the sheath.

Azithan owed him for this one.

He pressed forward into the crowd. Those nearest him glanced over, glaring at him.

This wasn't the way the job was supposed to go. Then again, none of the jobs ever went quite the way they were supposed to go. Most of the time, Fes ended up in some sort of trouble. Azithan sent him after difficult to acquire items, and given Fes's reputation, that made sense, but there were times when he wished that he didn't have that reputation and that he wasn't so successful. Of course, if he weren't so successful, he wouldn't be as useful to Azithan.

The edge of the market was just up ahead. All he had to do was get a little farther, away from Carter, and he could make a run for the palace.

A shout caused him to turn.

That was a mistake.

When he turned around, the priest from the tent was looking at him. How had he reached him so quickly?

There had to be a more accessible—and less crowded —way through the city.

Fes withdrew the dagger from his sheath, holding it out. "I'm sorry, but I have a job."

The priest glanced from Fes to the dagger. "The artifacts belong to the dragons."

"I'm pretty sure the fire mages would disagree."

"Would they?"

Almost too late, Fes realized someone barreled toward him. The size of the man and his clothing suggested he was hired by Carter. He spun, sending a kick that sent the attacker flying backward, but the dagger went flying from his hand... landing directly in front of the priest.

"That's mine," Fes said.

The priest held it out in front of him. Fes was tempted to reach for his other dagger but decided against it. He lunged for the priest, but the man backed away. "Where did you acquire such an artifact?"

"It's mine," he said again.

"And what you carry in your pouch is mine. A trade?"

A debate warred within him. He wanted the fee that Azithan promised, but he also didn't want to lose his dagger. He prized it, but mostly because it was the only thing he had of his family.

Still, the money—and the risk of disappointing Azithan.

Two men approached, nearing the priest. Carter trailed behind them.

It didn't leave him with any choice.

Fes spun, racing off toward the edge of the market.

When he reached it, he glanced back and saw the priest with several others around him, simply watching him. Carter and her men had disappeared. He would need to move quickly to stay ahead of her as he raced toward the palace.

Fes fixed the priest in his mind. He would find him again, and he would reacquire his dagger. That was worth much to him. Finding a priest in Anuhr couldn't be that hard, could it?

The priest watched him, holding on to the dagger. With the sunlight reflecting off the blackened blade, it seemed to glow somewhat. Fes rubbed the hilt of his other dagger and spun away.

Outside the market, he turned away, racing along the street until any thought of pursuit died off. From here, he could make out the palace in the distance, though he was still far from it. He ran through the narrow streets lined with two-story homes all crammed together, weaving around people walking through the side streets Fes preferred so as to avoid the chaos of the wider streets. As he ran, he reached into the pack and pulled the bone out. It was warm, which made him think it *was* a real dragon bone. And it had been offered in exchange for something else.

Did Azithan know what the merchants wanted from the priest? Most likely he did. If he didn't, that knowledge might be valuable to him, and more reason to keep Fes around.

He would be paid for this job. And he would see that Azithan paid even more than what he had agreed. Losing his dagger was worth an extra gold or two.

CHAPTER TWO

F es was holding onto the bone, rolling it in his hands, running it along the surface when the door to the room opened. The bone was mostly smooth, but there were strange striations in it that he could feel though he couldn't see them. It seemed as if the warmth he felt seeped from those striations. He'd held replica bones often enough, but this didn't seem to be a copy. The real thing, then.

"No. Don't get up on my behalf," Azithan said as he entered.

Fes looked over. He didn't bother to move his leg, which was draped over the arm of the chair. Like everything in the room, it was ornate, decorated with silver gilding worked into the arms. In Azithan's rooms, everything had a certain gilding to it.

"Why should I get up? Your chairs are much more comfortable than any that I have."

"I should think so. Considering what you have come from, that's not all too surprising."

Azithan stopped in front of him. He was draped in a thick maroon robe, and he wore a gold collar marked with symbols of the empire, including the dragon, the symbol for the emperor. Azithan reached for the bone, but Fes pulled it back, twisting in his seat.

"Not before you pay me."

Azithan looked hurt. "Have I ever failed to pay you?"

"It's not a failure to pay so much as it is the terms of our arrangement."

Azithan regarded him for a moment with a dangerous gleam in his eye. "Have you decided to change those terms?"

"I lost a dagger."

Azithan turned away, leaving Fes sitting with the bone on his lap, and made his way to the massive tile-framed hearth. A warm fire crackled within, and there came the scent of cinnamon on the air. That fit Azithan far too well.

"A dagger? That's what your change of focus is about? Why should I care about a dagger?"

"Because I care about a dagger," Fes said, peeling his leg off the chair and twisting so that he could see Azithan better. The man had his back to him, and he did something near the hearth that created a strange mix of smells. Not only was there the cinnamon, but now there was something else, almost a hint of mint or perhaps pine.

"How much was the dagger worth to you?"

Fes debated what number to throw out. If he went too high, he ran the risk of offending Azithan. The only reason he cared whether or not he did that was because Azithan continued to send jobs his way. He needed those jobs. They paid well, and the alternative was much worse. Besides, Azithan had been kind to him.

"Probably three gold shils."

Azithan glanced over, a trace of a smile curving his mouth. "Three gold? I have a hard time believing that you would carry anything quite so valuable on you, Fezarn."

Fes tensed. He hated it when anyone used his full name, but there was something almost possessive about the way that Azithan said it. "That's what it's worth. And I lost it. I could have traded the bone for the dagger—the priest was willing to do that—but..."

"You wouldn't have traded the bone for the dagger," Azithan said, turning back to the fire. There came a flash of light that faded. A trail of orange smoke drifted into the room. Had Azithan added something to the fire, or was this a demonstration of his fire magic? The man *was* a fire mage, though Fes never saw him use that kind of magic. "You wouldn't want to have failed in a task. I know you well enough to know that you would hate that, Fezarn."

Fes looked down at the bone. He ran his hand along the surface, feeling the strange grooves. Azithan was right. He always completed his tasks and had so far never failed. That was another reason that Azithan continued to hire him. "Did you know I'd find this?"

"Was it with the priest?"

Fes hesitated. "The bone wasn't *with* the priest. It was his payment."

"For what?"

"I don't know." Azithan waited, but Fes didn't have anything more to say. He hadn't learned of the task the merchant wanted of the priest and had thought the bone all he cared about. "Is it authentic?"

Azithan's face tightened a moment as he did something. Fes could feel it as tension in the air. "It appears to be."

"Five gold shils of value?" Fes asked.

Azithan chuckled. "Is it five now? I thought the agreement was for me to pay four. Between the increase in price along with what you are quoting me for your lost dagger, I'm beginning to question whether you are to be trusted, Fezarn." Azithan turned to him, clasping his hands before him. "You are a collector for the empire. Is that not worth something to you?"

"Is that what I am now?" He had been Azithan's

collector. Was he getting promoted? It wasn't that Fes would argue with such a promotion. There was value in serving the empire, even if he didn't feel any particular allegiance to it.

Azithan studied him. "You've served me long enough to know your worth."

It had been nearly a year since Fes had stopped needing to take other jobs. A year spent working with Azithan, assigned to track down items of various value, though none of them of value to Fes. A year where he hadn't needed to fear where money would come from... or whether he would have anything to eat. A year since he had needed to serve Horus.

"I don't really know what I'm worth to you."

"You work for the empire, which gives you a certain level of credibility that you wouldn't otherwise have. I think that matters more than you give it credit for." Azithan watched him for a moment before turning away and heading toward the back of the room. When he returned, he tossed a sack onto Fes's lap. "That should more than cover for your missing dagger. There are plenty of places that you can go to purchase a replacement. Now, if you don't mind?" He reached out for the bone, and Fes handed it over to him.

"I might be able to buy another dagger, but it won't be the same." Fes glanced at the coin purse in his lap. He untied the strings and flipped it open and began sorting through the coins that Azithan had offered. He reached ten, and there were still a few coins remaining. More than he'd agreed. Then again, Azithan had always been fair with him.

Azithan brought the bone close to his face, studying it. A strange tingling irritated Fes's arms for a moment before fading. Azithan smiled to himself as he brought the bone to the back of the room and set it down.

"Is it what you were hoping it would be?"

"A dragon bone is valuable."

"To a fire mage," Fes said, watching Azithan.

"You don't think others would find it valuable?"

"I don't know. Valuable enough the merchant thought the priest would accept a job for him."

Azithan straightened. "Do you have any idea what job that might be?"

"Not particularly. When I saw the bone, I thought that's what you were after."

The fire mage watched Fes for a long moment. "The bone has value. That's why you were paid, Fezarn."

"You wanted to know why the priest came to the city." Azithan had not only known about the bone, but he must have known about the meeting with the priest.

Azithan smiled tightly. "Now you begin to think. Yes. That would have been *more* valuable to me."

Fes glanced down at the bag of coins. How much more valuable would it have been? Azithan had paid a ransom for just the bone—would he have paid even more?

"I could go back to the merchant…"

"It will likely be too late. Now that they know you were there, they will have connected you to me."

"I could try."

Azithan frowned at him before returning to stand in front of the fire. "Tell me, Fezarn, what is it that you saw when you were there?"

"I told you what I saw."

"And you gave no thought to why a merchant would pay a priest with a priceless dragon relic?"

He should have. "How would the merchants have acquired an actual bone? I thought most of these were lost, scavenged long ago."

"Not scavenged," Azithan said, derision in the way he used the term. "Most of the fragments of bone were harvested by the dragonwalkers for the empire centuries ago, but there are those who still know how to find them. They belong to the empire to ensure its protection."

Dragonwalkers. If the stories were real, they had a place of esteem when they existed, prized for their ability to crawl through the Dragon Plains and claim the bones for the empire during the Great War a thousand years ago. Those bones had been the key to defeating the dragons and bringing peace. In the time since the last of the dragons, the entire empire had known peace. Though rumors regularly spoke of the threat of attacks, the mere presence of the fire mages held them at bay.

The dragonwalkers were gone, and those who still searched for relics were considered scavengers, not sharing the same esteem as the ancient dragonwalkers. How could they, when most scavengers sold replica dragon bones to the gullible?

"When was the empire really threatened?"

"More often than you know," Azithan said softly. "The threat of power maintains peace. We must always be prepared."

"For what? Toulen borders us to the west, and they want nothing but peace. We don't know what's beyond the northern mountains, and the sea borders us on the east and south. The empire is safe, Azithan." The small nations that had once existed had long ago been swallowed by the empire so that none really knew what they once had been.

"Some believe that the dragons will one day return," Azithan said.

"You're starting to sound like the priest."

"There are far too many stories that suggest the possibility. That is why the empire remains prepared."

"And the priests will return them? They might have some magic, but from what I've seen, I doubt it's enough for that."

"I suppose that would be true. The Priests of the

Flame believe the dragons never were completely exterminated, and that they simply have chosen to mask
themselves. No one disputes that the dragons had power,
though if creatures of such strength were to be able to
conceal their presence, it's unlikely they would have
managed to do so for the last thousand years."

"They're gone, and the priests think that bringing
their bones back together will cause the dragons to rise
once more."

"I'll admit it is unlikely." Azithan watched him for a
moment, and then he flashed a smile. "You did well,
Fezarn. Perhaps you even earned the gold that I paid you
this time. Next time, wait to grab the bone until you have
learned what they are *really* after."

"I lost my dagger to get that for you."

Azithan nodded toward the door. "Go find yourself
another dagger. You should have enough money to buy
whatever quality of blade you want."

The fire mage turned back to the fire and Fes glared
at his back. The money might be able to buy a quality
blade, but it wouldn't replace the dagger—*his* dagger.

Maybe he should have traded the bone for the dagger.
Azithan wouldn't have known. Fes glanced at the bone,
sighing briefly, and then made his way out of Azithan's
room. He headed out of the palace and back out onto the
streets.

In this part of the city, there was a chaotic sort of

activity. Shops had sprung up, one after another, each vying for the money that spilled out of the palace. Plenty of people served the palace, and plenty of wealth poured into the city. It wasn't quite as chaotic as it was in the Great Market, but there still was a certain sense of excitement. Most of the buildings were decorated with dragons, marking their allegiance to the emperor and trying to curry his favor. Those decorations became less frequent the farther he went from the palace.

Fes started toward his home. He didn't have much, little more than a room, but it was his. Were he not so dependent on Azithan and the jobs that he took, he might not have bothered to pay for even that, but for now, with Azithan hiring him as often as he did, Fes didn't want to be too far from the center of the city and didn't want to be too far from the offers of employment.

Azithan was right. He *did* need to replace his dagger. It wouldn't do for him to have only one, mainly as there were times when he had needed both. He knew just such a place that he could go but doubted that Tracen would have anything for him. He was a skilled metalsmith, and in high enough demand that it would be luck were he to have a dagger. At least he could put in an order. It might take a long time, but Fes didn't know when his next job would come.

As he meandered through the city, he passed through a busy section. There were carts out on the street, with people selling food or other items. It was an outdoor market, one that attempted to rival the Great Market, but there wasn't the same vibrancy within the city as there was at the edge of the city. From here, he could continue onward, reach the slums where he'd spent so much of his youth, but he'd avoided returning over the last year, wanting to stay as far from the slums as he could.

When he reached Tracen's shop, he stepped inside, getting away from the din of the street. He heard a hammering in the back of the shop, and Fes made his way toward his friend. They had known each other for years, back when Tracen had still been in the slums and before he'd managed to find an apprenticeship and get out. He was the only one Fes remained in touch with from those days.

Tracen looked up, his hammer paused before striking the metal. "Fes. No assignment today?"

"There was. I finished."

"Oh yeah? And what bizarre item did he have you tracking this time?"

"I thought it was a bone, but I think there was more to it." Azithan had been after whatever the merchants knew about, the reason they wanted the priest to do *something* for them. He might have to pay another visit to the market before the Bayars disappeared.

Tracen set his hammer down and looked over at Fes as he wiped a bead of sweat off his forehead. "As in a dragon bone?" Tracen whistled softly. "That's got to be worth… I don't even know *what* it would be worth."

"Well, I did steal it from a priest."

Tracen came around the forge and leaned on one of the tables that displayed the knives he'd made. All of them were of high-quality steel, though many were simple. A basket near the far corner contained swords that he had made. Neither was quite the right weapon for Fes. He preferred something of a little longer blade, but not so long that he had to worry about cutting himself with it, not the way that he would if he carried a sword.

"What are you doing stealing from priests? Do you really need that kind of luck?"

Fes chuckled. "What kind of luck is that?"

"It can't be good, not if you're stealing from a priest."

"I think I've already had enough bad luck."

"You can't keep using what happened to your parents as an excuse."

"No? I thought that I could use that as often as I wanted."

Tracen snorted. "It is tragic, but I think you need to move on."

"I have moved on. That's what brought me here." Not that he had anyplace else he could have gone. Had he not come to Anuhr, Fes suspected he would have died.

"No, you've thrown in with the emperor."

"Not the emperor. Azithan."

Tracen arched a brow. "They're pretty much the same, aren't they?"

"Fine, but I'd rather have the stability of a job and the safety of knowing that were anything to happen, I have a connection in the palace."

"A connection that may not care about you if things turn sour. Will Azithan watch out for you? The emperor? You need someone who cares about you and honest work."

Fes smiled at Tracen. "That's sweet of you, but I don't think that you're my type."

Tracen shot him an annoyed look and returned to the forge and picked up his hammer. He began beating on the metal, striking it with a steady rhythmic blow. Something was soothing about listening to him as he worked. He could never know the sort of comfort that Tracen had while hammering metal, shaping it into knives or swords or any of the dozen other things that he had made. Then again, Tracen led something of a boring life, and it was one that Fes wasn't sure that he could ever stomach.

"You know what I mean," he said while hammering. "You didn't want to stay with *her*—"

"It would never have worked, and we both knew it. Besides, this is a steady job."

"Steady doesn't mean that it's a good job. Think of all the things he's asked you to track for him."

Fes pulled out the coin purse and shook it. "But he pays."

Tracen glanced over. "There is that."

"Which is why I came."

"You didn't come to visit with me?"

Fes shrugged. "You know how much I enjoy chatting with you."

"You only come when you need something."

"That's not true, and you know it. Besides, you say that as if it's a bad thing."

"It's not a bad thing, but…" Tracen shook his head. "What do you need?"

"A dagger."

"A dagger? I could make you a sword. That's infinitely more valuable than a dagger. I wouldn't even charge you that much for it."

"Because you already have dozens of swords."

"I have plenty, but that doesn't mean that they weren't time-consuming to make. Everything that I create takes time. I put everything that I can into it, so it doesn't matter how long it takes to create."

"I wasn't criticizing."

"You weren't, but too many have and complain about the pace with which I make the swords. What can I say? I know how to work efficiently."

"Which is why I'm asking you for a dagger. I need something that will fit my sheath," he said, pulling the sheath off his belt, "and I need something with a sturdy blade. It doesn't have to be ornate or even all that fancy."

"And why?"

"I lost one."

"One of your daggers?"

Fes nodded. "When I was chasing the bone for Azithan. I lost one."

"And since you're coming here, it seems as if he paid for what you've lost."

Fes flashed a smile. "You are the best."

"I am. And it would be helpful if you would spread that rumor a little more to get me more business."

"I don't think you're hurting for business."

Tracen looked around the shop. With all of the items that he had stacked up, Fes could tell that Tracen remained busy. Maybe *too* busy. Would he have time to make the dagger?

"I'm getting to the point where I need to bring on someone else."

There it was. The comment he'd made about honest work finally made sense. "I'm not looking for work," Fes said.

"The offer is there."

"I like what I do. I'm good at it."

"You like what you do because you get to be by yourself. You don't have to be. It's okay for you to care about someone other than—"

Fes raised his hand, cutting off Tracen. "Can you make me a dagger or not?"

"I'll make you a dagger. It will be the nicest damned dagger that you'd ever imagine."

"That's what I'm hoping for."

"When do you need it by?"

Fes shrugged. "I haven't got another job, not yet. How long do you need?"

"Considering the quality that you'd be looking for, probably a couple days? I guess that means you need to avoid getting into a fight."

Fes slipped the other dagger out of his sheath and flipped it forward before sliding it back into the sheath. "I think I'm okay."

"Okay. With just that one? If I didn't know better, I would think that you were practically naked."

"Sometimes it feels like that."

"You plan to pay?"

"How much do you need for the dagger?"

"Normally I charge two silver rasn for something like that, but I could get by with charging you just one."

Fes flipped a gold coin to Tracen. He caught it before it came crashing down into one of the flames. "Keep the rest. I'm sure I'll have something else I'll need from you."

"He really does have you well paid, doesn't he?"

"What does that mean?"

"You don't even care how much you're spending on daggers. I could make you three for that price."

"Then make me three."

Tracen grinned and stuffed the gold coin into his pocket. "No. I think I'll stick with just the one. Besides, would you do with three daggers?"

"Be three times as safe."

"It's not you that I worry about. It's everyone else."

"No one else has any reason to worry about me."

"They do if you run around with three daggers." As Fes started to leave, Tracen called out to him. "Don't forget the offer."

"How can I forget it?"

Tracen grinned, and Fes left the shop, heading back into the chaos of the city to see if he could chase down his dagger.

CHAPTER THREE

The entrance to the market was less busy at this time of night. Fes watched, debating whether to reenter, but decided to just sit outside and watch for signs of the priest. He'd feared that finding him would be difficult in a city the size of Anuhr, but a priest *did* stand out. Thankfully Azithan had paid him well enough to buy information.

He shouldn't have come after the priest, but regardless of what Azithan said, the dagger mattered to him. Losing it would be like losing his parents all over again.

It was late and other than the moon, there was very little light. A faint wind blew through, swirling around his hair and his jacket, casting a cooler air to the night and carrying the market's exotic smells of spices and treats and dozens of other things that were not typically found in Anuhr.

Searching the market for the priest wouldn't be easy, but what did he have other than time, especially now that he had to wait on Tracen to make him a dagger? Besides, it wasn't that he had a job waiting for him, and if he discovered what the priest was after, he didn't doubt that Azithan would pay.

A group of men headed toward the market. Fes caught up to them, staying barely a pace or two behind them, but close enough that it would appear to an outsider that he belonged with that group. They were chatting about activity in the palace, and about women that they knew, but there was a comment that caught him.

"They're moving troops north, I hear."

"That's nothing but a rumor," one of the men said.

"There's a rebellion."

"There's always a rebellion. The emperor has ruled long enough that there is always someone who thinks to remove him from power."

One of the other men hushed him, but the speaker looked over. "It's not like I'm saying that I want to over-throw the emperor. Skies of Fire! Why would I want something like that?"

"You need to be careful with those sorts of comments. It's bound to get you into…" The man turned and seemed to notice Fes. His eyes widened slightly, and Fes flashed a smile. He doubted that it made him look any less threatening. He was tall—taller than many, though there were plenty of people in the city who were taller than him. Time spent running around had made him fit and muscular, which the cloak he wore obscured.

He didn't want to have these men questioning his presence, so he turned away and headed toward the nearest tent. Lights glowed from each of the tents along the street. Trading would go on all night, maximizing each trader's time in the city. Eventually, they would go and would be replaced by another. It had been that way for centuries. The Great Market constantly changing, constantly churning, and the merchants within it always changing over.

He found a tent that had more activity than most, and he stepped inside. Rows of tables were set up, and jewelry and linens and pottery were on the table. Why would this tent be so appealing to so many people?

When he saw the merchant, he thought that he understood. The man had dark skin and tight curly black hair, and the colorful jacket he wore practically shouted that he came from Toulen. It was the nation to their western border, and goods that came from there were often prized.

Fes scanned the table, looking at the various artifacts. The jewelry was interesting. Most of it was beaded and painted with bright colors, much like the Bayars' tent.

Some appeared to be carved out of bone, and one necklace had a large horn hanging from it, likely the tusk of some strange animal found only in Toulen. The stone carvings were incredibly intricate and made in strange poses with people set as if they were praying or with arms out as if trying to balance. Fes was drawn to one such sculpture and lifted it, finding the stone incredibly slick and smooth.

"What do you think of the totem?"

He looked up to see the merchant watching him. The man had dark brown eyes that were surprisingly warm. His voice carried the rhythmic accent of his people. Fes had interacted with the people of Toulen several times before and had always been treated fairly. Even in Anuhr, that was unusual.

"It's incredible craftsmanship."

"Thank you."

"You made this?"

The merchant spread his hands out, motioning to the table. "I made all of this."

That surprised him. Oftentimes, merchants would band together, consolidating so that they could bring an entire tent worth of items to the Great Market. Very rarely was a single merchant responsible for everything inside it. Then again, given the distance from Toulen, it was possible that he had taken the entire journey to make most of these items. And it would likely be worth it. A man like this, with items such as what Fes saw here, would be able to sell out of his supplies quickly, likely earning enough money to more than make it worth it to have ventured this far.

"What's the significance of the pose?"

The man smiled as he stepped closer to the table. He paused and looked around the tent, but others seemed content with merely wandering around the tables, browsing as they scanned the items. "There is much significance to each totem. Some are designed for luck." He plucked one of the sculptures, this out of a brown stone with the figurine appearing to kneel. "Others are designed for goodwill." This one was a figurine with the hands clasped together, bowing. "And still others are designed for strength." He pointed to the one Fes held.

This one had the arms outstretched, and Fes wondered why it would be symbolic of strength. There was nothing about it that screamed strength, but perhaps it meant something to the people of Toulen.

"You strike me as a man who doesn't need strength."

Fes replaced the totem back on the table, chuckling. "Who doesn't need strength?"

"Most men would benefit from wisdom."

"I'm not most men."

"Are you saying you have enough wisdom?"

Fes looked up and met the man's eyes. The man

smiled at him, and Fes couldn't help but smile back. "I don't know that many would accuse me of wisdom."

"Then why do you have no need?"

"It's not that I don't have the need, it's just that I'm not sure I'm a fit for wisdom."

"Ah, well that is entirely different. Perhaps with your understanding of that, you have shown more wisdom than most."

Fes motioned to one of the totems. It seemed the figurine was twisted, as if ready to spin. "What of this one?"

"That is one that calls for blessing with fighting."

Fes smiled to himself. "That's the kind of thing I could use."

"You find yourself fighting?"

"More often than I want."

"You don't have to embrace a life of violence. The Great Ones know that each of us can choose our own path."

"It's a little late for me to be choosing my path."

"So you allow another to choose it for you?"

"Not that, either. I'm just saying—"

The man smiled again. "I don't mean to challenge you. It's just that these totems are meant to help with reflection. And if you find that you need strength with fighting, then perhaps you do, but perhaps if you feel that you don't need wisdom, it's possible that might be a better fit for you."

Fes looked along the table, and as he did, he saw a man grabbing one of the items, and slipping it into his pocket.

"Excuse me for a moment," he said. He stepped away from the merchant and headed toward the younger man. "I saw that," he said behind him. "Most of the time, I probably wouldn't care, but..." He liked the Toulen merchant. Not that it mattered to the man, but it mattered to Fes.

The man turned, and he glowered at Fes. "Move."

"Is it worth your hand?"

The man continued to glare at Fes and tried to push past him.

"Is it worth your hand?" Fes asked again.

"You don't look like you serve the Dragon Emperor, so you would have no authority."

Fes smiled at the man. If only he knew. "No, but the people of Toulen have harsh rules for thieves. And in the Great Market, thieving is left to the individual merchant to determine how to deal, depending on culture and custom. I will ask you again: Do you value your hand?"

The man tried to push past him again, and this time Fes grabbed him by the wrist, spinning him around, and dipped his hand into his pocket, pulling the carving out and setting it back on the table. He checked his other pockets but didn't find anything else. When he was done, he pushed the man away from him, sending him staggering from the tent.

The merchant watched the entire thing with only a hint of amusement on his face.

"I haven't taken a hand in many years," he said. "Perhaps I should take yours for stealing my prize."

"I figured you wouldn't want the hassle of reporting it to the emperor," Fes said. That was the only requirement, though few enough bothered to report it. For that matter, few enough bothered to report thieving at all. It likely happened frequently in the Great Market, but there wasn't a whole lot that could be done to prevent it.

"Then I should thank you. Perhaps you have shown more wisdom than you believe of yourself."

Fes snorted. "That's unlikely." He looked down at the carving, wondering what the man might have grabbed that would have been so interesting. It was a sculpture of a dragon, and incredibly detailed. It was carved out of a reddish stone or possibly an incredibly dense wood. Either way, the carving was smooth, sanded or stropped so that it was silky to the touch. The dragon had its wings parted, spread out, and the four legs were arched, almost as if preparing to pounce.

"Did you make this as well?"

"Not that. That didn't come from here."

Fes squeezed his eyes shut. "I'm sorry. I grabbed the wrong item." Where had the man hidden the totem?

"It's likely that was stolen as well. I can speak to the guards and send word to the Dragon Emperor."

Fes shook his head. "It's not necessary. I know someone who can see that the merchant is compensated." He suspected that for a sculpture like this, Azithan would be happy to pay, and likely more than the sculpture was worth. If nothing else, Azithan was more than happy to spend the emperor's money.

"How much for the sculpture for wisdom?" he asked.

The Toulen man studied him for a moment. "I think that perhaps you would be better served by something like this," he said pulling a different totem from the table. It was one where the pose indicated movement, though as Fes stared at it, he wasn't entirely sure why he felt that way. Something about the totem tugged on him, almost as if he was meant to have it.

"What is this one for?"

"There are many possible benefits for this totem, but in your case, I think that it is perhaps for insight."

He arched a brow at the man. "Are you saying I lack insight?"

"Many of us lack insight, but what I suggest is that you would benefit from looking inward. We can all use a certain measure of self-discovery."

"And how much?"

"Consider it my gift."

"But I didn't stop the thief."

"You didn't, but you tried. To the people of Toulen, that is often just as valuable."

Fes took the sculpture and twisted it in his hand. He didn't have many belongings, and certainly nothing quite like this. "Thank you."

The sound of chanting came from outside the tent, and Fes turned, frowning.

"They often come through here after dusk," the merchant said.

"Often?" Fes asked, turning to him. It was surprising that the merchant from Toulen would know what happened in the market often. "How long have you been here?"

"Two weeks. Long enough to have recognized a pattern. The priests lead people through here."

That might be why the priest had returned to the market. They wouldn't be quite a tolerated in the rest of the city, but in the Great Market, few would object to the presence of priests. "I'm surprised that you would have been here quite so long."

"Items sell quickly, but they are replaceable, and I have plenty of product," the merchant said with a smile. "Besides, I have to be prepared for when thieves decide to dip into my supplies." The merchant chuckled. "Thank you."

"Thanks to you, as well."

Fes reached the entrance to the tent, peeking his head

outside. A priest led a line of people through the market, but not the one he looked for. Several of the people walking with the priest carried lanterns while others carried torches, and they all held them up, letting the fire and the flame glow in the night. It pushed back the darkness, the same way they believed the dragons once pushed back the darkness.

Fools, all of them. When the dragons had lived, they would have been terrible creatures, and there were plenty of stories of the dragons hunting and destroying cities, not pushing back the darkness or helping those less fortunate, not the way the priests seemed to believe. It was better the fire mages now used their magic for defense of the Arashn Empire.

The entire line moved past, and Fes stayed off to the side of the road, not wanting to get into the middle of the procession. He had never seen anything quite like it, but there was an element of ceremony to it. Others joined as the procession moved through, trailing after them, and their chanting added to that of the others.

It wasn't led by the priest he looked for, but maybe he could lead him to the other.

Fes weaved around a series of tents, coming between them as he tried to get ahead of the procession, wanting to watch. If he could see them, see where they were going, he thought that he could perhaps discover where the priest had gone.

They made their way to the edge of the market, and from there they stepped out into the empty plains. At night, there was something eerie about the darkness and the emptiness of the plain. Shadows swirled around the gathered wagons, and the horses that were corralled stomped and occasionally made snorting sounds that disrupted the quiet.

The priest led the procession beyond the wagons and out into the darkness. They formed a circle when they stopped, joining others who came out from a different place between the tents. Fes didn't see any sign of the priest who had taken his dagger.

The chanting continued, though it was in a language he didn't recognize. Every so often, they would punctuate the chanting, raising the fire into the night, and their voices would soar, rising higher and higher. Fes listened, annoyed more than anything. It was a waste. How much time and energy was spent on such things?

Too much. That was the easy answer.

The dragons were gone. As far as Fes was concerned, it should stay that way, with the fire mages providing the empire with their protection.

If only they had been around to protect his parents, but they'd been lost making what should have been a safe crossing through the empire, leaving him and his brother Benjan orphaned and forcing Fes into the streets of Anuhr to survive. This city had become his home, but it wasn't supposed to be his home. And after losing Benjan...

He forced those thoughts away. It was only times like this when he didn't have a task that he thought about what he'd lost. He needed to find the priest, reclaim his dagger, and wait for Azithan's next assignment. Sitting here wouldn't help him with either.

The chanting continued, the voices splitting the night, and Fes turned away.

CHAPTER FOUR

Fes wasn't typically the person to track people through the city—most of his jobs involved *things* rather than people—but Azithan had claimed it would be worth his time, and the jobs the fire mage hired him for were always worth his money. If nothing else, it distracted Fes from his failed search for the priest.

It had been nearly two days since he'd seen him, long enough that he could have disappeared from the city. Taking another job might distract him, but his heart really wasn't in it. The longer he went without finding his dagger, the more irritated he became.

The job was simple. Follow the woman through the city.

"Follow her only," Azithan had said.

"Just follow her?" That had been an odd assignment. "Nothing else."

"If all goes well, that will be all you will need to do."

"And if all doesn't go well?"

"Then you may intervene."

"You want her to travel safely."

Azithan had nodded.

"Then why not hire someone else? I'm not an enforcer."

"No, but you have other skills. Besides, I think you are more than adequate for this assignment."

Fes hadn't argued. Not with the price offered, but as he sat here, he had to wonder what about the woman was worth Azithan's protection.

"What does she mean to you?" he'd asked.

Azithan had frowned. "She has something to do with your last assignment. As you were mostly successful there, I thought you would prefer a chance to prove yourself again."

"The priest?" he'd asked, hopeful.

"I don't think she's with him, but it's possible they are connected."

Now that he saw her, he decided that she didn't look like the merchants. They had a particularly colorful style of dress and hers didn't seem any different than others in the city, mostly unremarkable.

Other than her dark raven colored hair and her

incredible beauty. She was incredibly striking. Fes had never seen anyone quite like her but didn't think that it was her attractiveness that had appealed to Azithan. The fire mage didn't strike him as someone who was all that concerned about external beauty. Azithan cared more about items of power. With those, he could probably buy or coerce his way to acquiring beauty like this.

Fes had to go about it the old-fashioned way, which meant that he rarely had a chance with someone like this. The last beauty he'd been with had left him. Or he'd left her. Either way, he hadn't seen Alison in the better part of a year. It was best that way for both of them. He took jobs that actually paid, and he didn't get in the way of her progressing with Horus.

As he tracked Azithan's woman, Fes decided that it *was* possible she was someone Azithan had hired. Fes didn't harbor any misbeliefs that he was the only person who was hired for jobs, especially when there was value in the end result. No, Azithan had a stable of people who he hired, and while Fes liked to think that he was the most skilled of them, that didn't mean that there weren't others who had a similar level of skill. Not all would be trackers. Some would be informants, and some would be enforcers.

She turned down a side street, disappearing into an alleyway. From here, there weren't many other places that she could go. There were shops, and there were other homes, but there would be limitations to how easily she could escape.

When she disappeared into one of the buildings, Fes waited, lingering on the street. She was gone for an hour, maybe more, before she reappeared. This time, she was carrying something in a small pack that she hadn't been carrying before.

If that was what Azithan had been after, he could have said so. Instead, he'd instructed Fes to follow. Nothing more.

Could that be what Azithan wanted? Was she a courier?

Fes trailed after her. When she turned a corner, there was a flicker of movement out of the corner of his eye that caught his attention.

Two men approached, and one of them had a sword unsheathed. They were street thieves; at least, he thought so at first. The way they headed straight toward the woman made him wonder if they might be something else.

Could Carter be after the same things as Azithan —again?

Fes swore under his breath. And here he had begun to hope the job would be easy.

He positioned himself so that they would have to come through him to reach her. He continued to trail after her, not wanting to lose sight of her as she headed through the city, and when she turned a corner, moving out onto a busier street, the men tried to lunge around him, but Fes stuck out his foot, knocking one over. The other spun, swinging his sword around.

Fes jumped out of the way, reaching for his dagger.

The other man had righted himself and unsheathed his sword, whipping it around toward Fes. Definitely not simple thieves. These were the kind of men Carter employed.

He slipped off to the side, getting out of the way of one of the attackers, before slicing forward, sliding the dagger along the flesh of the man's arm. The man dropped his sword, and Fes kicked it out of the way.

There was more movement, and Fes rolled, knocking down the first attacker. He went flying out into the street, and the crowd had to part around him, moving out of the way. If they took too long, not only would Fes lose sight of the woman, he'd draw the attention of a patrol.

The other man stood in a ready posture, the kind that told Fes that he had experience with the sword. This wasn't a man to spend much time trifling with.

With his dagger, he doubted that he would be able to combat him very easily.

So he threw it at him.

It flipped end over end and caught him in the stomach.

The man dropped to the ground, reaching for the

dagger, but Fes got there first and pulled it free, giving it a twist as he removed it. He kicked the sword out of the way, keeping him from attacking again, and quickly wiped his dagger on the man's shirt.

The fight had lasted a moment, and he still feared that he'd lost track of the woman, but he found her heading into a busier section of the city. It made it even harder to follow her. Maybe that was the reason Azithan had wanted him to follow her. Had he known that she would disappear into the city? If this were only about keeping an eye on her, it would be challenging.

Fes squeezed through the crowd, shoving his way forward. Every so often, he'd pause and make certain he could still see her, but she hadn't gotten away.

When the crowd finally thinned enough for him to catch up to her, he noted three men trailing after her.

He wasn't a fighter and hadn't been since leaving the slums. Horus might have used him in that way, but that wasn't the reason Azithan hired him.

One of the men moved forward the woman and grabbed the pack.

Fes kept his dagger sheathed and stumbled forward, pretending to be intoxicated. "I'm sorry," he said, knocking the man over before he could grab the pack. He'd used that trick before in the slums.

The man shoved him, and Fes managed to twist, falling forward into the man and pushing him back. The other two with him helped restrain Fes, trying to grab him, but he threw his arms up as if he were falling, and they weren't able to hold him.

One of the men tried to kick Fes, but he grabbed the man's leg and twisted, shoving him away.

The woman glanced back, and her eyes went wide.

She started off, racing forward through the street.

He couldn't let her get too far ahead. Jumping toward the next attacker, he drove his fist into the man's nose, crushing it. As he spun around, his elbow caught the next man, dropping him.

Where had she gone?

So far, there had been five people after her, and if that was the way this was going, he needed to catch up to her before any others thought to attack.

He hurried along the street, trying to catch up, and found her lying on the ground, motionless. Blood poured from the side of her head where it had struck the stones, and she moaned, apparently in pain. The pack was missing.

Fes searched around the street but saw no evidence of where it had gone.

He returned to the woman and crouched down next to her. "Where did they go?"

She blinked, trying to look over at him but didn't seem as if she could focus. "Who are you? You can't have it."

"What was it? Where did they go?"

"No," she said, trying to scramble away from him.

It drew the attention of others in the street and Fes looked around, realizing that he had better do something or people would begin to approach. Plenty of people in the city were unwilling to keep street thugs from attacking, and the way he was crouching next to her, with her head bleeding as profusely as it was, it likely appeared as if he had been the one to assault her.

"Let me help you," he said. He tried to pitch his words loudly enough that anyone else who might be thinking that he was trying something with her would realize that he was only offering his aid. He wasn't sure that he was successful.

"Please, don't hurt me again."

The crowd behind him was beginning to murmur, and regardless of the job, he would need to take off and get away from her before they became unruly. It was hard enough for him to handle facing off against two or three men individually, but trying the same against an entire crowd?

He stood and started backing away.

Fes slipped into an alley and watched her get up, her hand pressed against her head, and turn back the way she came. He followed her until she reached the building where he'd first found her, keeping a safe distance. There were no other attacks.

They'd been after the pack.

Which meant Azithan had been after the pack.

Why not simply tell him?

Azithan had some explaining to do.

Fes made his way to the palace. When he reached Azithan's rooms, he took a seat in his usual chair, waiting for the man to appear. He looked around but didn't see the bone that he had brought him earlier.

Even the fire was cold. How long had it been since Azithan had been here? A stack of books on the table looked as if he had been here and researching recently, but there was no other sign of the man.

When the door opened, Fes was near the back of the room, his gaze drifting along the surface of the desk where Azithan kept the stack of books, making every effort *not* to snoop.

"Fezarn. I was not expecting to see you quite so soon," Azithan said. As he made his way into the room, his hands slipped into the sleeves of his maroon robes, and he fixed Fes with a strange expression. "Did you finish the job?"

Fes shook his head. "I followed her. The woman was attacked—"

"Attacked? Your job was to follow her."

"And I did. I prevented two attacks, but the third got in front of me."

Azithan frowned. He took a step toward Fes and heat began to radiate from him. Fire mage magic. That was what he had to be, but Fes had never been quite so close to it.

"Who attacked her?"

"I don't know. They were more than simple street thieves." He hesitated before deciding to tell him about Carter. "Carter followed me when you sent me after the bone. And since this job was related…"

He frowned, turning his back to Fes and looking at the hearth. "She remains far more involved than she should."

"She does. I don't know who she works for."

"No. Neither do I, which troubles me." He turned back to Fes. "The woman you were asked to follow would have had an item on her. Did you see this?"

"She was carrying some sort of package, but I didn't see what happened to it. She was bleeding on the street when I found her."

"She was alive?" Azithan asked.

"I followed her back to her home. She's alive." As Azithan stayed near the fire, flames sprang from the coals. Fes couldn't help but be impressed. He didn't get to see fire mages working their magic that often. Few outside of the fire mage temple ever really got to see it anymore, not like they once had. With the empire safe and secured, there was no reason to flaunt that magic. "Who is she to you?"

"It's not who she is to me, but what she was carrying."

Fes didn't know that he believed Azithan. "If you would have sent more than me..."

"More than you would have drawn even more attention."

"Why? What did she have?"

Azithan sighed and turned back to face him. There was a sense of power from him, and Fes wondered why he should feel it so clearly. "I don't know. She follows the Path of the Flame."

"A priestess?"

"Again, I don't know."

"Is she connected to the priest?"

"You mean the one who has your dagger?"

Fes glared at him. Azithan didn't care about his dagger, but Fes *wanted* that blade back. He needed it. "Is she?"

"Probably."

"Then I need to find her again."

"You won't."

"I know where she lives."

"That's not where she lives. It's where she's staying. The priests don't like to linger in Anuhr for too long. They fear the fire mages."

"Fear or dislike?"

Azithan shrugged and turned back to the fire. "Does it matter?"

"Or so much as it impacts the jobs you offer me."

"There might be a way for you to find him again, but you won't like it."

"Because there's no money in it?"

"There's always money, but in this, I think I can offer you something more than what you're looking for."

"More than the dagger?"

Azithan turned to him. Power swirled, making Fes take a step back. Why should he detect that power? "I can help you find the reason you value the dagger."

He tensed. That had been one thing he'd been careful about with Azithan. He didn't need the fire mage knowing about his past, nothing more than what he had already discovered when he had plucked Fes from the slums for his ability to sniff out dragon relics.

But the way he said it suggested he knew something more.

What did Azithan know about his parents?

"It's a family heirloom. Nothing more."

"Nothing?" He arched a brow and Fes understood that Azithan *knew*.

"What do you know, Azithan?"

"Only that there are answers to questions you haven't asked yet."

"What kind of answers?"

Azithan crossed over to him and jerked back his jacket, revealing the remaining dagger. He lifted it by the hilt and twisted it in his hands for a moment before slipping it back into Fes's sheath. "The kind that would tell you why you're in possession of a priceless dagger."

He'd known they were valuable but had never contemplated finding out *how* valuable. There had been no reason. "The priest knows?"

Azithan shook his head. "Doubtful, but there are things I can tell you. First, you need to learn what he's after. Then I'll provide you with answers."

"That's not how our arrangement works."

"No? You would prefer I pay rather than answer your questions?"

"It helps."

Azithan chuckled, turning his attention back to the fire. "I suspect this will be well worth your time. But you must see it for yourself."

"You suspect? You don't know?"

"As I said, you will have to see for yourself."

"See what?"

"Whatever the priest is after."

"You don't know?"

"Not this time, Fezarn. There are… reasons… that it's difficult for me to learn."

Fes debated what to do. Azithan offered to pay, but

only if he completed a job that might not have an easy endpoint. If he did it, he might get more than a payday. He might get answers.

As long as he'd been in the slums, he'd wanted answers. Not only about what had happened to his parents, but about why they had traveled where they had in the first place. Anuhr had been the closest city for Fes to reach, but that wasn't where his parents had intended to end up.

And the daggers *were* priceless, for more reasons than Azithan knew.

"How can I find him?"

"I believe the answers will be with someone you know well."

He tensed, not liking the sound of that. "Who?"

"Horus."

"No."

Azithan tipped his head. "I know you don't want to see him again—"

Fes squeezed his eyes shut. "You don't understand."

"You told me that he used you."

He sighed. "He used me. And worse." And Azithan had saved him from it. Now he'd need to go back to him?

"If you don't want to do this—or can't—I understand."

There was something more within what Azithan said. Fes might not need to take the assignment, but he would

miss out on something more if he didn't, something
Azithan knew.

"You promise to tell me what you know?"

Azithan nodded. "I do. When you find him, just don't
tell him I sent you."

CHAPTER FIVE

This part of the city was dark and more than a little dirty. After spending as much time as he had lately near the palace, working with Azithan, coming back to the slums and being exposed to the filth in the south-western part of the city was somewhat jarring. It was home to thieves and worse, but there had been a time when Fes had called it home.

When his parents had died, leaving him and his brother as orphans, this had been the only place he hadn't been exiled from. The patrols pushed the strays out of the center of the city, sweeping them to the outskirts of Anuhr as if that solved the problem.

And it was because of this part of the city that he'd lost his brother.

Even after losing Benjan, he hadn't been able to leave. Where would he have gone?

Fes had vowed not to succumb to the darkness within the empire the same way his brother had, even if it meant working with the very thing that had killed Benjan. Surviving had turned him into something his parents would not have wanted, but at least he had the opportunity to use the rage that always seemed to boil beneath the surface.

Fes paused while making his way along a darkened street and spun. "Are you going to keep following me, or are you going to show yourself?" A cloaked figure appeared out of the darkness, and Fes forced himself to smile. "Alison. It's been a while."

She stalked around him, dressed all in black. It matched her straight hair, which was longer than when he'd seen her last. Had she lost weight? Maybe it was only that she had become leaner, more muscular over the previous year.

She was smaller than him and quite compact, but there was a feisty strength to her that had appealed to him from the moment he'd met her when they were both kids prowling the streets. It still did. "Only because of you."

"You know why I left."

"You want to start this now, or should we wait?"

He grunted. "Wait, preferably." And never, if he had his way.

She leaned toward him, inhaling deeply. "You smell like him."

"I'm not sure what that means," Fes said.

"A mixture of cinnamon. You smell like the palace."

"I can't help that."

"Sure you can," she said. "You don't have to take those jobs."

"It brought me away from here." And it brought him away from the man he was about to go see. Didn't she understand that?

She glared at him. "For how long? They'll use you like they use everyone else. And then where will you be?"

"I would have been worse off had I stayed." She didn't want to admit it, but it had been the truth. They both knew it, which was why Fes had taken the job Azithan offered. How could he not?

Fes turned away from her, looking along the street. It was late enough that it was mostly empty, but if Alison was here, it was unlikely that she would be alone. It wasn't that she was afraid to come here alone —she was far too capable with the sword she had buckled to her waist—but it was safer to come with others.

"You don't have to worry. No one followed me here."

"I doubt that," he said.

"You can doubt all you want. I'm not letting anyone follow me."

"Even if you weren't aware that they were following you?"

She jabbed him with her finger. "Do you think that I wouldn't be so aware of people following me?"

"I've snuck up on you more than once."

"It's been a long time, Fezarn. Or do you go by something else now?"

"Just Fes."

"That doesn't change what you've done."

It didn't, but Azithan hadn't cared about any of Fes's past transgressions, even if he knew about them. He had wanted Fes's skill, and the time spent on the streets had made him skilled. Useful. If Fes had anything to do with it, those skills would make him wealthy, too.

"Does he know?"

Fes glared at her for a moment. "Does he know what?"

"Does he know who you are? Does he know *what* you are?"

"I'm not sure that it matters."

"It matters. Don't try to convince yourself that it doesn't."

"I haven't convinced myself of anything. And it's because of Horus that I became what I did."

She jabbed him in the chest again and circled around him. Fes should have expected to come across her when

Azithan had him come for Horus, but he hadn't thought to see her *quite* so soon.

"You've convinced yourself that you're better than the rest of us."

Fes shook his head. "Again. I haven't convinced myself of anything."

She only glared at him. "You keep telling yourself that. Why have you come here today?"

"Do I have to have a reason?"

She shrugged. "It would help."

"I came for a job."

"He doesn't have any opportunities for you."

"That's not what I heard."

"You stink of the palace and think you can just return?"

Fes stared at her a moment. "It was good to see you again, Alison." He started off down the street, planning to move past her, but she butted up in front of him, blocking his way.

"That's it? That's all you have to say to me?"

"What else is there to say?"

"You just left us here."

"I was offered an opportunity. Freedom."

"There is no freedom. Not within the empire."

"There is for me," he said softly.

She glared at him. "You left *me* here."

Fes met the anger in her eyes. It had been a year, and

that anger still hadn't faded. The way she looked at him made him wonder if it ever would fade. "I took an opportunity."

Alison looked as if she wanted to say something, but she bit it back. "Just go back to the palace and serve the empire like a good little dog." She stepped off to the side and let him move past.

He continued through the streets until he reached Horus's building. Most buildings here were run down and dilapidated, but Horus managed to take pride in his holdings, making it almost appear stately. There was nothing conspicuous about his home, but then, Horus controlled enough power that he didn't have to be conspicuous.

When Fes knocked, a grizzled man with a peppered beard greeted him. He didn't look any different than when Fes had seen him last. Maybe a little older. Harder, if that were possible. "Fes. I'm glad to see you here," Horus said.

There wasn't any surprise on Horus's face. The man was well connected, but how had he known Fes was coming?

When the answer came to him, he almost laughed. Alison hadn't been there to confront him. She had delayed him.

Clever.

"Rumor in my part of the city is that you might know

how to find someone I'm looking for." Let him have a reminder that Fes didn't belong in the slums, not anymore.

"And who might that be?"

How direct should he be? "A priest."

Horus arched a brow at him, his gaze focused solely on Fes. Probably a half dozen others were standing behind him, watching as well. "There are many priests in the city."

"Many? That's not likely."

"No? Do you believe the empire can control access to Anuhr so tightly?"

"I think the priests would be careful about their presence. They favor the dragons much more than the empire."

"You say that as if it's a bad thing, Fezarn."

Fes liked it even less when Horus said his name than he did when Alison did. At least with Alison, there was an existing relationship between them, even if it had soured long ago. With Horus, Fes felt much the same as he did about the way that Azithan said his name. Both men had a similar way about them, a similar way of making him feel as if they thought they owned him. At least with Horus, he had managed to get away. Well, mostly away. With Azithan, Fes wasn't sure that he would.

"Why are you really here? I heard you had better employment opportunities," Horus said.

"What can I say? It pays well." Let him think that the only reason, not that Fes had grown tired of the violence.

"For how long? When will you be out of favor?"

Fes didn't know, but that was always the risk. Eventually, Azithan might grow tired of him. And then what would he do? Return here and take jobs that paid a fraction of what Azithan offered? It was why he saved everything he could. Eventually, those jobs would end, and he wanted to be free of both the empire and men like Horus. He'd already saved quite a bit and, in time, he thought he could be completely free—regardless of what happened with Azithan.

"Do you know anything or not?"

Horus studied him a long moment. "Why do you think I might? You have different connections now. Some would say better connections."

Azithan had warned him not to reveal that he'd sent him, but it wasn't necessary to name him to find out what Horus might know. "They aren't better. Different. And they aren't helpful when it comes to what I'm looking for."

"Why do you want to find this priest?"

"Because he has something of mine."

"Intriguing." Horus paused before motioning for Fes to join him. He followed into a wide entry room. Wooden benches ran along each wall. A lantern glowed with a soft light. The thick carpet rolled across the floor was worth as much as two Azithan-paid jobs. "I would like to tell you that you would be out of luck, especially since you abandoned us here."

Fes glared at him for a moment. "You would like to tell me that, but it sounds as if you won't."

"No. But before I help you, there's something I will need from you."

"I'm not available for any jobs. Not again."

"Then I'm not available for information."

What would one job matter?

A lot. Especially if they were the kind of jobs Horus had offered in the past. The kind that wanted to use Fes, to change him and turn him into something he wanted to avoid. "What's the job?"

"I have a contact who hired me to reclaim an item of value. Given your recent connections, it's possible that you are the exact right person to take on this job."

"And why is that? Why can't you go?"

"My place is in the city, and there are certain items that I can't get close to."

Fes didn't like the sound of where this was going. "What sort of items are you looking for?" he asked carefully.

"The kind of items that I can sell, of course."

"And what kind of items are those?" Fes looked at him for a moment, feeling a sinking sensation in the pit of his stomach. "I'm not going to break into the palace for you."

Horus waved his hand. "The palace? Why would I ever think to ask you to break into the palace?"

"I have no idea what you might think to ask me," he said. "But you've mentioned my recent connections, so it seems to me you think to use that."

"You'd be wrong," Horus said, leaning toward him. His breath stunk of the bitter coffee that was preferred in this part of the city. "What my client is looking for is not in the city."

Fes looked around Horus's room. It was decorated with items that Fes suspected were all forgeries; none of them could be true dragon relics, but they would be excellent replicas. "If it's not in the city, then where is it?"

"As I said, the job will take you out of the city with my client. There is a certain item that must be acquired."

The connection between Horus offering to help him find the priest and the need to leave the city couldn't be a coincidence.

Had Azithan known?

Knowing what he did of the fire mage, Fes thought he had. The coincidence was too much to be otherwise.

"What's the item?"

Horus shrugged. "Probably nothing, but my client thinks it could be valuable. He's paying quite well, which means I will pay well."

"You've never paid well. Not me, at least."

"I'm hurt, Fezarn. Truly I am."

"You could offer Alison. You always favored her anyway."

"I think you might be better for what I need."

Fes stared at him, debating what he would say to Horus. He *wanted* to refuse, but there was the promise of what Azithan had said, and he *did* want to find his dagger. "Why wouldn't I just go directly to the client?"

Horus smiled widely. "That's not how these things work, Fezarn. I arrange the deals. You take them. Or not." He shrugged. "You could simply return to the palace and your new employer, but I suspect he'd be disappointed if you didn't try to learn the details of the job."

Horus knew Azithan sent him. This had been arranged. All of it. It had to be.

Why, though? What kind of game had he fallen into?

"What's the payment?"

"I can offer thirty gold shils."

Fes's breath caught. "Thirty? Now I know you're not serious."

"This time, I am."

How long had he lived in the slums, hoping for a score like that? Most of the time it had been coppers, nothing more, just enough to keep him strung along, forced to take another job, and then another.

Why would it change?

The answer was obvious when it came to him.

Because Horus knew he had another option. Which meant whatever he wanted Fes for *was* valuable.

"You've never paid anything close that before, so what would make you inclined to pay it now?" It would take a half dozen jobs working for Azithan to come close to that amount, and who knew when the next job might come?

"The client is quite eager to have this job done right. It's fortuitous you showed up here tonight," he said with a wide smile. "Without you, I would have had to hire two to three times as many people."

Fes thought fortuitous didn't *quite* fit. Planned, more likely.

But by who?

"Who's the client?"

"Does that mean you'll take the job?"

"For thirty gold?" Horus nodded. "Then I'll take it." Thirty *plus* whatever Azithan paid when this was all played out. That was almost enough to excuse whatever else he might be asked to do.

Horus departed. When he returned a few moments later, Fes wasn't surprised that he brought the priest Fes had stolen the bone from. He had the same striped hat and the same wrinkled eyes. Which meant that he had Fes's dagger. And it meant Azithan knew.

Why go through all of this?

The priest looked at Fes as if he didn't recognize him, but that had to be an act, didn't it? The priest had to recognize him, the same way that Fes recognized the priest.

"What's the job?" He asked it carefully, trying to feign ignorance when it came to the priest, not confident whether he had succeeded. The priest watched him, a serene expression on his face.

"Talmund has requested an escort acquiring an item."

"Just an escort?" Horus nodded. "What's the item?" Fes asked the priest.

"We can discuss the particulars on the road," Talmund said.

Fes turned to Horus, hating that he had to ask the next question, but now that he had the priest in front of him, it probably didn't matter. He could wait for him to leave Horus's home and grab the dagger. Only... the gold gave him reason to pause.

"If all you needed was an escort, you have better people for the job."

"Perhaps, but you were requested."

"Requested?" He shifted his focus to the priest. Talmund watched him now, no longer hiding the look of recognition.

"Do the job, and you may have your weapon back," the priest said.

Fes snorted. He'd had it wrong. This hadn't been all Azithan's doing at all. The priest had *wanted* him to know where to find him. "Quite the setup to get me here. Why me?"

"Let's say that I admired your particular skill."

"That skill isn't available for hire," he said, looking at Horus.

The priest glanced from Horus to Fes. "Perhaps you misunderstand. I need the skill I encountered in the market."

Fes frowned. Did he know how Fes had a way with the discovery of dragon relics? That it was the reason Azithan had hired him in the first place? The way he looked at Fes suggested that he might.

"And you'll hold your end of the bargain?" he asked Horus.

"I'll pay twenty percent upfront. The rest will be paid when you return."

The priest watched him, and for a moment, there was a flicker of more than simple recognition, but then it was gone.

Why him?

It had to do with whatever the merchant had wanted the priest to do, but what was it? And how much would Azithan pay when he was done?

"If I take this job, how long do you expect it to take?"

"A month, maybe two."

"A month? For thirty gold? You're not paying enough."

Horus watched him, and the irritated smile that he'd

been wearing spread wider. "Fine. Forty gold. I can't pay any more than that."

Fes glanced at the priest. Was he good for that much gold?

Even if he weren't, Azithan would pay for whatever he was after. Maybe not forty gold, but enough to make it worth his time. And with that kind of money, he could avoid taking another job for a while. A long while.

Was it worth it to work for Horus again?

It wouldn't be working for Horus, though. It would be working for the priest.

After pausing a moment, Fes nodded. "I'll do it."

"Good," Horus said, almost as if he had expected nothing else. "You will meet us in the morning."

"Meet where?"

"Near the market. There is another party that will be accompanying you."

Fes gritted his teeth. He could easily imagine what the other party would be, and if he was right, it meant that he would be traveling with the same family he'd stolen the bone from. How long would it be before that became awkward?

But then, the priest had hired him.

"I'll meet you in the morning."

He headed outside and found Alison waiting in the shadows. She looked over when he appeared outside of Horus's door, rising from her crouch. "Are you doing it?"

He frowned at her. She knew of the job, which meant she was involved. "It seems you'll find out soon enough."

"If you attempt to steal this and run off…"

"Why would I attempt to do that? Horus has made it quite clear what this job is and what it will pay."

"Yeah? How much did he offer you?"

Fes frowned. Could she have been offered more than him again? Horus had a soft spot for Alison, but doing so meant the priest was paying significantly more than what Horus would pay Fes. He had a hard time believing the priest had access to that kind of money.

What exactly were they going after? "What do you know about the job?"

She glared at him. "It seems you'll find out soon enough."

CHAPTER SIX

Fes returned to the palace after leaving Horus, sneaking in through the side entrance Azithan had shown him and up to the fire mage's private room, pausing every so often to admire the sleek dragonglass sculptures along the way. Most were of dragons, though some were of strange figures that reminded him of the totems the merchant from Toulen had shown him.

"You knew," Fes said after entering Azithan's room.

The fire mage glanced over from his seat near the hearth. Smoke curled around him and the haze in the air left Fes's skin tingling. "I knew what?"

"That Horus had been hired by the priest. You knew."

"I knew it likely."

"Why not tell me? Why throw me in there for the surprise?"

Azithan turned and stared at the fire crackling within the hearth. He crossed his hands over his lap, and Fes noticed something clutched between his fingers. It wasn't a dragon bone. The shape was small and round, far too smooth to be a bone like the one he had stolen from the priest.

"There are things I cannot fully ascertain, Fezarn. Your prior connections are valuable."

It troubled Fes that Azithan said something similar to what Horus had said. "He's after something. I was asked to provide protection as he travels north."

Azithan nodded. "From what you told me of the Bayars, I suspected that would be the case."

"Do you know what he's after?"

"I know what he *might* be after."

Fes made his way into the room until he faced Azithan, forcing the fire mage to look at him. "You care to tell me what it might be?"

"Think of what you've already seen. What do *you* think it might be?"

It wasn't hard for him to come up with an answer. It was what Azithan had sent him after in the first place. "A dragon relic."

And not just any dragon relic, not if Azithan was so interested in it. As a fire mage, he had access to authentic dragon relics. Plenty of them. They were what fueled his magic. Whatever Azithan was after would be something rare.

"A relic," Azithan agreed, "and perhaps one that we have not often discovered."

"Why me?" He glanced over at the fire, turning his attention to the flames much as Azithan did. "The priest wanted me. Was it only because I stole the dragon bone from him? Or does he want me for the same reason you wanted me?" They didn't talk about Fes's ability, but neither denied it. There was no point in it.

Azithan pressed his lips together. One hand squeezed the item he held for a moment, the knuckles going white. "It's possible."

"Not possible. Probable. That's the reason you want me to go, isn't it?"

Azithan glanced up at him. "You have a quick mind, Fezarn. You will learn much about yourself on a journey like this, much that will be useful."

"Useful to you? The empire? Or to me?"

Azithan turned to stare at the fire once more. "Yes."

They fell into a silence. There was no sound other than the steady crackling of the flames. Smoke drifted out of the hearth, and it was pleasant, a scented aroma that wafted into his nostrils, making his head swim.

"I take it you want me to claim the item the priest is after for you."

Azithan nodded.

"What's it worth?"

Azithan looked up. "More than you can imagine."

Fes chuckled. "I can imagine quite a bit, Azithan."

The fire mage stared at him. "Don't worry, Fezarn. If you manage to bring it back, you will be well compensated."

"That's not what I mean."

Azithan sighed. "I know it's not, and if what I suspect is right, you might be the perfect person to bring it to me."

"What if they stop me?"

"I trust that you won't fail me. You haven't so far."

Fes left and wandered the city for a while before returning to his home and resting. He had a restless sleep, and by the time morning came, he had an uneasy sensation in his stomach. Maybe it was nerves. Perhaps it was something else. He felt as if he were forced into taking this job, though he wasn't— not really. Azithan didn't require it of him, and neither did the priest, but they were paying him enough that he really had no choice in the matter. Besides, if he didn't take the job, he wouldn't be able to recover his dagger. That might be the greatest prize in all of this.

When Fes arrived at the market, he was prepared for the Bayars' anger at him stealing the bone from the merchant but found none. They had their tent packed, and their carts were loaded. No one seemed to pay any mind to him.

"You showed," Alison said.

Fes glanced over at her. She was dressed in dark leathers, almost as if she intentionally tried to contrast with the maroon and gold the empire soldiers wore. "I did."

"Your master let you play?" she asked with a sneer.

Fes glanced over at the distant palace. From here, it was little more than a massive structure rising in the center of the city. Over the last year, Fes had become comfortable making his way in and out of the palace, though he still snuck in, feeling more like a thief than a servant of the empire. Perhaps he never would feel like a servant to the empire and the Dragon Emperor.

And why should he? The empire didn't care about any individual. It hadn't protected his family. Azithan might pay well now, but how long would that last? There would come a time when Fes was left alone again, and he had to be prepared for that.

No. He had no allegiance to the empire. He cared about ensuring his own safety and future, and that was it. But first, he had to get through this. When he did, he might finally have enough.

"How long before we leave?" he asked.

"We've been waiting for you," she said.

He was the holdup? That wouldn't endear him to anyone, either. "I don't have a horse."

"Your master didn't lend you one?"

To be honest, Fes hadn't thought about asking for a horse. He probably would have, but considering the quality of the animals he saw lined up ready to depart the city, he suspected that any horse he might have been lent would have stood out. Maybe it was best that he hadn't asked.

"I don't have one. How about you let me ride with you?"

Alison glared at him. "I'm sure the Bayars can find something for you to ride. Or you could steal one from them. I hear you're good at that."

The priest rode up before he could answer. He tipped his head at Alison before glancing at Fes. "Horus thought that you might back out."

"Even though he offered to pay forty gold?"

"He wasn't sure whether your ties to the empire would overrule your desire for compensation."

"You know, you could just give me my dagger back, and we could be done with this."

"And then you would have what you want, but I would not have what I want."

Fes glanced at Alison and then the priest. "You wanted an escort. It seems you have one."

"They will travel with us some of the way, but our journey will go beyond where the Bayars will travel."

Beyond? The Bayars lived in the northern plains, and beyond there... "The dragon plains?" he asked, and the priest nodded.

Skies of Fire.

He had known they would be after a dragon relic but hadn't expected they would go as far as the dragon plains. "There aren't any relics there. Not anymore. The dragonwalkers pick them over."

"Perhaps, but perhaps not. What does it matter to you? You'll be compensated either way."

By Horus, but not by Azithan if he didn't bring the relic back to him. And while Fes didn't have any real loyalty to the empire, he *did* have some to Azithan. The fire mage was the reason he had managed to escape the slums.

"I suppose it doesn't." He smiled at Alison. "Now. About that horse."

She grunted and shook her head but dismounted and stormed off.

When she was gone, the priest turned to Fes. "I understand the two of you once had a better relationship."

Fes watched Alison. She was speaking with one of the merchants and waving her hands as she did. He could only imagine what she was saying to wrangle a horse for

Fes. "It was better, but I'm not sure that you would call it a relationship."

"No? What would you call it?"

Fes stared at the priest. "Not a relationship."

The priest studied Fes. The way that he looked at him made Fes wonder what Alison had told him. Could she have shared how they had been together for more than a year? Could she have shared with the priest how Fes had been unwilling to continue taking jobs from Horus for meager pay, bolting at the first opportunity for something more? After Azithan had offered the job, Fes had tried taking her with him, but she had refused. She could have had more, but she preferred what Horus could offer over what Fes had been promised.

When she returned with his horse, he took it without a word, climbing into the saddle. They headed off, quickly putting distance behind Anuhr and making decent time.

As the procession headed through the countryside, Fes glanced every so often at Alison or the priest, but neither of them said much. He was hired help, which meant that there wasn't much for him to say.

Alison had procured him a dark brown stallion, and Fes sat stiffly in the saddle. He didn't have as much familiarity riding and would prefer to have remained on the ground, walking alongside, or even riding in one of the carts that trailed behind them, but that wasn't to be his place.

The merchants moved quickly. He would've expected a slower pace as the wagons rolled along the countryside, but with three horses to each, they were able to keep a relatively rapid clip.

As they rode, the priest glanced over at one point, and he nudged his horse closer. "You're quiet."

Fes looked over briefly. The priest wore the same striped hat, and even his cloak had red embroidered along the sleeves. He squinted in the bright sunlight, and it made the wrinkles along his brow more prominent.

"What's there for me to say? You're paying for my presence. Isn't that enough?"

"Is there somewhere else that you would like to be?"

Fes turned away and looked into the distance. If he were able to remain in the city, working for Azithan, that would be preferable. "There are lots of places that I would rather be." He let his horse slow to avoid more conversation and tried to get behind Alison in the line, but the person riding behind him nearly ran into them.

Fes glanced back, apologizing briefly before kicking the horse to go faster. The horse began to gallop and moved far more quickly than he wanted. Fes pulled on the reins, hating how inept he felt while riding, but that did little other than twist the horse around.

When he was turned, he saw a trail of dust in the distance.

Alison reached him and grabbed the reins, turning the horse and slowing him back to her pace. "You're welcome."

He shook his head. "Do you see what's coming?"

Alison glared at him for a moment. "That's all that you have for me?"

He twisted in the saddle, ignoring the barb. Now wasn't the time for them to deal with their past issues. He'd rather not deal with them at all, but with as long a journey as they had before them, he wasn't sure he'd be so lucky. "Look back there. Do you see the trail of dust?"

Alison turned, but she wasn't as tall as him. "I don't see anything."

"It's coming from the south and moving quickly."

"I don't see it."

"Just because you don't see it doesn't mean that it's not there," he snapped, instantly regretting it.

"There are plenty of people who take this path," Alison said.

Fes didn't argue. He hadn't been outside of the city nearly as much as she had, so he didn't know what travel on the hard-packed roads leading toward and away from Anuhr might be like. He tried to twist in the saddle to position himself so that he could get a better view but wasn't able to see anything other than the very distant trail of dust.

"You need to relax," Alison said.

The priest frowned and veered his horse off the road, slowing enough that he got behind them before twisting around and moving at a faster clip again. "I only see a hint of a haze. I don't see anything else."

Fes shrugged. "Fine. I see what I see, and if you don't care, then I won't worry."

Only he found that he was worrying. Azithan had learned the priest was after something valuable, and if he could learn that, others might also.

Others like Carter.

She had chased many of the same things he had, but he'd not learned who she served. Whoever it was had money—and enough for Carter to be as well-established in the city as she was.

If it was her, he needed to know.

He pulled on the reins and circled around outside the caravan, ignoring Alison's protests as he did. From here, he had a much better vantage of everything behind them. The procession was incredibly long, all members of the Bayars, and all traveling back toward their home.

When he was free of the procession, the distant trail of dust in the distance was clearer—and moving quickly.

He hurried the horse and reached the others. Alison

glanced over, looking as if she intended to grab the reins of his horse before shrugging when he twisted away from her. "Someone is coming."

"This road is heavily traveled, Fes. It's nothing," she said.

Could that be what it was? Maybe it wasn't anything more. If that were the case, there wouldn't be anything for him to worry about.

"I'll have the wagons send scouts," the priest said.

"Talmund—"

"It's better to be cautious." He rode off, leaving Fes and Alison in an uneasy silence. Neither of them seemed willing to break it. When he returned, he motioned to the back of the caravan where word spread through the caravan. "They decided to speed along until we know for certain."

It took a moment, but the caravan began to move more quickly. Fes twisted so he could watch other riders as they left the procession and then returned. A murmuring passed along the line of wagons, and then they surged forward with even more speed.

"Who else might have followed?" he asked.

The priest glanced over. "Even merchants aren't always safe on the roads."

"The empire has soldiers patrolling—"

"Their patrols can't be everywhere."

Fes stared at him for a moment before smiling. "I

spent enough time in the palace to know the empire is generally secured."

"Is it? I've heard rumors to the contrary."

"Such as what?"

The priest looked away, not meeting Fes's eyes. They rode at a gallop now, moving quickly across the rolling countryside. Fes considered the priest, wondering what he might know. Considering the beliefs of those who followed the Path of the Flame, it wasn't difficult to determine what that might be.

"The rebellion? They wouldn't be so close to the city."

"There are those who question the rule of the empire."

"The empire has kept the people safe for over a thousand years."

The priest glanced over, and darkness clouded his brow. "At what cost?"

Fes laughed. "Those like you still get hung up on the dragons. They've been gone for centuries, no longer a threat. *Because* of the empire."

"What if they were wrong?"

Fes stared at him, uncertain how to even respond to that statement.

When he glanced back, he noticed riders wearing darkly colored clothing were moving swiftly toward them. There were limits to how fast the caravan could push the wagons. It wouldn't take long for the riders to reach them.

"What are they after?" he asked the priest.

"Money, probably," Talmund said. "I'm sure that's something that you know quite a bit about."

"Why would they think that there is money to be had here?"

"With all of the trade that takes place in the city, each wagon carries considerable wealth."

Fes peeled off, wanting to see for himself how many were approaching. He slowed his horse long enough to count probably a hundred riders. All of them were armed with swords and bows, more than enough to overtake the caravan. How had they not caught sight of them before?

None of them was Carter. At least there was that.

When he returned to Alison and Talmund, he said, "I counted at least a hundred. All wearing dark clothing. Is that the rebellion?"

Alison said nothing.

"It doesn't seem like enough to be from the rebellion, at least not the rumors I'd heard. But we won't be able to outrun them." And he didn't think the caravan was equipped to fight.

A shout sounded behind them. The battle had started.

There were screams, and the sound of metal on metal rang in the air. Fes looked over to see the priest sitting rigidly in the saddle.

Alison nudged him. "Our task was to get him safely to the north. From there—"

"We can't leave them."

He didn't dare slow his horse. If he did, they would be set upon even faster. The rear of the procession had taken the brunt of the attack, but it wouldn't be long before the rest of the attackers reached them.

"If you want to get paid, we need to keep him safe."

Fes glared at her for a moment. She was right, but that didn't make it any better.

"Grab his reins," he said, hating himself.

When Alison grabbed the reins of the horse, the priest shook his head. "I can't leave them. They need—"

Alison jerked him forward. "They have their own protection. You have yours."

They kicked their horses at a faster pace and streaked away. As they did, Fes glanced back to see the merchants under attack. Their guard engaged, but the soldiers were skilled, and they attacked in unison, quickly overwhelming the caravan. There was no way that the merchant guard would be able to suppress the attack.

"Come on," Alison urged.

Fes tore his gaze away.

Thundering hooves chased them, and he glanced back. A cluster of riders made their way after them. He considered turning to face them, but all it would take was a stray arrow to end him.

"Hurry," Alison urged.

They raced off, putting distance between them and

their pursuers, and eventually saw no sign of them. The priest still sat rigidly in the saddle, and every so often he would turn back, almost longingly, but he said nothing.

When it seemed no one followed, they stopped. A haunted expression remained fixed on Talmund's face. "We shouldn't have left them. Not like that."

"We didn't have any choice," Alison said. "If we would've stayed, we would have been overwhelmed the same as the rest of the merchants."

It was harsh, but not untrue. And Fes should have seen it too.

"But the Bayars—"

The image of the attack and the slaughter of the merchants flashed into his mind. If the attackers *were* thieves, they didn't seem as if they intended to leave anyone alive. "I'm sorry," he said.

They guided the horses to a stream and allowed them to drink. Fes climbed out of the saddle, looking around them. The landscape here was flat but otherwise fairly green. Clumps of trees grew, and there was still no sign of the distant mountains. When they neared them, they would be closer to finishing their task, but they had a month or more before they got there. It was possible that they might be able to make it more quickly, but there were limits to how fast the horses could go. And now that they no longer had the merchants for protection, it was down to himself and Alison to protect the priest.

The priest had a somber expression, and he rested one hand on the side of the horse as it drank from the stream. Day had begun to fade, and the sun was hazy overhead. Wind gusted, carrying the smells of grass and earth.

"I saw the way they attacked," Fes said. "Why were they slaughtering them if they were only after money?"

"There are evils in the world," the priest answered, as if that were enough.

Fes looked over at Alison, but she merely stared at him blankly. "Did Horus expect this?" He turned to the priest. "Did you?"

That might explain why he had offered to pay so much. Fes should have asked more questions and been prepared for the possibility that there was more to it than he had seen.

Neither answered.

"Why drag me along? If what you needed was protection, there are better ways of arranging that." Mercenaries could be hired for relatively cheap. He'd seen it often enough in Anuhr. Carter always kept a crew hired for various jobs, so it was possible.

"You will be more than capable."

"And we need to move quickly," Alison said. "A larger group couldn't have done that."

Fes stared at them, practically unable to believe that Alison would be so cold.

"Wait here," he said.

He climbed into the saddle, which seemed to stir Alison more than anything else. "Where are you going?"

Fes turned his attention to the east. "I'm going to see what happened after the attack."

"We know what happened," she said.

Fes looked over at the priest. "If there are attackers out there, I want to know what we have to avoid. Wait here."

"No promises."

"You don't want to do this without me, so wait here."

He galloped off, heading directly east. He rode the horse hard, keeping low and clinging to the stallion's neck. It was late in the day when he found the remains of the caravan. Flames consumed wagons, leaving most of them completely destroyed. Nothing remained other than the charred remnants of the brightly colored tarps. He found fallen bodies, burned the same as the wagons.

Everything was destroyed.

Fes dismounted and began to wind his way through the destruction. So many lives lost. It sickened him. It shouldn't—he'd seen people die often enough, especially living where he had in the city—but he couldn't help that he hated seeing a scene quite like this.

It made no sense. Why destroy the entire caravan?

And *how*?

The ground still steamed in certain places, and he meandered carefully through, not wanting to burn his boots. His cloak hung too low to the ground for his comfort, so he pulled it up, keeping the hem from dragging across the scalding earth so that it didn't ignite.

One of the bodies was less burned than the others. Fes approached carefully and turned away. It was a merchant who he recognized. Not the one who had identified him in the tent, but still it was one he had seen in the market.

The entire Bayars family lost.

They had come to the city to trade, no different than any other merchant hoping to strike wealth while in the Great Market. And they had found devastation instead.

Near what would have been the head of the procession, he came upon a flash of maroon. That was different than the clothing that the merchants wore. Maroon was the color of the empire and the emperor.

The emperor wouldn't have had anything to do with this, would he?

Not from what he'd seen. It had been men in dark clothing, not the colors of the empire. Had they come to protect the merchant caravan, only arriving too late?

Fes rolled the man over. He had a long sword still gripped in his hand, holding onto it through his dying moments. His face was charred beyond recognition, but there was no questioning the style of the blade or the cut of his clothing. A leather cloak twisted about him, making it difficult for Fes to fully determine, but that had to be what this was. This had to be the emperor's men.

Fes looked at the burned remains of the wagon with a new light.

Fire mages wouldn't do this, but what other answer was there?

He crouched, trying to piece together what he knew, but there wasn't enough for him to go on. The caravan had been attacked and, from the looks of it, soldiers of the empire had come to intervene, but had not been enough. Anyone willing to risk the might of the empire was reason to be careful.

Could it have been an arm of the rebellion?

Maybe he should have listened better when Azithan was speaking about the rebellion, but he was more concerned with what the next job would be and how much he would get paid.

Fes had started toward his horse when he saw a flash of blue.

It came from near one of the wagons. There wasn't much of the wagon remaining, only traces of what had been the wheels and twisted remains of what appeared to be a metal box. The box had been opened, and the contents splayed across the ground.

Fes hurried over to it. He leaned down, examining it, and realized with a start that it was the inert dragon pearl that he had seen in the market. The necklace that it had been attached to was gone, but the pearl itself remained intact.

Fes picked it up and nearly scalded his hand. The pearl remained too hot for him to safely handle.

He slipped his hand inside his cloak and grabbed the pearl. If it burned his hand through the cloak—or somehow burned the cloak—he would have to leave it, but it didn't.

He examined it. It was mostly black, though there were streaks of blue within it that seemed to catch the fading daylight. That was odd. He wondered what the colors meant, if anything.

He slipped the pearl into his pocket, turned away from the dead, and headed back to Alison and the priest. There was more to this job than he had anticipated. While the priest and Alison might not have expected this kind of trouble, they hadn't been surprised by it.

It was time for answers, but would they give them to him?

CHAPTER SEVEN

It was late when he found Alison and the priest. Fes hadn't been sure whether they would wait for him and had been a little surprised that they had. They remained camped near the stream and had built a small fire that crackled softly, consuming branches and leaving a trail of smoke that drifted into the night.

"That will be noticeable," he said as he jumped out of the horse's saddle.

The horse quickly tried to abandon him, going to the stream to drink. Fes let go of the reins at the water's edge before changing his mind and rushing over to grab them. If the horse decided to bolt, he wouldn't have anything to ride.

"We haven't seen any sign of movement since you left

us." Accusation dripped with her words. "You're lucky we waited for you. And I think we're safe enough here."

"You didn't see what I did."

"What did you see?"

Fes took a seat away from the fire but near enough that he could see what they were doing. "The caravan was destroyed."

"Destroyed?" Alison chewed on dried meat, staring at the fire rather than looking up at him.

"They were burned. Everything was burned. The whole thing was destroyed. There were empire soldiers there too, but they were dead." Fes let the words hang in the air for a moment. "Why destroy the wagons? Is it because of what you're after?"

Talmund sighed. "If what I've been told is true, we are after an item that could change many lives."

Fes chuckled. "That seems awfully dramatic. I thought we were coming after something that would be worth fifty gold or more."

"And wouldn't it be worth fifty gold—or ten times that much—for something that has the possibility of changing the lives of everyone within the empire?"

"And what is that?"

The priest studied him for a moment. In the faint firelight, his eyes seemed to dance, flickering with the flame, moving more vibrantly than what Fes would have expected. It was almost as if the flames were inside him rather than only reflected in his eyes.

"Tell me about yourself, Fezarn."

The change in topic startled him, and Fes stared at the priest for a long moment. Had Horus given the priest his full name? He hated it when people did, mostly because his full name was a reminder of everything that he'd lost. His parents had called him Fezarn, as had his brother, and when they were all lost, he had become Fes. It was less painful that way.

"That has nothing to do with what you're after."

Talmund leaned forward, practically leaning over the fire, and fixed Fes with a hard expression. "On the contrary, it has quite a lot to do with what we are after. And why you're here. What can you tell me about yourself?"

Fes glanced from him to Alison before shrugging. "What's there to tell? I'm an orphan and was raised in the slums of the city."

"Until you caught the attention of Azithan?" the priest asked.

"Until he abandoned us for the fire mage," Alison said.

Fes ignored her. "What does it matter to you?"

"I am someone your master has sought to suppress."

Fes laughed bitterly. "I don't think Azithan cares so much about the dragon priests."

"I believe he cares far more than he admits. Azithan searches for power. You have seen it."

"He's a fire mage," Fes said, shrugging. It didn't matter that he acknowledged that now, especially as it seemed as if the priest already knew. The fire mages used the ancient dragon relics to draw power, using the magic stored within the bones to fuel their spells. "And this isn't about Azithan."

"Perhaps not to you."

"Neither Azithan nor the emperor would have attacked the caravan. The temple has more real artifacts than anything the Bayars might have."

"I'm well aware of the stolen artifacts the fire mages possess," he said, reaching beneath his cloak and pulling something out.

Fes's breath caught. It was his dagger.

"It was a job. I've been working for Azithan for a while now. He pays well, and—"

The priest cocked his head, a half smile on his face. "Are you under the impression that I'm somehow angry?"

"I'm under the impression that you don't care for Azithan."

"And why should I?" the priest asked.

Fes stared at him for a moment before laughing to himself. "I suppose that you have no reason to."

"There is no reason to, and if you truly understood the empire, you would recognize that there has been a battle waging between the empire and people like myself for far longer than most realize."

"A battle? With the priests?" Fes shook his head.

"Where do you think your fire mage friend's magic comes from?"

"Everyone knows where it comes from. And why the fire mages have it. Without them—"

"Yes. The empire would have fallen to the threat posed by the dragons. Only, what if that's not entirely true?"

Fes glanced from Alison to the priest. "Is that what this is about? I have no interest in being a part of your plan to overthrow the empire, regardless of what you might pay."

The priest smiled. "And how would I be able to overthrow the empire? This is about finding something of value. That is all."

"Then why this line of questioning?"

The priest spread his hands out in front of him. "To get you to ask different questions. Nothing more."

"Such as what? About myself? That's what you're asking about, after all."

"Why won't you tell me about your family?"

"It has no bearing on this task," Fes said. He didn't talk about that with anyone, and certainly not with some strange dragon priest that he had been hired to escort north. He wasn't going to share anything with someone like this. Those were his secrets and his shame.

But then, Azithan had suspected the priest wanted him for his other talent, that which allowed him to find dragon relics. Could that be what Talmund was after?

"Then tell me about this knife." The priest tapped the dagger on his lap, and Alison leaned over, her eyes widening slightly.

"He has your dagger?" Alison asked, cocking a brow at Fes. She chortled loudly, the noise of it far too loud in the night. "You lost a dagger? Oh, that's just wonderful. I would never have suspected that you would lose something so precious to you. I know how proud you are of those stupid things."

"They're not stupid," Fes said.

"They're not always practical, either. What good is a stone blade when metal won't be damaged quite as easily?"

"What good is it? The good in it is that the blade never needs sharpening. The good in it is that it doesn't break. The good in it is that—"

"Only a few people have them," the priest said.

Fes turned his irritation from Alison and looked over at the priest. "What?"

The priest nodded, handing the dagger over to Alison. "Dragonglass is rare. The fact that you have them—and didn't sell them—is part of the reason I wanted you to accompany me." The priest twisted the dagger in his hand. He had a strange familiarity with the blade. "There have long been rumors that the ancient Settlers possessed such knives."

It was Fes's turn to laugh. "The Settlers? As in the Dragonwalkers?"

The priest nodded. "They called themselves by a different name, but yes."

"What did they call themselves?" Alison asked.

"A name that has been lost over the generations. The Settlers remained even after the dragons were slaughtered, their blood seeping into the earth and the dragon fields. The people who lived there, those known as the Settlers, inherited something unexpected. They have a connection to the long dead dragons, and that connection grants them power that others do not have." He nodded at the dagger that Alison still held, twisting it in her hands. "Blades like that are a marker of that connection."

He said the last softly, and he looked over at Fes. There wasn't any hint of an accusation. There was nothing other than curiosity.

"You never wondered why the tasks that your master assigns you are tied to dragon relics?"

Most assignments *had* been about the dragon relics, but how would Talmund know? "Why should I wonder?

Dragon relics are valuable to the empire and fire mages in particular. But why are they valuable to *you*?"

"The Priests of the Flame search for a different reason."

Fes chuckled. "I've heard of that reason. Can you really believe that bringing the dragon bones back together will somehow resurrect the dragons?"

"What I think is of little consequence. It is what will happen that matters."

Fes looked over at Alison, shaking his head. "Do you see that? Do you see what Horus has gotten us into?"

Alison shrugged. "It doesn't matter. What I want is to have enough money to not worry."

It was the same reason Fes had. The same reason he and Alison hadn't worked out when they had been together before. "And he paid his twenty percent, otherwise I wouldn't be here, but is this really what we want to be doing?" Alison looked away, and Fes turned his attention to the priest. "I will get you north. I will ensure that you find whatever it is that you're after, but I'm not getting caught up in your belief that the dragons will somehow return. Even if they did, what would that change?"

"Everything."

Fes looked at him, saying nothing. The priest was mad.

Fes stood and left the fire. Every so often, he would

glance over, and he would see that Alison still held onto his dagger. If what the priest said was true, then he was descended from the Settlers. The Dragonwalkers. He should be pleased by that knowledge since the Dragonwalkers had once been honored.

Had Azithan known?

Maybe he had. That might be the reason Azithan had pulled him away from the slums, giving him a chance to be something more. An opportunity to show that the empire still prized those who had that ancient connection.

Maybe there was nothing else to it other than the fact that Fes was skilled.

He eyed the priest a little longer, knowing he shouldn't let him get to him.

There was a reason the emperor banned the priests from Anuhr. They were a cult, crazy people who believed that the dragons were worthy of worship rather than something to be feared. It was better that they were gone. The dragon relics had *saved* the empire.

More than ever, he wanted to finish this job, but seeing the way the priest looked at him, he wondered if it would be even harder than he had thought.

CHAPTER EIGHT

The next morning, Fes stopped them atop a hillside and looked back. In the distance, there was movement. It wasn't the same movement they had seen when the merchants were attacked, but there was still enough activity to tell him that dozens of riders were behind them. They were near enough that he could make out the colors on their cloaks.

They were all brown. Leather.

That had been the same color of cloak that he'd seen on the man with the merchant wagons. Maybe they were rebels, but he feared they were mercenaries. Either way, they couldn't linger for long.

"It looks like we have company," Fes said.

"We need to stay ahead of them," Alison said.

"I'm aware of that," Fes said. "What exactly are we after that's so valuable? And how do so many know about it?"

"Others search for the same thing as your friend Azithan," the priest said.

"Like the rebels?" When he didn't answer, Fes pressed. "What kind of relic is this? How powerful an item are we talking about?"

"To the right person? Incredibly powerful."

"The priests?"

Talmund eyed him a long moment. "If what I've been told is correct, we might find an item that will help with a thousand-year-old task."

"The dragons." The priest nodded. That was what Azithan must have hoped he'd find—and return to him.

"Have you changed your mind about helping?"

"I've already told you what I require to do this job."

"At least you're honest," the priest said.

"Yes. That's our Fezarn. He's nothing if not honest," Alison said.

"I was never dishonest with you."

"No? You weren't ever terribly honest with me, either. You could have worked with me. You *used* me. We could have both gotten out."

"Will your history together cause a problem?" the priest asked.

"Fezarn decided he didn't need the people he'd worked with his entire life. When a different offer came along, he bolted. He was more interested in gold. That's all he's ever been interested in. He has no interest in anyone other than himself."

The priest looked over at him, and Fes said nothing. He wasn't about to reveal anything more, even if it might appease Alison. What did it matter? She was right—he *had* left. It was the only way to get out.

"We need to get moving and get ahead of these soldiers."

They turned their horses and headed north, moving quickly. The priest, a skilled rider guided them. His skill became increasingly evident the longer they went. Fes was saddle sore, uncomfortable from the days spent riding, and stiffened up each night. The priest showed no signs of that, though neither did Alison.

"They're gaining on us," he said late in the day.

"So it appears," Alison said.

"I think we need to try to lead them off."

Alison shook her head. "By that, you mean splitting up?"

Fes shrugged. "Split up, take the priest. One of us needs to create a different trail. If they continue to follow, we need to distract them."

"Fes—there's only the two of us with him. If one of us goes off, he'll be left in danger. That wasn't the job."

"The job was to get him to the dragon fields and let him acquire whatever it was that he wanted to acquire. We can't do that if we don't survive. We have to keep him alive." Fes looked back. It was easier to get a better count of their pursuit now. Maybe a dozen, maybe less. Still more than they could manage.

"I'll stay," Alison said.

Fes shook his head. "You're the better rider. You need to go with him and move as quickly as possible. Besides, you're lighter than I am, so your horse should be able to go faster."

"If you're trying to protect me—"

"I thought you said I didn't care about anyone."

She frowned and studied him for a moment. "You don't. Which makes this all the stranger."

"Just go. Let me try to lead them away, and then you two can continue north."

"What happens if they capture you?"

"Then I have to use the abilities Horus prized me for."

Alison studied him. Would she remember how much he hated Horus using him for his fighting prowess? She said nothing.

He held his hand out. "I'll need my dagger."

Alison glanced over to the priest, and he nodded slightly.

Fes almost swore at her. What was she doing, looking to the priest for permission to return his dagger? When she pulled it from beneath her cloak, she handed it over hilt first. Fes sighed, running his thumb along the blue sphere at the end of the hilt. There was something that was always comforting to him about that. He slipped it into the sheath as the priest watched him, saying nothing.

"Go," he said.

"What do you intend?"

Fes shrugged. "I don't know. I'm going to try to make enough of a path to convince them to follow. Find dry ground, anything that will mask the passing of the horses. It needs to be difficult for them to trail after you. I'm going to do the opposite."

Fes watch them angle slightly easterly, no longer heading directly north. From here, he could tell the ground would be rockier in that direction, but it also had sweeping hills that might conceal their passing.

How could he guide the mercenaries away without them realizing that he was doing so? They had to think they were still together but concealed just enough to draw their attention.

Fes veered his horse in the same northeasterly direction and headed toward the rock. When it started to slope upward, he wound around it. There was no sign of Alison and the priest passing, which he thought was good. Hopefully, the soldiers following him didn't have some other way of tracking them.

He continued to head in the same direction and

reached a peak. He looked out from here, searching for movement, and found the soldiers down below. Fes made a show of trying to get behind the rock, trying to conceal himself, and then began heading west.

Would that work?

If they were trailing after the priest, it might not matter. It was possible the soldiers knew which direction they would be heading and would try to head them off, especially if they knew what they were after. Fes had to find some way to lead them astray.

He slowed the horse to draw them to him.

He meandered around the rock, going slowly and looking back every so often. When he did, he occasionally caught sight of the soldiers. There were fewer now than when he had first seen them.

Maybe that was only his imagination.

Now they were close enough that they should see him. He had to be prepared to take off and keep them from going after Alison and the priest. He wasn't sure it would work, and even if it did, he wasn't sure how long he'd be able to outrun them. Not on horseback.

There was something he could do.

Fes led the horse around a bend in the path and looked for a way to tie him up. There was a strange rock formation, and he used that to secure the horse.

Fes unsheathed his daggers. It felt good holding both of them again. It felt good that he was once more in control of them, and it felt good having both in his hands. There was something right about it. He had felt *off* without the second dagger, and he knew that he shouldn't, knew that it shouldn't matter, but somehow it did.

It was a part of him, the same way that the anger he often felt was a part of him.

That anger had saved him. Had given him a purpose when he'd been younger. Horus—and others like him— had taken advantage of it. Used it. Become a fighter. A killer when needed. And had made him into something he had wanted to escape.

Now he would need to use it again.

Calling on the anger was easy enough. All he needed was to think of the caravan burned and destroyed, and the anger simmered beneath the surface. It was these men who were responsible for what had happened to the Bayars.

There came a flash of dark leather and Fes leaped at it, slashing with his pair of daggers, leading to a spray of blood and a grunt. He rolled past the fallen man, coming out into the open, and saw two other soldiers. Where were the others?

Fes jumped at the nearest man as he was attempting to ready his bow, but the man wasn't quick enough. Fes jabbed one dagger in his stomach and twisted as he pulled out, already moving off to the last man.

This man he needed to keep alive. He needed questions answered.

He yanked on the man's leg, pulling him from the saddle, and jabbed daggers into each shoulder. "Who are you?"

The man looked up at him. "You made a mistake."

"No. You made a mistake." The image of the burned caravan came to mind again, and he kneeled on the man's stomach, knocking the wind out of him. "Why did you need to destroy those people? Why did you need to kill everyone?"

"You don't understand. There is—"

An arrow sunk into the ground near him and Fes rolled off to the side, kicking the man in the head as he did so that he could keep him from following. He popped to his feet and looked around. Another pair of mercenaries approached. One had his bow out and was nocking another arrow, and the other had a sword in hand.

Fes sprinted toward them. Anger boiled within him, the same sort of anger that sometimes caused him to lose control. The same anger Horus had loved to take advantage of. It was that anger he had wanted to get away from.

This time, he embraced it.

Fes jumped and slashed at the nearest man. The man brought his sword around, but Fes was quicker and carved through his chest with the twin blades. He split him apart and, in that motion, he blocked the oncoming sword and then climbed on top of his saddle, launching from there to the other soldier. He landed with his knee crashing into the man's head, and they tumbled together from their saddle, with Fes coming to land on top of him.

Catching his breath, he looked around, searching for signs of other attackers, but there were none.

Fes wiped his blades off. He made his way back to the man he'd stabbed in the shoulders, but he was either unconscious or dead. With the way his head twisted off to the side, it was possible he was killed.

That wasn't Fes's plan. He hadn't intended to kill the man, but he didn't feel guilty about having done so. With what they were doing, the way they were coming at them, Fes couldn't allow himself to feel guilt. They wouldn't need to keep him alive and would have done the same to him as they had to the merchants.

He climbed onto the rocky point, looking to see where the other soldiers were. If they were behind him, he needed to be ready. He had taken out five, and thought that he'd seen at least a dozen, but where were the rest?

Unless they had split off.

Fes swore under his breath. Why couldn't the soldiers make this easy?

Then again, he wouldn't be easy. Not with this. It would force him to attack and to embrace violence that he sought to suppress. And it wasn't even that he disliked violence—he was far too good at it to hate it—but he didn't like the way the rage boiled inside him. It was a sensation that he tried to ignore, but he was never good at it, not nearly as good as he wanted to be. When that rage burbled up within him, bad things happened. People died. Sometimes too many people died.

Horus had used that part of him, and Azithan had rescued him from it.

There was no sign of the other soldiers.

He hurried down the rock and jumped into the saddle and directed the horse off. He needed to move quickly, but he wasn't a skilled enough rider to make the speed that he needed.

As he rode, he tried to suppress the anger inside him. It was surprising how mad he'd been at the sight of the charred caravan. He hadn't thought so at the time, but since then, he had felt a growing anger at what the soldiers had done.

Why would he have cared?

Because they didn't deserve to die. That was all there was to it.

He let his mind go blank as he rode, keeping his focus on the rocks around him, searching for movement but seeing nothing. Riding quickly, Fes raced along, urging the horse for increased speed, and still didn't see any signs of Alison or the priest. They couldn't be that far ahead of him. He had delayed, but he hadn't delayed that long. Then again, they were riding quickly. They weren't waiting for him.

Near dusk, he saw a campsite in the distance.

It was smoke at first. There was nothing other than that, but it was far more substantial than what it should have been. It wasn't Alison and the priest. He hadn't expected it to be them because they wouldn't have taken a break, not this early. There was still too much light in the sky, which meant that there was too much time in the day for them to be traveling.

That meant someone else.

Who else would be out here in the countryside? There weren't many places this far away from the city for people to travel, not in this direction. There were other cities, and some villages, but he hadn't come across any of them so far.

As he approached, he decided he needed to be careful.

Fes found a clump of trees and tied off the horse. He approached on foot, keeping his daggers ready, not confident whether these were other mercenaries or whether this would be something more benign.

It was a wagon.

Not just a wagon, but a merchant wagon.

"You can come out of the dark," a voice said.

Fes frowned. He'd heard that voice before, but where?

He made his way forward, moving hesitantly at first

until he caught sight of the person near the fire. It was the Toulen merchant who had been kind to him.

He reached into his pocket, fingering the figurine the man had given him, wondering again what it symbolized and why the man had thought to make a gift of it. There had to be some other reason, and he had thought that he would never know.

"I know you. You're the man who helped stop the thief."

Fes frowned. "What are you doing so far from the city?"

"I departed not long after you visited. My sales had been drying up, and it was time for me to return."

"This way?" Toulen was more to the west, and they were heading far too north for him to think that the merchant was heading in the right direction.

"You must not travel outside of the city very much," the merchant said, motioning for him to join him by the fire. Fes was surprised to see that the merchant wasn't alone. There was a young girl with him. She couldn't be more than ten, maybe twelve, and she sat with a knife in hand, carving a chunk of wood. Fes smiled to himself. Perhaps that was how the merchant had made so much.

"I don't," Fes said.

"If you had, you might be aware of activity along the borders that make passing difficult. Certain places are better than others, and as we need to return to Toulen, it's easier to head toward the northern pass and then back south again."

"That would have to add quite a bit of time to your travels."

"It adds time, but it is quite a bit safer than any other way that we could have gone." The man looked at him for a moment. "You come on foot?"

Fes nodded to the darkness. "I left my horse tied up by some trees. I wasn't certain what I would come across."

"Why?"

"It's not safe here, either. I've come across soldiers." When the man arched his brow, Fes nodded. "Not empire soldiers."

"There shouldn't be any other soldiers in this part of the empire. Your emperor has kept these lands as safe as they can be."

"I just ran across five of them not more than a few hours back."

"Five? And what happened to them?"

"They won't be following, if that's what you're worried about."

The merchant stared at him for a moment, and then he stuck out his hand. "I'm Theole."

Fes shook the man's hand. "Fes."

"Fes? That's an interesting name for someone from the empire."

"Blame my parents."

The man smiled and motioned to the girl. "This is my daughter Indra."

"It's just the two of you?"

"Just the two of us. We left my wife and my younger son in Toulen. Trading is so good at the Great Market that we just had to come, but the timing was not ideal."

"You came even though the journey was as dangerous as what you said?"

"What choice do I have? I need to provide for my family, and trade in Toulen isn't what it is here. The people of the empire love their trinkets from Toulen."

"Most think they have some sort of power imbued in them."

"What's to make you think that they don't?" Theole asked.

Fes reached into his pocket and began to run his hand along the figurine that Theole had given him. "Are they magical sculptures?" he asked, eying the girl.

"Perhaps not quite as magical as what the people of the empire would prefer. Most think that if it's not a dragon relic that it's not as valuable."

"Apparently," Fes said. He needed to catch up to Alison and the priest, but he didn't like the idea of leaving these two here, with the soldiers who might potentially attack. After what happened to the Bayars, Fes didn't like the idea of anything happening to Theole, especially because the man had been kind to him. "I don't think that you should stay here," he said to Theole.

"We don't have much choice. Our horses are tired, and we needed to rest for the night. You're welcome to join us. We don't have much to offer—it is only the two of us—but I will share what I can."

Fes squeezed his eyes shut. "I'm not hungry," he said, though his stomach rumbled and attempted to betray him.

"You might be hungry if you knew we had Toulese cheese. You haven't lived until you've had our cheese. I have some flatbread, and you can have a few bites. It's filling."

Fes looked out into the night. It would be difficult to search for signs of Alison and the priest in the dark, but if he stayed, it was possible that they would get even farther ahead.

Not only that, but he still didn't know what happened with the seven other soldiers he'd seen.

He looked over at Indra and decided he couldn't leave them alone. At least the priest had Alison, and she wasn't entirely helpless. She was skilled with her sword and would provide protection that their ability to outrun the mercenaries couldn't. Indra, on the other hand, didn't appear to have any sort of protection other than her father, and he didn't have the look of a fighter.

"I suppose it wouldn't be all bad to have a fire to rest near tonight."

Theole beamed. "Wonderful. Indra and I could use the company."

"Let me go bring my horse over."

Theole nodded, and Fes hurried off to the clump of trees and grabbed his horse, walking him back to the wagons. When he returned, he heard Theole and Indra discussing something and caught only the tail end of their argument.

"But we don't know him," Indra said.

Theole glanced over and smiled. "We know him well enough. This is Fes. He stopped a thief in the market."

Fes forced a smile. He might have stopped a thief, but he'd been a thief often enough that any good he might have done halting the thief for Theole was canceled out by all of the times that he'd stolen for Azithan—or for himself.

"Come, sit. Let the fire take away your worries."

Fes took a deep breath, glancing out into the night once more before joining them at the fire. He didn't think that the fire would take away his worries. More likely than not, it would add to his concerns and remind him of what the soldiers had done to the Bayars, and the anger that occasionally threatened to boil up within him would return.

He looked over to see Indra watching him, her movements paused as she stopped the carving, staring at him with a flat expression. Fes forced a smile, but he wasn't sure how convincing he was.

If he left, what would happen to Indra and her father?

Nothing good. At least if he stayed, he could offer some measure of protection, if only for the night. And then they would have to find their own—or he would have to hunt down the rest of the soldiers.

CHAPTER NINE

F es jerked awake at a snapping sound. The fire was burning down, and he wondered if perhaps he only heard the fire beginning to fade. When he looked up, he saw Indra sitting in front of the fire, watching him.

Fes rubbed the sleep from his eyes. It was late enough that the moon wasn't visible, leaving only stars shining overhead. Theole snored nearby, resting near the wagon, one hand on one of the wheels. Did he think that Fes would try to steal the wagon while they were sleeping?

"Who are you?" Indra asked softly.

"I'm someone passing through."

"You're more than that. Why are you out here? Father said he saw you in the city, and that you stopped a thief, and that's good enough, but that doesn't explain why you're out here."

"I took a job that brought me here," Fes said, sitting up and crossing his legs. He shifted so that he kept the daggers from digging into his side.

"What kind of job?"

"The kind of job that's worth a lot of money."

"How much money?"

Fes shook his head. "It doesn't matter."

"It must be an awful lot of money if you're willing to come all the way out here. How long did it take you to get here?"

Fes shrugged. "A week and a half. Maybe a bit less."

"We've been at this for two weeks." She looked over at her father, watching him for a moment. "Father thinks that we can make it to Toulen again, but the stories out of the city made it seem like that might not be possible."

"What kind of stories?"

"Stories of the rebellion."

He hadn't heard enough stories—nothing concrete enough to act on. "They're just that—stories. The empire has enough soldiers to ensure safety within its borders." The words sounded hollow to him after seeing the empire troops cut down while trying to save the Bayars.

"The rebellion moves along all the borders. At least, that's what my father tells me," she said. "We came through it on the way here, but we nearly didn't make it. Father had to move more quickly than he wanted to, and we didn't take many breaks. We lost one of the horses..."

Her gaze drifted over to the line of tied-off horses. "And we didn't make nearly as much in the Great Market as we had hoped."

"Why is that?"

"I don't know. I haven't been to the Great Market before, but Father says that sales weren't as good as they had been before. Maybe the people of the empire no longer care for Toulen carvings."

Fes reached into his pocket and pulled out the carving that Theole had given him. He set it on his lap, looking at it.

Indra gasped softly. "Where did you get that?"

"Your father gave it to me. When I stopped the shoplifter, he thought that I might like this. It's quite an interesting figurine—or totem. I'm still not sure I know the difference."

"In Toulen, a figurine is designed to be decorative while a totem is a call for a blessing."

"What kind of blessing?"

"With that? That is a blessing for power."

Fes looked at the figurine. There seemed to be a strange sense of movement to it, though maybe it was nothing more than the firelight dancing along it. The carving seemed to twist, the body spiraling with the arms splayed out similar to another figurine that he'd seen. "Well, your father gave this to me after I stopped the thief."

"Father shouldn't just give those away, especially not that one."

"Why?"

"That's a powerful blessing. It has to be given to the right person."

"What if I am the right person?"

Indra stared at him for a moment, seeming to try to determine whether he was or not. "I don't know. Maybe you are, but he still shouldn't have given it to you. Blessings are difficult to create, and that one particularly."

Fes looked over at the knife and the hunk of wood that was lying near her. "Is that what you're making? Are those totems?"

Indra glanced down and picked up the hunk of wood and the knife. She ran her thumb along the carving, almost a loving gesture. "These aren't totems. I'm not skilled enough yet to make them. My father and my mother are the ones who have the necessary ability."

"Then what do you make?"

"Figurines," she said, smiling at him.

She stood and went over to the wagon, pulling open a door and rifling through it for a moment before returning. When she did, she set three figurines on her lap. Each of them was incredibly detailed, depictions of people and something that looked like a wolf. They were almost lifelike, and in the fading, flickering flames of the fire, the shadows danced around them, practically bringing them to life.

"You made these?" Fes asked, looking across the fire at her.

"Once I demonstrate the necessary skill with these, I can progress to work on even more intricate work. Eventually, father says I will be able to make totems."

"Why is there such skill needed to make totems?"

"I've already told you. Totems are blessings."

"And by blessings, you mean..."

She smiled. "We have many different blessings in Toulen. The ability to imbue totems with power is but one."

Fes looked down at the totem. It seemed to be made of stone rather than wood and very detailed though, surprisingly enough, not nearly as detailed as what he saw resting on Indra's lap. The figurines that she had carved were even more detailed than the totem that Theole had given him.

Power. That was what she had said.

"What kind of power?"

"When we make totems, we put a part of ourselves into the creation. That helps to grant the blessing and gives it strength."

She said nothing more, and Fes had the sense that she wouldn't. "Why does this one seemed to be less intricate than yours?"

"Because it is," Indra said. "Part of the blessing takes away the detail. It blurs it. Otherwise, the blessing would be too powerful."

"I don't understand."

Indra stared at the totem for a moment before shaking her head. "That answer is for those of Toulen."

Would any in the empire know? Azithan might. When he returned, he would have to ask about the totems. They couldn't be *that* powerful if they were willing to sell them at the Great Market. "Am I in any danger carrying this with me?" he asked, smiling.

She gave him a look of disgust. "It's a great honor to be given a blessing, especially one like that."

"But your father was selling others like this."

"He wasn't selling them, not in a traditional sense."

Fes started to laugh but realized that she wasn't joking. "If he wasn't selling them in a traditional sense, how was he selling them in a nontraditional sense?"

"They were meant to be traded."

"Traded for what?"

She looked over at her sleeping father. He was breathing heavily, snoring occasionally, and had a firm grip on the wagon wheel. "For things that we can't acquire in Toulen."

"What kind of things?"

"Things."

Fes waited for her to elaborate, but she didn't. He only shrugged. "If you want it back..."

Indra shook her head. "If he gave it to you, then he meant for you to have the blessing. I was just surprised that he would, especially as he doesn't know you."

"And he has to know me to give me a totem?"

"In order to find the right totem, he would need to know you."

"He wouldn't know others coming to the Great Market."

"Not at first, but that's why we stayed as long as we did."

Fes held up the totem, running his finger along it. There was something smooth that reminded him of his dagger, though it was probably the stone. The totem itself was cool, though not unpleasantly so.

He stuck it back into his pocket, careful not to break it. "Can I use the blessing?"

"You don't get to choose. The blessing will decide when—and if—it will work for you."

Fes smiled. "It sounds like there's something magical to the totem."

"Because there is," she said, motioning around them.

He looked around and saw for the first time that there were similar totems set all around the campsite. "Why are they there?"

"To protect us. We can't travel through here by

ourselves safely. Father thought that setting the totems around would protect us."

"Is it to ward off others?"

"It prevents them from seeing us."

"But I saw you."

"And you shouldn't have been able to. I think it's because you had one of our totems that you were able to see us. Otherwise..."

Interesting. Could they be useful in other ways?

He could think of plenty of ways to use something that would mask his presence. Would it work with the soldiers? But for him to do so, he'd need to take the totems from Indra and her father, and considering what they went through, he didn't want to do that. They needed to get to Toulen, and with soldiers along the road, it might be dangerous.

Fes rolled over, needing to get back to sleep. In the daylight, he could go looking for Alison and the priest. Hopefully, he could find them before the soldiers. He didn't want to embrace the rage again, though he already knew that he would if it came to that.

The rest of the night passed with an interrupted sort of sleep. Fes awoke a few times and each time that he did, he thought that he saw Indra watching him. She didn't trust him, but why would she be the one to sit up through the night to hold watch? Why not Theole?

He had dreams, though they were faint and in the

back of his mind, and they left him troubled, feeling as if he were missing something. In those dreams, he saw rings of smoke and flashes of color, but nothing that made sense. When he awoke an hour or so before dawn, he sat up with a cold sweat. Indra was asleep, but Theole was up.

"You don't need to be awake on my behalf," Theole said.

Theole sat with his back against the wagon. He was running his thumb across something, and it took Fes a moment to realize that he was using a piece of stone, almost as if he were smoothing it with his thumb. The air nearly had an energy to it, like lightning following a storm.

"Indra told me about the totem," he said.

Theole paused and flicked his gaze toward him for a moment before looking back down. "Did she? I wonder what she told you."

"She told me that the totems carried blessings and that the one you gave me represented power."

"I gave you a totem that represented what was in your heart," he said. He continued to press on the stone, and every so often, Fes noticed a crackle, almost of insects but seeming to come from the stone.

"How do you know what was in my heart?"

"It doesn't take long to know a man, especially one who carries around a dragonglass dagger."

Fes breathed out. "How did you know?"

"I can feel it. There is a certain heat to it. You didn't need a blessing to be blessed, but I thought that perhaps having the blessing might help you augment what you already possess."

"And what is that?"

"That is the power that burns within your heart. I can't see it, not clearly, but I can feel it."

Burns. Like the anger he'd always tried to suppress. "I don't know what you're feeling."

Theole pressed on the totem, which emitted a soft rumbling. "Perhaps it is nothing. I have been at this for so long that it becomes difficult for me to fully understand sometimes."

"Why *did* you give me the totem?"

"Because you needed it."

"I didn't need it. I wasn't at your tent to purchase anything."

Theole studied him a long moment. As he did, the friendliness on his face faded, if only briefly. Darkness replaced it and then was gone. "There may come a time when you will have need of that blessing, when you will have need of that totem."

Fes looked over at Indra. "She said she is only able to carve figurines for now."

With this, Theole looked upon Indra with a loving gaze. "She will be more talented than me. She has such exquisite control at her age, and in time, that will only get better."

"If the totems have power, why do you sell them?" It was the same question that he had asked of Indra, but he hadn't gotten much of an answer from her.

"Did I sell it?" Theole smiled and turned his attention back to his work. "There are plenty of other items that I had for sale, but the totems are unique. They are not meant for most people."

"Why have them there?"

Theole continued to stare at Indra and didn't answer.

Fes looked around. In the growing dawn, it was easier to see the totems that were arranged around the campsite. They were almost an equal distance apart, forming a circle around them. They were different, each of them unique, and he wondered if that was important.

"Do they really work? She said they help you avoid detection."

Theole nodded to Indra. "We will see. If we make it back to Toulen, then they have worked. For now, they help her relax. Otherwise, I don't think she could sleep."

He pressed on the stone again, and this time Fes felt a distinct rumbling. He looked up to see thick storm clouds rolling in out of the east. Thunder rumbled again, though it was distinct from what he had just heard, almost as if whatever it was that Theole was doing to his totem had elicited the thunder.

"You may stay with us if you would like," Theole said.

"I need to get back to my job."

"But you're alone," Theole said.

"I hadn't been, but with the soldiers..."

"I see. You offered yourself up."

It had been something other than that. He had no intention of sacrificing himself. "I didn't offer myself, but I was willing to try to draw them away."

"And it worked," Theole said, nodding knowingly. "You see? It doesn't take long to know what's in a man's heart."

"Others remain. I did everything I could to try and limit the damage, but I wasn't able to stop all of them."

"And that's what you intend to do?" Theole got up and began to collect the totems around the campsite, putting them into a pouch that he carried on his waist. "You will complete your task with these soldiers?"

"I don't know if I can stop them," he said.

"And yet, you stopped the others."

"Only by..." He shook his head. It didn't matter how he had stopped the mercenaries, only that he had. "They did something. They harmed others."

"Perhaps they are mercenaries and not soldiers at all. Or perhaps they are the rebellion. There is danger in these lands."

"There's danger everywhere."

"Perhaps," Theole said. He stopped in front of Fes and

handed him something. Fes frowned as he realized that it was another totem. "This may help you on your journey."

This was a figure that appeared to be kneeling, almost as if bowing in prayer. The features were soft, smooth, and he couldn't imagine that Theole had created them with only his fingers, but he hadn't seen him carving with anything else. What else could he have used?

"Use it carefully, Fes. You have power within you. I could sense that when I first met you. But there is something else that longs for freedom you keep bottled up."

Fes stared at him. Did he know about the rage that threatened to erupt? "There's nothing in me."

"More than you allow. And like all things, it will reveal itself in time. Take this."

"I don't know that I should. Indra said they were powerful."

"All totems are power. That is how they were made. They are blessings, and shouldn't a blessing carry with it a certain sense of power?"

"What kind of power does this have?"

"The kind that will help you on your journey."

Fes took it and stuck it in his pocket with the other. He looked down at Indra while she was sleeping, looking peaceful. A girl like that didn't deserve to be put into danger on the road. "Be careful," Fes said. "If the northern pass is too dangerous, turn back. Don't risk the rebellion simply to force your way back home. There are other ways."

"There are always ways home," Theole said, "only some are more difficult to find than others."

"If we meet again, I'll do whatever I can to help you."

Theole studied him. "If we meet again, I would ask only that you protect Indra."

Fes glanced at the girl. "I will. I promise."

He grabbed his horse, climbed in the saddle, and nodded to Theole. As he left, he glanced back, struggling with how he was feeling. Theole had been kind to him twice. Both times had been unnecessary, and even after the last year spent with Azithan, not knowing the same hardship of his youth, that was something strange. He patted his pocket, feeling the heaviness of the totems within. They served as a reminder that perhaps there was some good in the world.

CHAPTER TEN

I t was late in the day when he saw the husk of the
forest. Fes paused, staring at the remains of the trees,
little more than fingers of what appeared to be rock,
though he knew better. This was the Issana Forest, a
place burned to husks centuries ago by the dragons and
one of the areas closest to Anuhr where someone could
see the effect of those ancient creatures. Fog hovered
over the ground like a haze of smoke, adding to the
impact. Seeing a place like that made it all too easy to
imagine how dangerous the dragons once had been.

He turned away and continued north. As he rode,
dark clouds rose in the distance. Fes had been riding
hard, trying to outrun the sound of the thunder rolling in
from the east. Every so often, a drop of rain would strike
him, and he swore to himself, trying to move more

quickly. He wanted to outrun the rain, at least put enough space between himself and the rain so that he could find a place to hunker down for the night.

Had the rain come, he would've missed the dust cloud in the distance.

Could that be Alison and the priest?

It was too large. Even without getting close to it, he knew that. That meant there was another explanation, though the only other reason that made sense would be the other soldiers.

Hopefully, there were no more than seven. If there were, would he be enough to keep them from catching up to Alison and the priest?

He slowed, wanting to keep a certain space between himself and whoever might be in front of him. When it was darker, it would be easier to approach, and he wouldn't have to fear quite as much about who was there and what they might be after.

It was nearly dusk when rain started.

It came down gently at first. It was a drizzling sort of rain and more uncomfortable and unpleasant than anything else. Thunder followed, practically pushing the rain faster and faster, forcing it toward him. Fes wrapped his cloak around himself for warmth, but as the drizzling rain changed over to a steadier rainfall, even his cloak wouldn't be enough. And then it began a sheeting rain.

There wouldn't be any place for him to camp out for

the night, not where he could get out of the rain. The land around him was mostly flat, and there were no trees, nothing to provide much protection. He thought about hiding beneath his horse, but the stupid creature would probably trample him while he was sleeping.

He crested a gently rising hill, and lights flickered in the distance.

A village.

It wasn't a large village, no more than a couple dozen homes, but even a village of that size would have someplace for him. And for the soldiers.

Would Alison and the priest be there too? There was no reason Alison wouldn't stay in a village overnight, especially as it would provide a certain level of protection. If they were there, the soldiers would reach them without them having a chance to react.

Fes kicked the horse up to a gallop and reached the village shortly after full dark.

Lights flickered in some windows, and he climbed off the horse and walked it inside the village. He looked for signs of an inn, anything where the soldiers might stay for the night, and found it near the center.

He tied the horse up before entering.

There was a dining hall, if it could be called that. It was simple, a row of two long tables with benches on either side. A smattering of people sat on the benches, some grouped together and murmuring while others ate alone. A hearth at the far end of the room crackled with a warm fire and Fes made his way toward it, wiping the rain out of his hair and dripping in a pool across the floor.

He took a seat at the table, and a waitress approached. She was full-figured and cast him with a strange gaze. "Where you coming from, stranger?"

"Desyl," he said. It was a city near enough to where he thought he might be that it should be believable. He didn't want anyone to know that he came out of the capital.

"What are you doing here then?"

Fes tried to think about what he could remember of the maps of this area. What answer could he give it would be believable? "I'm heading toward Hovn." It was a city on the other side of the empire, and far enough that he would have to stop along the way. Hovn was known for its goods, and well enough that it shouldn't draw too much attention to the fact that he was heading that way.

"That's a dangerous journey, friend," a man said from the table near him.

Fes looked over. He was an older man who was missing two of his front teeth, and he grinned at Fes while taking a bite of vegetables.

"Why is it dangerous?" he asked.

"Not many make that journey, not with the rebellion being what it is."

"I don't put a lot of stock in the rebellion," Fes said.

The man scooted closer to him and leaned in. "No? Most people around here might not put much stock in the rebellion, but I can guarantee you that folks who come from Desyl would. From what I hear, the rebellion has already made its way there. Even the emperor's men can't tamp it down."

Could the rebellion be strong enough to risk attacking the army?

If so, *could* that have been the rebellion that had attacked the Bayars? Talmund hadn't thought so, and Fes was inclined to believe him, but what if it had been?

Could he be chasing rebellion troops back to their stronghold?

The waitress returned with a plate of food and set in front of Fes. He picked at a lump of overly done meat, shredding it off before stuffing it in his mouth. His stomach had been rumbling, and it was good to have food.

The other man kept watching him. He'd have to engage him in conversation or find some other way of placating him. "Are you from there?" Fes asked in between bites.

The man shook his head. "No. I come from Boldon."

That was to the south, almost to the capital. "Then you don't know. There might be rumors, but that's all they are. Rumors. Those of us who live there know the truth."

The man grinned. "I suppose that's right, though I suppose if I were from there, I would know that the rebellion has begun to press in, pushing in on the emperor's lands." He leaned closer to Fes again and flashed another smile. "Rumor is that they are after the dragon fields."

Fes snorted. "Who isn't after the dragon fields?" He glanced over at the man. "The emperor has long used the dragon fields to hold power. A fire mage like him would be able to use those artifacts to push back the rebellion." He shrugged. "Those of us from Desyl don't care so much about that. The emperor doesn't make himself known all that much, and so long as trade keeps coming through, what do we care?"

"There were others that came through here earlier in the day," the man said

"What kind of others?"

Man shrugged. "The kind of others I don't mess with. I see them, I see their swords, see the hint of crimson on their cloaks, and I know better."

Crimson. That meant the empire.

And not the soldiers he'd feared.

Could they have taken care of the other soldiers? If so, then he didn't have to worry about the priest. The empire's soldiers would ensure their safety. "Yeah? The emperor sent men through here? It seems a little out of the way."

"Not if the rumors out of Desyl have any meat to them." The man took another bite and sat upright. "Then again, as you're from there, you would know, wouldn't you?"

He ignored the man as he began to eat, digging into his meat. The food was stringy and tough, and the vegetables were mushy, but it was food. It was better than the dried jerky that he had been eating on the road, and the mug of ale set in front of him was warm and pleasant. The fire felt wonderful against his skin, helping dry out his cloak. All he needed was a few hours here, and he could get back on the road, let the storm pass, and be back after Alison and the priest.

"Anyone else come through here?" Fes asked.

"No one that matters. A group of men and a woman, but they didn't stay long, trying to get ahead of the rain." He scratched his chin. "Though there was a priest. We don't see too many priests down in Boldon, though I know they're there. Most of the time, they stay to themselves, or they make their way up to the dragon fields, doing their weird worship of the remains."

Fes snorted. He tried to hide his interest. "How long ago was the priest through here?"

"They said he came a day ago. Didn't stay long. Had something to eat and hurried down from here. Kind enough man, though you know the priests, they have a bit of a temper to them."

"I can't say that I do know the priests."

"That right? Even in Desyl?"

Did the priests have more of a presence in Desyl? Maybe he'd made a mistake throwing that out as his homeland, though it had seemed safe enough. What were the odds that someone would know rumors of Desyl here? "How can you ever know really know the priests?" Fes asked, deciding on diversion.

The man shrugged. "That's a question I can't answer."

Fes tried to pull away, getting tired of having this conversation with the man. Now that he knew both soldiers and the priest to have come through, he wanted nothing more from him.

When he finished eating, he took a chair and dragged it over near the fire, sitting close to it with his cloak wrapped around him. He might have drifted off and jerked awake when a minstrel began playing.

The inn was emptier now, not nearly as many people sitting around the tables, and Fes wondered how late it had gotten. The waitress who had been serving him was nowhere to be seen. When he stood, stiffness left him sore. As he reached the door and peeked outside, he saw that the storm had mostly passed.

It was muddy, and as much as he might want to leave, he was bound to turn an ankle and lose the horse if he ventured out tonight. It was better to wait until morning, better to wait until there was more daylight, which meant that he was holing up here for the night.

When he turned back, three men stood in front of him.

"You have the look of someone who works for the emperor," one of the men said. He was tall, almost as tall as Fes, and had a muscular build. His hands were stained, and there was a quiet sort of strength about him. He was a man to be careful with. The other two with him were shorter, and they stood off to the side, deferring to the first man.

Now he was getting accused of working for the emperor outside the city? It was bad enough in the city, especially when people like Alison felt that lessened him, but what about him looked like an empire soldier here?

"Is that a problem?" Fes asked. "Last I heard, we're part of the empire."

"We might be part of the empire, but that don't mean that we have to have love for the emperor."

Fes leaned close, unmindful of the fact that the man could punch him. These fools needed to be careful, especially as there had been actual empire soldiers through here recently. "Is that right? No love for the emperor? What happens if he sends his men up here?"

"I thought you said you didn't work for them."

"Well, now I seem to remember I didn't answer that

question. You came here accusing me of something, and I simply said nothing."

"Like the empire. It's done nothing here. They let *them* move through here, openly attacking—" One of the other men grabbed his arm, cutting him off, but the man shook him off. "If he's with the empire, we're going to get them to pay attention to us."

"I'm not here to argue," he said.

"No? Then what *are* you here for? And if you're not with empire, are you with *them?*"

Fes frowned. What was taking place here?

"Just step back and let me leave." He pulled open his cloak and grabbed each of his daggers.

The man snorted. "You don't scare us. There's just you. No soggy man coming into the middle of Jalden all alone like this is to be feared. Now, the woman with bright red hair and angry gleam to her eyes? That's a different matter."

Fes squeezed the hilt of his daggers more tightly.

The man at the table had mentioned a group of men and a woman. And now the red hair? That was Carter. It had to be.

She *was* here.

Attacking a caravan wasn't the kind of thing Carter would typically do—and it wasn't the sort of thing she would have the *power* to do.

That meant something else.

Could her master have been drawn out after this item?

Fes had wondered who employed Carter for the last year and had gotten no closer to getting any answers. Would they finally come now that they were outside of Anuhr and away from the emperor?

What had Horus gotten him into?

It was time for him to go, but he had to deal with this first. "Go sit down," Fes said.

"Sit down? I think it's time for you to be leaving."

"It's middle of the night. I'm not going anywhere," Fes said.

"You can sit outside and sleep just as well as you can inside."

Fes looked past the man, intentionally ignoring him. "Is this your tavern?"

The man shook his head.

"Then you have no reason to be throwing me out. Even if it was your tavern, I haven't done anything."

"Don't matter. We don't want you here. There's been too many strangers coming through here. And too much happens when they do."

Fes pulled the daggers from their sheath and stepped toward the man, jabbing the daggers up toward his neck, stopping short of slicing into his throat. "You'll step back and head home. Or to your rooms, if this isn't your home." Based on their comments, Fes suspected it was. "Either way, the only other option is dying."

The other two men acted more quickly than Fes would have expected and reached his arms. They pulled him back, lowering his daggers from the other man's neck.

The first man punched and connected with Fes's stomach, knocking the wind out of him. He held onto his daggers, refusing to let them go.

He struggled to catch his wind but needed just a moment. Let the man get closer...

He kicked.

He caught the man in the chest, driving him back, so he stumbled over a table. The two men holding onto Fes's arms tried to pull him off to the side, but Fes twisted and managed to bring his wrists down, and the daggers sliced through their forearms.

Anger began bubbling within him.

Fes resisted the urge to let it consume him. It would do no good for him to get into that place here. These men were fools, but that was it. They didn't deserve to be slaughtered.

The men on either side of him grabbed for their wrists, clasping their hands over them as blood spurted.

"You might want to have those looked at," Fes said.

He stalked toward the first man and slammed the hilt of each dagger into his chest. It was enough to hurt, but not enough to do anything more. The man fell back, and Fes followed him, kicking him again and sending him toppling into the tavern.

Checking to ensure the man wasn't dead, Fes wiped his daggers on the man's jacket, then stuffed them back into their sheaths.

He looked around, but no one else in the tavern seemed to be paying much attention to him.

He took a deep breath and made his way back to the hearth. He knew better than to let someone get him riled up, but maybe now he could rest peacefully. At least until morning. Then he'd have to go and see what Carter was up to—and maybe finally learn who she worked for.

CHAPTER ELEVEN

F es left the tavern in the early daylight. The ground was still muddy from the rain the day before but was already starting to firm up and dry out. He was thankful for that and rode the horse carefully, sticking to the main roadway leading out of the village. As he did, he glanced back. The village seemed smaller in the daylight, though maybe that was only the overcast sky. A couple hundred people probably lived here, not much more than that, and they were far enough away from Anuhr that they wouldn't have the same protections as larger cities or those closer to the capital. Would that be why the three men had acted the way that they had? Could they resent the empire?

Fes had resented the empire for most of his life. It was

only when Azithan had pulled him from the slums that he'd begun to feel differently about it, though would he continue to feel that way if his jobs suddenly ceased? It wasn't as if he had an allegiance to the empire. It was to Azithan.

Tearing his gaze away from the village, he rode swiftly, heading north toward the dragon fields. That would be how he'd find Alison and the priest, though by now he might be far enough behind them that it wouldn't matter.

There was no one else out on the road yet this morning, which he was thankful for because it let him keep a good pace. More importantly, there was no other sign of Carter and the soldiers—or Alison and the priest.

He had taken too long coming this way. The delay with Theole and Indra had kept him for a night, and then there had been the delay in the tavern from the rain. They would have been far ahead of him.

He needn't have worried.

It was evening on the second day after leaving the village when he came across a group of riders far in the distance. When he crested a small rise, movement in the distance caught his attention. At first, Fes hadn't been sure what he saw, but the longer he rode, the more it became clear. Mercenaries.

Would that mean Carter?

If Carter was up ahead of him, there might not be anything he could do, especially if she outnumbered him. He wouldn't have put it past her—or the person who employed her—to hire dozens of soldiers. But would they have been enough to destroy the caravan? That seemed beyond even Carter.

Fes put the horse to a gallop to investigate, prepared to run were it necessary.

He reached them far more quickly than he should have. None wore the crimson and gold of the empire. All were dressed in dark leathers much like those he'd seen attacking the Bayars. There were ten in total, and two had bows pointed at him. There were far more of them than he had planned on.

Fes unsheathed his daggers and leaped off his horse as the arrows streaked toward him. They sunk into the side of the horse and the creature collapsed.

He'd have to take one of theirs, but that meant he'd have to survive.

Fes leaped at the nearest man. He was holding a bow and was preparing another arrow, but Fes reached him before he could. He sliced through the bowman's arm, the blade severing bone as easily as it cut through flesh.

The man screamed as he fell from his saddle.

Fes dropped to the ground, rolling underneath the horse, and came up springing at the next man. This one had a sword which he brought around. Fes deflected, jabbing with his left hand while blocking with his right. He cried out, and the air filled with the sound of his anger, heat boiling through him, the rage of the attack surging.

Fes welcomed the anger. He embraced the rage.

He jumped and crashed into one of the men while kicking at another. They'd been sitting too close together, and the one fell from his saddle while Fes swung around, jabbing his dagger into the first man's chest.

That left six people.

The mercenaries had recovered, and they converged on him.

One nocked an arrow and Fes started toward him, but two men blocked, both bringing their swords up.

That was too much for him. He couldn't stop them, and as much as he wanted to blindly attack, he knew better than to rush toward them.

Was there another possibility?

Fes reached into his cloak and pulled out the dagger that Tracen had made for him. It was well-made and excellent steel, and he threw it at the man with the bow.

He was the one who could do the most damage, at least from a distance.

That left five.

Five against him. Five armed with swords, pressing in with a circle as they squeezed toward him. The swords had a much better reach than his daggers, and he knew better than to confront them like this.

How was he going to handle five swordsmen?

He needed every bit of that anger, every bit of that rage, and he needed to find some way to let it fill him, consume him, and draw upon the strength that always came when it did.

Thinking back to his parents, he tried to remember what it had been like when he'd let that anger fill him. He'd been overwhelmed by it then, losing control, and only Benjan had managed to bring him back from it.

It nearly gutted him thinking back to it, and he hated that he had to, and hated that he used it this way, but losing them had been the most devastating thing that ever happened to him, and it was when he had lost them that he first fell into the rage.

Everything went blank.

Fes leaped, and he somehow cleared a slicing sword and jabbed his dagger into one man's eyes. He spun around, slicing with the other dagger, and he decapitated the next man. His hands were warm and sticky, and that angered him even more. The daggers didn't deserve that kind of blood, yet they seemed to welcome it.

He twisted, kicking out, and his boot connected with the stomach of one of the men, who doubled over. Fes jabbed up with his knife, catching him in the eye. Two more.

He twisted, coming around, and he caught this man in the chest.

Where had the last gone?

He was missing.

Fes looked up, wiping away the blood that had sprayed all over his face, and saw the man riding off, galloping east.

Fes stood rooted in place as he looked around.

The rage began to ease, beating in time with his heart as it slowed, and he shook, trying not to think about what had happened. He'd killed, much like he had the night his parents had died. He couldn't keep allowing himself to fall into the rage—it was the reason he'd wanted to get away from Horus—but it was easy out here. Almost as if Horus had known that he'd need to reach for that part of him again.

Fes took a moment to search these men. He forced himself to do so, knowing that he needed to see what they were after. Two of them had nothing more than a few silvers. He pocketed that. It was no use letting money go to waste, especially when he had earned it.

One of the men had a woven bracelet in his pocket. Fes tried not to think about what that meant but failed. It was an engagement charm, given to him by the woman who he now would no longer see ever again.

When he reached the fourth person, he found something surprising in his pockets. This was a carving, and it took Fes a moment to realize that it had come from the Bayars. The style was similar to what he'd seen in their tent.

These men *had* been involved in that attack.

And they were likely with Carter. That still didn't explain the fire, which meant there were others. But why would a fire mage work with Carter?

The rest of the men had nothing.

Fes stood and grabbed two of the horses. They had remained here while he had killed these men, which told him that they were seasoned horses. He needed to find the priest and Alison, but more importantly, he needed to get ahead of Carter.

But what if he was too late?

It was possible Carter already had reached Alison and the priest. As much as he wanted to avoid her, he needed to know. And the man who had ridden off would lead him to her.

Fes climbed into one of the saddles and headed east.

The rain helped him track the other rider. The man must've been riding the horse hard, likely terrified of the fact that one man in a fit of crazy rage had managed to kill ten—well, nine. Fes was thankful for the fact that he was able to track him, and was grateful for the fact that the rain had granted him that ability, and he kept a rapid pace. As long as there was daylight, he didn't think that he would lose sight of the other man.

Near evening, another village appeared.

The tracks led directly to the village. Fes knew where he had to go, just as he knew that Carter would be there. How many more mercenaries would there be? Would he be able to get to Alison?

They had seen dozens when the merchant caravan had been attacked. Did that mean that there were still dozens remaining?

If so, where were they?

It was possible that they had been sent back to the capital, but why leave only a small contingent, unless they didn't expect any difficulty?

Maybe they hadn't expected Fes.

This was all Horus's fault.

He must have known; it must have been the reason he'd wanted Fes's involvement, but then this hadn't only been about Horus. It had been the priest who'd wanted Fes. Had he known what they would encounter? If so, why send only two of them? Why wouldn't he have wanted more? Two wouldn't be nearly enough, not against dozens of mercenaries. And not against Carter.

Carter would be at the inn, if there were one.

He came upon it near the center of the village.

It was louder than the last, and Fes was careful to tie up the two horses he had stolen near the back of the tavern. If he had to escape, he could head out the back and make quick work of getting away.

Hesitating at the door, he considered turning back. Alison and Talmund might not even be here. They could have gotten ahead of Carter, but something told him they hadn't.

And there was another advantage to coming in this way. Carter would know that he followed. If nothing else, she would hesitate.

Or so he hoped.

He pushed open the door and stepped inside.

It was arranged similar to the last tavern, with rows of tables and benches along them. The tables were crowded, dozens of men in here, and his gaze drifted around until he came upon the one person that he least wanted to see —and the one person that he most needed to see.

Fes searched the inside of the tavern as he made his way over to Carter. She was laughing loudly while eating, waving her hands in the air while talking to three men around him. Her bright red hair was braided and hung down her back.

There was no sign of the man who had gotten away, but he had to be here.

Which meant Carter had to know that Fes would be on his way.

A direct approach. That was the only way to go about this. If Carter would know that he was coming, it only made sense for him to approach her directly.

Unsurprisingly, Carter sat at the end of a bench. It was an easier way to get out, with only one person on her side to get away from. Fes found an empty chair and dragged it over, slamming his fist on the table as he took a seat.

Carter looked over at him lazily. A sneer parted her lips. "Fezarn," she said, drawing out the name.

Fes glared at her, and when someone to his left reached for him, Fes grabbed his wrist and snapped it quickly. "Have your men stay back."

"Impressive. I didn't know that Fezarn had such anger inside him. I could have used you long ago."

"You were never going to be able to use me," he said.

"No? Others would say differently." She smiled, tilting her head so that the flames caught her bright red hair, almost matching it. "I didn't think that you'd actually leave your master like this."

Fes gritted his teeth. She wanted a reaction out of him, and he had to do everything in his power to avoid giving her what she wanted.

"Why are you here?"

"I imagine I'm here for the same reason as you. Why are you here, Fezarn?"

"A job."

"Job?" Carter asked with feigned ignorance. "Why would Fezarn need to take a job? Why would he be out here when Azithan is back in the empire?" She leaned toward him. "Unless this is for Azithan. And if it is, I must ask why you had to come all the way out here?"

"A job," he repeated.

"A job that has to do with a priest. And dragon relics of incredible value." Fes must have reacted because Carter smiled. "Yes, I'm well aware of your job. Probably more than you."

"You followed us."

"I followed the priest. I wonder, what do *you* know about your job?"

"What's that supposed to mean?"

"Only that you aren't prepared, Fezarn. You are skilled, and the men you've killed will cost me, but you can't cross the dragon plains with only a priest and another thief."

"Why not?"

"You know so little, don't you? A shame they hired you. Anuhr is much more interesting with you there." She winked at him. "But without a mage, you can't even reach what you seek."

"Why is that?"

She smiled, and something was condescending about the way she did it. "What you're after takes more than a dragon relic thief. More than a priest. It requires a *mage*."

Fes stared, unblinking. Could Carter be telling him the truth?

Why would she lie? She obviously believed that he

couldn't reach what he was after, not without help they didn't have.

Had Azithan known?

If he had, why not say something? Or better yet, come with them?

He looked along the table. The men watched him, and he had the uneasy sense that he wasn't going to be getting away from this easily. There were more here than he could fight and escape.

The only way was to bluster and make them afraid of him. With what he'd done already, they had reason to fear him. "I'm going to get to it before you do," Fes started. "Regardless of what you think, I'm not going to stop until I get there, and—"

Carter shrugged. "Go ahead and try."

With that, she nodded.

Fes jumped to his feet. Everyone at Carter's end of the table—nearly a dozen—all got to their feet and converged on him.

He stared at Carter, glaring at her for a moment.

A dozen. Could he take out a dozen?

He'd just managed to survive against nine, and that was when he allowed the rage to consume him. Could he do the same against more than that?

Carter watched, as if trying to determine what Fes might do. For what it was worth, Fes was trying to decide what he would do. Was it worth it to attack? Or should he wait?

He took a deep breath, backing up. Now wasn't the time to fight Carter. Now that he knew she was here, now that he knew that she didn't have the priest and Alison—if she did, he would have said something by now —he needed to get out of here and regroup. He needed to prepare for the next move, though he wasn't sure what that would be.

He located the back door to the tavern, thankful he had tied the horses up there rather than leaving them out front.

Spinning quickly, he bolted for the back door and into the alley outside, grabbing the reins of the horses and jumping into the saddle. Surprisingly, the men didn't follow him.

Then again, maybe it wasn't surprising. Fes had killed off a dozen of them, so they would be cautious.

He rode off, going quickly. He headed north, cutting across the ground, no longer trying to stick to the trails. He wanted to make good time. He was willing to ride throughout the night, and with two horses, he thought that he could.

And what had he learned? He had learned that Carter knew of the dragon relic and that it was incredibly valuable. And he had determined there was a fire mage with her, though he hadn't seen them.

With a fire mage, they would be able to cross the dragon plains. And they'd be able to recover the relic. If what Carter said was right—and he had no real reason to doubt it—how did the priest intend to do the same without one?

CHAPTER TWELVE

His whole body ached. He'd been riding hard throughout the night, changing up horses so that each didn't grow too tired from the strain of bearing him. By the time daylight streaked across the sky, Fes thought he was more tired than the horses. He still had not come across any sign of Alison or the priest. How far ahead would they have gotten?

They should have gone north and toward the dragon plains, but maybe he'd been mistaken. Maybe whatever the priest was after would be found somewhere else.

He nodded off while riding, his head bobbing forward. Every so often, he would jerk awake and look around the landscape before drifting off again. When the sun was high in the sky, he calculated that he had traveled much farther than he had anticipated, and reached a road leading to the north.

Movement startled him awake. Maybe it was only his imagination, but the more that he looked, the less he thought it likely.

Could there be more of Carter's men? He didn't think that Carter had gone ahead of him, but maybe she had other mercenaries scattered all over these lands. She had resources, but even that seemed more than what he'd expect from her. The attack on the caravan was more than what he would have expected from her.

Fes shifted, trying to get into a more comfortable position, but any way that he shifted on the saddle remained incredibly uncomfortable. He was ready to be out of the saddle and be at the destination, but he was only two weeks out of the capital.

Could he handle another two weeks—or more?

No. The better question was whether he could handle another six weeks. Once he reached his destination, he still had the return trip.

And somehow, he had to stay ahead of Carter. Even when that was done, then he had to deal with the way that he intended to get back, and somehow reach Azithan or Horus.

He continued to ride, moving carefully as it became clear there were others along the road. As he neared, relief swept through him.

Alison.

She was alive, and the priest appeared unharmed, which meant that they had managed to stay ahead of Carter and her mercenaries. After the days he'd spent searching for her, he hadn't been sure that he'd even be able to find her again. They could have taken many different directions. Thankfully they'd headed this way.

When he approached, Alison spun and nearly attacked before sheathing her sword. "Fes." Was that annoyance in her tone? "Do you know what I almost did?"

"I'm glad to see you too."

"How did you find us?" She looked behind him, and he turned, worried that Carter had sent soldiers after him, but the road was empty.

"I kept going north."

The priest studied him. "What happened?"

"What do you mean?"

"You're covered in blood. It looks to be dried, so I presume that you are unharmed, but I am curious as to what happened."

Fes looked down. His cloak *had* been covered in blood. He hadn't paid much attention to that, though he would have gone into the tavern coated with it. It was surprising that he hadn't elicited much more of a reaction than he had. "The mercenaries."

"How many?" Alison asked.

"About a dozen fewer than we had before," he said.

Alison cocked her head, studying him. They had stopped in the middle of the road with open plains on either side, the mountains far in the distance. They were out in the open, far too exposed for Fes.

"A dozen? You killed off a *dozen* mercenaries?"

"Not all at once," he said. "And there's more. Carter is here."

She swore softly. When Alison swore, there was something almost sweet about it, though that was rarely the case with her. It reminded him of the days long ago when they had been together.

"I take it that you know him?" Talmund asked.

"I know her," Alison said, watching Fes as she spoke. "Those of us who still work for Horus have had far too much experience with her. Can we stop her?"

Fes shook his head. He doubted that Alison had the same experience with Carter as he did. Since working for Azithan, he had gotten to know Carter far better than he wanted. "She has too many men with her for us to stop."

"It's not about stopping. It's about getting ahead of her," the priest said.

Fes considered him a moment before revealing what had bothered him during the last day. "She said we need to have a fire mage to reach the plains." Would the priest answer? Would he deny that to Fes?

"Normally, she would be right."

"Normally?"

"There is something Carter has not planned on that allows us to reach the dragon plains."

Fes studied the priest, meeting the man's dark eyes. Was he telling the truth? He wanted Fes to accompany him, and had maneuvered him into doing so, but why? What reason was there for him trying to draw Fes into all of this?

"Whatever you're both after is incredibly valuable. Enough so that she managed to hire a fire mage."

"Are you sure of that?" Alison asked.

"I saw the Bayars caravan after the attack. It was destroyed. Burned. I don't know much about fire mages—"

"More than most of us since you work for one."

He let the comment roll past him. "But I suspect an attack like that requires a fire mage. And with what she claimed..."

"How would she have managed to hire a fire mage?" Alison asked.

Fes shook his head. That was a good question. He thought the fire mages all worked on behalf of the emperor. To involve a fire mage in this meant it was valuable. Incredibly valuable.

Unless the fire mage was the one who had hired her.

"We are after something with incredible power," the

priest said. "There is much power in the dragon fields, but you must know where to look."

"Power enough to bring back the dragons, but why would anyone want the dragons to return?" Fes asked. "Do you intend to use the dragon to attack the empire?"

It was a thought that hadn't occurred to him before, but it made a particular sort of sense. More than anything, that might be reason to send Fes out of Anuhr, and with the priest. If true, it meant Fes was serving the needs of the empire more directly than ever.

Alison looked over. "Fes—"

"I've wondered about the intent of this mission all along. With Carter's involvement, it tells me something incredibly valuable is out there." And more than that, if Carter were out there—and with a fire mage—it was possible *she* was serving on behalf of the empire.

But then there was the issue of the slaughtered soldiers.

"Something like what you've described *could* be used to overthrow the empire."

"You don't know what you're talking about," Talmund said.

"No? Then why would anyone want to bring back the dragons? The stories about them are terrifying. Stretches of land that still smolder, all these years later. We even passed one on the way here! Places where life refuses to return. Destruction unlike anything we have ever known. That's what would happen if the dragons returned."

"It's what the empire has done with the dragon remains that is terrifying," the priest said. "They have taken something noble and pure and have twisted it, turning it into a way to control and enslave."

"Enslave?" Fes asked. "That seems to be quite the extreme way of putting it."

"You might not consider yourself enslaved, but you are. Everyone who once settled the dragon fields has been enslaved. The only people who oppose this enslavement are the priests."

Fes chuckled as he looked over at the priest. "I don't hold any particular love for the emperor—" Alison laughed, and he shot her a hard glare—"but the Arashn Empire provides protection."

"Protection from what?" the priest asked softly.

Fes shrugged. There had been peace for so long that it was hard for him to know what the empire protected against. "You might not like the empire, but what's the alternative? Letting places across the sea rule us? Toulen?"

"The empire only wants us to believe that we're protected. It's how they have subjugated many for as long as they have."

"And if the dragons were to return?" The idea of it was impossible. Fes didn't know much about those times

—he wasn't the kind to care about the histories—but stories of the dragons still remained. They were powerful creatures, and wild. Why anyone would think to worship them was beyond him.

"The world would once more know their majesty," the priest whispered.

Fes didn't argue. He needed to see this through, if for nothing more than to bring whatever they were after back to Azithan. He might not know the emperor, but he *did* know Azithan. He had offered Fes an alternative to life in the slums.

"Let's keep moving," he said.

The priest studied him before nodding. They moved swiftly toward the north, and every step jostled him uncomfortably. The longer they went, the more he began to think it might have been better simply refusing this job to avoid time on horseback.

"One thing I've never understood is how dragon artifacts can be used for power," Alison said after they'd been riding for a while.

"Alison—" Fes started.

She shot him a look. "Not all of us went off to take a job with a fire mage, Fes. Some of us don't have the same experience with fire mages."

"Do you really still blame me for taking that job? It got me away from Horus. It gave me the opportunity to make money—real money—not the kind Horus was willing to pay."

"It took you from me," she said softly.

"Horus would have done that eventually," Fes said.

She turned away from him, focusing on the priest.

The priest considered them for a moment, and Fes imagined that he debated whether he would reveal a secret before glancing at Fes and pulling a small item from his pocket. It appeared to be a curved piece of stone. From where he was, Fes could see the striations along the stone, and there was a faint shimmering of deep red around it.

"This is a dragon claw," the priest said. "It came from a smallish creature, probably no more than two years old when she was slaughtered."

Fes leaned forward, curiosity getting the best of him. As often happened when around dragon artifacts, he felt a tugging sensation. Even if he didn't see the striations along the bone streaked with a hint of color, he would have known the relic to be real.

"Now watch," the priest said. He held the claw between his fingers, almost as if he intended to slash at Alison. Fes wasn't sure what they were supposed to watch for, but as he stared at the dragon claw, it began to change. First, it began to steam, almost as if it had been sitting out in the sun all day and then submerged into an icy bath. The hints of reddish glow became apparent, oozing from the striations.

It lasted only a moment. Long enough for both Fes and Alison to see it, but then it faded, returning back to the same appearance that the claw had before the demonstration.

He'd seen Azithan use his magic only a few times, but Alison hadn't been around a fire mage.

"That's it?" she asked.

"It? I just showed you the power that a one-thousand-year-old bone has, and you question whether that is it?"

She shrugged. "It just seems like there would have been... more. If all it does is glow like that, why is there such an interest in bones?" Alison said.

"It glows for him, but a fire mage would be different," Fes said.

She eyed him, annoyance burning in her gaze, before turning to the priest.

Talmund twisted the dragon claw in his hand before slipping it into his pocket. "That was nothing more than a small demonstration. That dragon claw has been with me for decades. I have drawn upon the power stored within that claw many times."

"Does using it deplete it?" Alison asked.

"There is only so much energy stored within these relics. When it is gone, so too is the residual power within them. The dragon priests are able to access that power, but we are cautious not to deplete it. We recognize that when that power is gone, there may not be any more. If we have any hope of restoring the dragons, there must be some residual power."

"And the fire mages?" Alison asked.

"The fire mages care little about restoring the dragons. They never have. Why do you think the dragons were slaughtered in the first place?"

"They were killed because they were dangerous," Fes said.

"Dangerous to who?" the priest asked. "If you ask the people of the dragon plains, they would tell you that their ancestors never feared the dragons. It wasn't until the first fire mage realized that there was power to be had by slaughtering the dragons that they began their hunt. Much power had been used over the years, and now... now very little remains."

Fes stared at the pocket where the priest had placed the dragon claw. He couldn't imagine the time when the dragons roamed free, and couldn't imagine the danger that must have existed, especially if that claw, nearly the size of the priest's finger, was from little more than a baby.

"That's why the Bayars wanted you to come?" Fes asked.

"He wanted me because I am one of the true priests of the Relash. We have long served the dragons, and we have long searched for a way to restore their power, and if that fails, to bring them peace."

"You don't think that the dragons have any peace?"

"The way they were destroyed took away any chance the dragons had for peace. The way their bones were torn apart, ripped from them, has taken away any chance they had at peace. We attempt only to bring them back together, to help the dragons find whatever lasting peace that they can. That is what we will do."

"It seems all a little bit..." Fes waved his hand. He didn't quite know how to describe it, other than he felt as if the priests and what they searched for was strange.

"Only because you don't believe," Talmund said.

The landscape had begun to change, and Fes stared. Mountains were rising in the far distance, but near enough that he could start to make them out. The northern mountain chain was immense and incredibly rugged, which made Fes thankful that he wasn't traveling that far. He was content to reach only the plains that stretched in front of it.

The dragon plains.

The dragon plains were said to be difficult to cross. The ground still steamed from the blood of the long dead dragons, and though no more bones remained, there was plenty of evidence of the destruction—and the power—that once had been here.

"Have you ever visited?" the priest asked.

Fes glanced over to see the priest watching him with a curious expression. He shook his head. "No. I've never visited. There has been no reason for me to come here."

"Even though you are descended from the Settlers?"

"I don't know who—or what—I'm descended from."

"That's not true," the priest said.

Fes ignored him and focused on the road ahead of him. They were moving at a reasonable pace, but he still worried about what would happen were Carter to attempt an attack. The path led them around a bend, and in the distance, Fes caught sight of movement.

"Be ready—"

As he said it, two men jumped from either side of the path, crashing into his horse. Fes was spun around and twisted in his saddle but wasn't able to right himself quickly enough.

He heard the sound of fighting and saw Alison swinging her sword at another attacker, while still another tried to grab her horse's reins.

Fes jumped from his saddle, pulling the daggers free. He couldn't fight from horseback, and these men were on foot, which meant that he would be better off facing them on foot.

He jumped toward the nearest attacker and jabbed the dagger into his shoulder. He twisted as he did, and the man screamed.

The person Alison fought called out as well, and he

looked over to see that person falling, dropping to the ground with half of his arm missing.

They were Carter's men. He could tell it from the style of fabric, the dark browns and blacks, but surprisingly, they weren't that skilled at fighting. There weren't even enough of them to do enough to Fes or Alison, let alone the priest...

Fes looked over to see what they had done to the priest, and too late he realized that the attack on himself and Alison had been nothing more than a diversion. They had planned it so that they could draw him and Alison off, and now that they had, the priest was isolated. One of the attackers held him tightly, and a knife was thrust into his side. The attacker kicked the horse and sent it surging forward.

Fes reached for his own horse and climbed into the saddle, only to discover that the horse had been lamed. One of the legs was injured, and the horse could barely walk.

He looked over at Alison. She had quickly dispatched her attackers but was in the same situation as him. There was no way for them to go anywhere.

Fes stared at the priest, watching as he was led away. He started after them, attempting to run after the mercenaries, but they were on horse, and he was on foot.

He turned back to Alison. She had rammed her sword

into Fes's attacker. She knelt over him, glaring at him with rage burning in her eyes.

Fes hurried over to her and touched her on the hand. "It won't change anything."

"It makes me feel better," she said.

"We have to go after him," Fes said.

"How?" She looked at Fes, and there was something more than irritation on her face. "On horse, it would be hard enough to catch up to them, and on foot... I don't think we have a chance."

"We know that Carter is the one who has him. And we know that she wants to bring the priest somewhere north, so you can use that and figure out how to catch him."

"On foot? Fes, they will get Talmund to the dragon fields and return before we even have a chance of reaching them."

Which meant that their job was going to fail. Which meant that the money that he had been promised from Horus was gone. Which meant that it was useless for him to continue heading north. He knew that it didn't matter —that it shouldn't matter—but he couldn't help himself.

"If we can reach the next village, we could find alternatives."

"Alternatives? They will be so far ahead of us that it won't matter at that point."

"Do you have a better idea?" He didn't think that

Alison intended to abandon the priest, though her reasoning seemed to be about more than the money involved. What reason would Alison have in going after the priest if it wasn't only about money?

She looked back at the fallen mercenaries. None of them breathed, and their blood was spilled on the ground. What a waste. It was an intentional sacrifice made by Carter to allow her to grab the priest. And it meant that she felt the priest was important, for whatever reason. Fes needed to understand what that reason might be.

"If only we had gotten a little farther," she whispered.

"Why?"

"It doesn't matter. Not now that they took Talmund."

"What are you getting at?"

Alison fell silent as they started walking. By late in the day, the sound of thunder rumbled toward him. When he looked up to see the clear sky, he realized that it wasn't thunder at all. It didn't take long for him to realize that riders approached.

"We should hide," he said.

But it was too late. They were out in the open, and there was no place for them to go. If they were more of Carter's men, then they needed to be ready for an attack. Carter might need the priest, but she didn't need Fes.

When they neared, he counted two dozen, and all

dressed differently than Carter's men had been. Not her mercenaries.

Fes looked over at Alison, expecting to see her reaching for her sword, but she didn't. She made no effort to grab for her weapon.

They were outnumbered.

But... by who?

CHAPTER THIRTEEN

When they grabbed his daggers, Fes resisted the urge to fight. The only thing that would happen were he to fight would be his death. They made no attempt on Alison, which implied something.

"You were expecting this?" Fes asked Alison as the two men grabbed him by the arms. Each man had pocketed one of his daggers, and he took a moment to memorize their features, determined to know who to go after to reclaim them.

She didn't answer. The men made quick work of binding his arms, trapping them behind him. Surprisingly, they didn't search his cloak. Considering the way they left Alison alone, he suspected she was in on whatever this was.

Could it be her way of taking for herself all of the money Horus might pay?

No. That didn't seem quite right. For her to deceive him like that, she would have needed to be paid significantly more. She had been all too willing to go with him as he accompanied the priest, which meant that losing the priest had changed something.

They guided him away from the road, marching him across the ground at a rapid clip. In the distance, a campsite became visible. Fes saw it as cook fires and a row of neatly arranged horses.

Fes glanced at his captors every so often as they dragged him through the campsite. There had to be three dozen or more tents here, all of them arranged neatly, a coordinated series of rows. A military encampment.

No one here wore the colors of the empire. Alarm bells went off in Fes's head. If there wasn't anyone here from the empire, that meant that these people served a different lord. After the talk about the rebellion, he hadn't expected to see any sign of it, but could they have been caught by them?

He glanced over at Alison. Unlike him, she walked free.

"What is this about, Alison?"

She glanced over. At first, Fes wasn't sure that she would answer, and then she shook her head. "This is about making a choice, Fes, the same way as you made one." She glanced over at him before turning away. "You weren't the only one who wanted to get away from Horus. I made my own choice. You need to make one now."

What she asked of him became evident as they made their way through the camp. He understood what it was that Alison was asking him to choose and where they were bringing him, though not how Alison had gotten involved in it. The rebellion.

That was why they had only wanted Alison and Fes. They hadn't thought they would need more, not if the plan had always been to meet up with the rebellion.

"How long have you been a part of it?"

"Long enough to know that it's the side you should be on."

"The rebellion is the side I should be on?" He looked around, and the two men marching along either side of him shot him a hard look. They had the numbers, but they didn't appear any more intimidating than most of the people in the city. If he met them one on one, or if he came across them while traveling, he wouldn't have hesitated to attack them.

"If you understood what the rebellion was after, you would know."

Fes shook his head. "How is Talmund involved in the rebellion?"

"It will all make sense soon."

Fes doubted that. Somehow, he had been drawn into this. The priest had wanted Fes—but why? "How long have you been working for them?"

She stared at him blankly for a moment.

"How long?"

"Ever since you left."

Fes looked away. He tested the bindings at his wrists, but they were securely fastened. "All this time you accused me of betrayal for wanting something else, you've done the same."

"The same?" She started toward him, and one of the men—a younger man with a flat expression—touched her arm, and she shook her head before rejoining him. "I've been working for a much more important purpose than you with Azithan."

"I'm sure you have," Fes said. "I'm sure that the rebellion"— he looked around at the procession, and shook his head in annoyance—"has a very important purpose. As far as I can tell, they're no different than Carter."

Alison glared for a moment. "Do not equate them to Carter."

"And why not? Why do you think they are so different than Carter? All she wants is power. Isn't that the exact same thing the rebellion wants?"

The man walking next to him jerked on his bindings, and it forced Fes to take a few steps away from Alison. He hadn't even realized that he was scooting toward her, and it seemed as if the man intended to protect her from Fes.

He laughed bitterly. "I'm not going to hurt her. If you know anything about me, you'll know that I would have no interest in hurting Alison."

The man glanced over at Alison, who nodded.

Fes chuckled. "See? Even Alison admits that."

"The rebellion is about much more than simply power," Alison said, looking over at Fes. "What they are doing is important. It's about freedom."

Fes glanced over. "Don't you mean what we are doing?"

Alison glared at him for a moment. "Fine. What we are doing is important. I don't care that you don't believe in the work—you don't have to—but that doesn't change what we are doing, or the reason that we are doing it."

"Don't you tell me why you're doing it," Fes said. "Tell me what you think is so important."

"Because people have been enslaved by the empire for generations. Your ancestors. Mine. We've been forced to serve, and for what? What has the empire ever given us? They use dragon relics to maintain power, holding us in our places. The rebellion would change all that."

Fes glanced at the others with Alison, but they stared straight ahead, unconcerned by him. And there was no reason that they needed to be concerned about him. Fes was completely trapped, and there was nothing he could do at this point. Then again, what did he want to do? He had no interest in hurting Alison. And he couldn't fight his way free, not with as many people as were here. At least with these soldiers, they wouldn't have to fear Carter and her men.

"How long have you been planning to betray me?"

"Betray you? I haven't betrayed you at all."

"You led me into your plans. You forced me to be a part of this."

"No one has forced you to do anything," an older man said, joining them. He was dressed in a dark jacket, and his silver hair was slicked back on his head. He glanced at Alison warmly. Fes could only shake his head. "You made a choice, Fezarn."

"I wish you people would stop calling me that."

"Is it not your name?" the man asked.

"It might be my name, but I don't care for you using it."

"Is there a reason you don't care for the name that your parents gave to you?"

Fes stared at the man for a moment, debating how he would answer. The man was baiting him, and he had long ago learned how to ignore men like that. He was older, with a deep crease that furrowed his brow, and there was something strange, almost a sense of energy that seemed to emanate from him.

"I would imagine that your parents spent considerable

time and energy choosing a name. A name makes a man, some would say."

Fes grunted. "The name makes a man? No. A man makes a man. The name is nothing more than that. A name."

"And what kind of man are you?"

Fes looked away from the man, turning his attention from the intense stare. This man—this rebel—considered him with an unsettling sort of attention. There was activity in the camp all around them, and more and more people were coming in, joining the several dozen rebels. Even with these numbers, there wouldn't be enough to pose much of a threat to the empire. The empire had thousands of soldiers—thousands upon thousands—and far more than the paltry numbers that he saw here.

"I'm a kind of man who knows what I am meant to do."

"I would argue that you are the kind of man who does not know that. If you knew what you were meant to do, you wouldn't resist working with us."

Fes turned his attention back to the man. "And that's what this is? Some sort of recruitment?" He looked back around the camp. "From what I can tell, this is little more than a capture."

The rebel forced a flat smile. "Perhaps that is all it is. Regardless, you will work with us."

"And how, exactly, am I to work with you?"

"You will help us find Talmund."

Fes grunted, laughing again. "All of this to force me to do what I was going to do anyway?"

"This wouldn't have been necessary had you managed to get him to us before."

Fes glanced over at Alison. "Was that always the plan?" He thought so, but wanted to know.

She stared at him a moment. "Not at first." That surprised him. "After the Bayars were attacked, I sent word."

"You have me here, and I've already told you that I intend to help, so what now?"

"That's it?"

"Should there be something more? I didn't figure there was a need for anything more, but maybe I'm wrong." The man glanced from Fes to Alison, seemingly uncertain what he should say. Fes only laughed to himself. "You don't need these," he said, motioning to the restraints. "If you intend to go after Talmund, then I'm with you. What choice do I have if I want to get paid?"

A part of him wondered if he should head back and warn Azithan. If the fire mage knew that he'd been captured by the rebellion, it was possible that he'd send more help. Even if he did, it would be too late. Whatever they were after would be gone.

For Fes to know how deep the deception had gone, he

needed to stay and learn. Which meant working with the rebellion for now.

The man nodded to one of the men on the other side of Fes, and he untied the ropes. When he was done, Fes turned to him and held out his hand. When the man arched his brow, Fes step toward him. "My daggers."

"What?" the man asked.

"My daggers. I will have them back."

The man glanced from Fes to the leader of the rebellion. He frowned, flicking his gaze to Alison for a moment before turning his attention back to Fes. "Let him have it."

Fes waited, holding his hand out until he received one of the daggers. The other man didn't attempt to give him the other, so Fes darted toward him and jabbed the dagger up toward his neck. "The other one, too."

Movement came around him, and Fes grinned, removing the dagger from the man's neck. He took a step back, twisting his dagger in his hands until he could slam it into the sheath at his belt. The other man hesitated a moment before handing over Fes's other dagger. When he had them both, he breathed out a sigh of relief.

The rebellion leader watched him, studying him for a long moment before turning away and motioning for them to follow.

Fes looked over at Alison before following her. As he went, he glared at her, and she made a point of not looking over at him. When they neared an enormous tent, she finally glanced back at him. "I don't want to hear it, Fes."

"Don't want to hear what?"

"I don't want to hear you making any judgments. You have your motivations, and I have mine."

"Mine haven't been quite as secretive."

"Neither have mine. Not if you were paying attention."

"You wanted more than you could get in the city. The same as I did. That doesn't mean the rebellion." She started away from him, but he grabbed her arm. "You would have me believe that you weren't trying to hide your involvement in the rebellion from me? That everything you've done with Horus has been about the rebellion?"

She glanced over before ducking into the tent. "Like I said, I haven't been hiding anything from you. Not if you were paying attention."

Fes stared at her back as she stepped into the tent.

When he went to follow, one of the men beside him grabbed his arm. It was someone he hadn't seen before, and Fes hadn't heard him approach. That would bother him, but it wouldn't be difficult for anyone to sneak up on him given how distracted he'd been.

Fes spun, almost reaching for his daggers, but the man stepped back, raising his hands. "Whoa, no need for that."

"Then don't touch me."

"I was just trying to keep you from having a sword through your belly."

"If they wanted to put a sword through my belly, they could have done so when they first found me."

The man shrugged. "Probably, but you're not going to be allowed in that tent."

"And why not?"

"Because that's where they're making plans."

"And let me guess: They don't want me to be a part of them."

The man flashed a smile. He was slightly wider than Fes, though not nearly as tall. A long scar ran across his chin, leaving the skin slightly dimpled. There was an easy-going affability about him, and Fes suspected the man was good in a fight.

"You know how it is."

Fes looked around, glancing at the man before shaking his head. "I very much *don't* know how it is. I don't know anything about what's going on other than the fact that I have somehow joined up with the rebellion."

The man flashed a smile. "You've joined? Good. I think they were worried they were going to have to kill you."

Fes stared at him, trying to determine if the man was joking, but didn't see any sign of that. "I didn't join."

The man shrugged. "Well, then I hope you decide to join so that they don't have to kill you."

"You can stop saying that," Fes said.

The man chuckled. "My name is Micah." He stretched out a hand, waiting for Fes to take it. When he did, the man's grip was firm—almost like getting squeezed by a vice. Yes, this man would be *very* good in a fight.

"I'm Fes."

"Fes? That's an interesting name. I'm sure you get that a lot."

"Actually, most the time people don't say anything about my name."

"All right, if you say so. Why don't you come with me while they're in there, chatting?" Micah said.

"Where would you have me go?"

"Well, this is a campsite, so you might as well come to the campfire, have something to eat, and maybe something to drink."

Fes's stomach rumbled. It was easy to overlook how hungry he was, and it was easy to forget how long it had been since he'd eaten, at least regularly. He had food, but not nearly as often as he would were he in the city.

Fes allowed Micah.

They wound their way through the camp and Micah waved at people as he went, obviously friendly with many people here. Every so often, he would pause and step aside, whispering something to someone, and then begin laughing before moving on. The camp had doubled in size since Fes had come and was now at the size where he knew he had to be careful. Even before, he had known he would have to proceed with care, but with nearly seventy soldiers, all rebels, he was a little concerned about how others might perceive him and what they might do.

"You come from the capital? Anuhr?" Micah said as they neared a larger campfire at the center of the tents.

Fes nodded. "I come from the capital. I took a job, and here I am."

"Some job."

Fes breathed out heavily. "That's the truth." Would he have done anything differently had he known that this would've happened? Would he have avoided taking the job, regardless of what it paid? With Carter's involvement —and now the rebellion—he would rather have stayed in the city. It would have been safer, regardless of what he might get paid.

"How did you get mixed up with her?" Micah asked, motioning toward the command tent.

"I've known her for a while."

Micah arched a brow, a wide grin spreading across his face. "Have you? Not too many men get to cozy up with her."

"Probably for good reason. She gets under your skin and gets angry when you don't do things the way that she wants, and even if you do exactly what you tell her that you're going to do, she still..." Fes shook his head. It didn't matter. He'd let his connection to Alison go long ago, and this wasn't going to do anything to change that.

Micah motioned for him to sit, so Fes found a barrel resting near the fire and took a seat on it. There were others around the fire. A woman who worked a spit eyed him suspiciously for a long moment before turning back to what she had been doing. Another man stood near a massive pot and stirred it occasionally.

"You came with the priest, then?"

"We were escorting him, and I was supposed to bring something back, when—"

Micah's eyes narrowed. "We heard about the attacks and the mercenaries. I can't believe they would have attacked the Bayars like that."

"The woman who did it is a real bastard," Fes said.

"I hear she's been attacking other merchants that make their way north," Micah said.

Fes's heart caught. If anything happened to Theole and Indra, he might actually cut Carter down. There was no reason to do anything to those two, and all they had wanted was to make it north, get through the mountains, and return to their family. They didn't deserve anything other than that safety.

"What have you heard?"

Micah waved his hand. "Stories, nothing more than

that. Half of the time, stories are just that, especially when it deals with attacks on people heading this way. The empire has patrols that come this way, but there's only so much that they can keep track of. You know how it is."

That was the problem. Fes *didn't* know how it was. He felt out of his element and had felt that way ever since leaving the city. If this was all about a valuable dragon relic, would it even be possible for him to reach it first?

"Are you hungry?"

"I could eat," Fes said.

Micah smiled and nodded to the man who was working at the pot. He spooned a steaming bowl of something and walked it over to Micah. Micah brought it to his nose and inhaled deeply. "Probably not what you are used to in the city, but it's pretty good, especially considering the alternative. We can't stop anywhere for too long; otherwise, we draw the attention of the empire. Can't have that, not with what we do. We're just a part of it, you know? Not the whole thing. Too dangerous to keep all of us together."

Fes looked around the camp. How many actually were in the rebellion? A camp like this wouldn't pose much of a challenge to the empire, but maybe that wasn't the point. They were able to move this way quickly, and they could avoid detection doing that. "And what is it that you do?"

"We are working to make a difference, trying to impact the way that the empire uses people. It's not easy, and most of the time, there's not a whole lot that we can do other than try to reach for small victories. We've had enough of those, especially lately, and if we can reach the dragon heart, it might finally start to turn things for us."

"That's what the priest is after?" When Micah nodded, Fes breathed out slowly. Dragon heart. That was the first he'd heard it named. "What *is* the dragon heart?"

Micah handed him the stew and Fes sniffed it before tipping it back and starting to drink. It was thick, and the meat was stringy, and any vegetables that were in the bowl were far chewier than he preferred, but it was food. There had been a time when he had first been trying to find a place in Anuhr when he had struggled for even a meal a day. Back then, Fes would have done anything for a meal like this, and now it was handed to him. After what he'd been through, he knew better than to object to the quality of what he was served, even if it did taste better than the jerky he'd been eating.

"I thought you were traveling with Alison."

"I am traveling with Alison, but I didn't know anything about a dragon heart."

"Maybe they called it something else," Micah said.

"Maybe," Fes said, taking another drink of the stew. "What is it?"

"It's an artifact of great power. I'm not sure that I

would even know what it is, but there are some who do, as long as they are sensitive to it."

"And the priest is sensitive to it?"

"Him and others like him. There are few enough who remain with the necessary sensitivities. That's why so much effort has been spent on getting him here."

"Are we close to the dragon fields?" He could see the mountains in the distance, but that didn't help him know whether the fields were nearby.

Micah shook his head. "We still got a ways to go before we reach them, though I've never really traveled there myself. We haven't had the right people with us before to do so."

How had Talmund thought to succeed without a fire mage?

"You seem troubled," Micah said.

"Shouldn't I be?" Fes asked. "I didn't realize that Alison was working for the rebellion. I didn't realize that I would get forced to do this."

"The dragon heart gives us a chance to push back. That's about all I know about it. But with it, we won't have to worry about the emperor sending his mages at us, not if the priests get behind us."

"Do you think they will?"

"For the dragon heart, they will."

Fes turned away and stared toward the command tent. Answers would be found in there, as would the person who likely was coordinating all of this. Horus was involved, though maybe only peripherally. Maybe the rebellion had used him, too. And Carter had Talmund and might have attacked Theole and Indra.

Somehow, the rebellion would have to get Talmund, but that might mean an attack.

Was that something Fes wanted to be a part of?

As he sat staring at the tent, he started to smile. Even with all that he'd been offered by Horus, he wasn't getting paid enough. Not nearly enough.

CHAPTER FOURTEEN

A hundred or more people traveled with them now. Other smaller groups continued to join the longer they rode. Most rode horses, though a few rode in the wagons, carted along with all of the supplies. They moved slowly, not nearly at the pace that Fes wanted, but there was a particular cadence to it, almost as if they weren't concerned about how quickly they reached the dragon fields.

But then, Fes and Alison couldn't be only interested in arriving at the dragon fields. They needed to rescue Talmund. He was the one who knew how to find the dragon heart.

"Why aren't we going any faster?" he asked Micah.

Micah had stayed with him, and it was either because he had been assigned to keep an eye on Fes or because he knew Fes needed someone to explain the rebellion to him. Alison had remained distant.

"There's no way for us to go any faster, not with the wagons."

"We could send scouts ahead. Carter will be moving much faster than this and since she has Talmund..."

Micah shrugged. "We've done that, but it leaves the wagons in a difficult spot. They need for us to provide a guard. Without us, the wagons are at greater risk of attack."

"The empire?"

"It's more than the empire you have to worry about when you get into the outer lands."

"Really?" Fes looked around him. With over a hundred soldiers, they would pose at least a challenge to anyone who thought to approach. With the numbers the rebellion had, there would be enough to intimidate almost any attackers other than the empire. "Seems like there's not a whole lot you'd have to be worried about."

Micah shrugged. "You'd be surprised. The rebellion started as nothing more than a way for us to protect each other. We banded together, wanting to offer protections that the empire wouldn't."

Fes didn't think arguing about how well the empire would protect everyone within its borders would work, not with Micah. He had the sense that he'd been hurt before. "And what do you think the empire owes you?"

"After what they've taken from us? Everything."

"And what has the empire taken from you?"

Micah smiled. "You haven't been around us long enough to understand. If you had, you wouldn't need me to explain it to you. Most of us come from the same sort of place. We have ancestors who were pushed out of their homelands, destroyed in attacks."

"How long ago was this?"

Micah arched a brow at him. "Long ago."

"You're talking about attacks that took place over a thousand years ago!"

"That doesn't change that they happened. Entire people were destroyed, pushed out of their lands. You don't think we should try to reclaim what was lost?"

Fes looked away. It was better not to argue with someone like Micah. This was a man who believed that they needed to counter what the empire had done centuries before. It was better to let go and make a living however you could. That had long been Fes's plan. Working with Azithan made it easier.

"You do what you need. If you think you can push the empire away from your ancestral lands…"

"With enough help, we will. Then we can begin to get the empire to stop enslaving our people."

Fes laughed. "I'll admit that most of my time has been spent in Anuhr, but I haven't heard of the empire enslaving anyone."

Micah eyed him a moment. "You have the look of the Settlers to you. Don't you know they were the first forced to serve?"

Fes couldn't say anything. He didn't know anything about this *look* he had, but even Talmund had suggested it. Could that be the secret of his parentage that Azithan had known? Was *that* the reason Azithan had wanted him to make this trip?

They continued their steady pace throughout the day, and gradually the details of the mountains looming in the distance became even more evident. The farther north they went, the more that Fes became aware of them. It was a pressure upon him, almost the way he felt when around dragon relics. The mountains were massive, and the snow-capped peaks seemed impossibly far away.

When they stopped for the night, a group of ten riders streaked off, galloping north.

"What's that about?" Fes asked Micah.

"Probably nothing."

"I thought you said they didn't send scouts out. That it was too dangerous to those who remained behind?"

"With as many as we have now, I wonder if maybe they decided it was worth the risk."

Fes stared after them. If they were making a run at the priest, he wanted to be a part of it, not anything like this where he was held back. That was why he'd left the city in the first place. Not to be pulled into the rebellion. And Alison knew it.

"Come on. You can help us make camp," Micah said.

"That's exactly what I was hoping you would say," Fes said sarcastically, but he followed. There wasn't anything else for him to do. At least they didn't seem interested in trying to confine him, but he wondered how friendly they would be if he made a run for it. Probably not nearly as friendly as they had been so far.

Fes helped set a few tents and worked with Micah to get a fire going near one of them. The same woman who had been roasting meat the night before made her way over to the growing fire and began to roast a clutch of hares. The meat smelled better than it had the night before and Fes found his mouth watering. Two other men prepared a stew, mixing in meats and vegetables, working quickly as they did.

"How was the ride?"

Fes glanced over. Alison stood next to him, staring at the fire intently. "About as well as I could expect."

"You don't have to be like that," she said.

"No? What would you prefer me to be like? You brought me here, forcing me into the rebellion—"

"There wasn't anything forced on you."

"I wasn't given a choice in this, Alison, and you can't tell me that you weren't planning this all along."

"I *wasn't* planning this all along."

"No?"

She shook her head, staring at the fire without any change to the intensity on her face. "I was content with hiring you. The two of us should have been able to move quietly enough to avoid notice. We thought staying with the Bayars would get us free of the city, but we hadn't expected an attack."

"Carter knew everything you were doing. Which meant she knows what you're after."

"She shouldn't have known," she said.

"You don't know Carter."

"We have experience with her."

"I doubt it's the same experience I have. I don't know who she's working with—but if what I suspect about the Bayars attack is right, there's a fire mage involved." It might not even be that the fire mage employed her. "Regardless, why did you really want me to come? Horus has to have others who would have been more capable of keeping Talmund safe. Is it because of my connection to Azithan?"

She looked down. "That's not it."

Fes took a step toward her. He was frustrated with how she had used him, but the least she could do was tell him why. "Then what?"

She sighed and finally turned away from the fire. "It's about the connection you have to dragon artifacts. That's the reason that Azithan keeps hiring you, you know. He knows you have a connection, and he probably knows what it is."

Fes was surprised that Alison knew about that part of himself. "If I have one, I don't know what it is."

"You can be so oblivious, can't you? Why else do you think your master wanted you?"

"He wanted me because I can complete jobs. I stayed with him because he paid what I was worth. Unlike Horus."

"I bet you don't even know there's a term for your kind."

He shot her a hard look, already knowing where she was going. "I'm not a dragonwalker."

"Maybe not the way they once were, but you might as well be. When the empire wants an artifact, they call you, don't they?"

"Not the empire. Azithan."

"And isn't he the empire?"

"He's only one fire mage."

"One who serves the emperor in the heart of the palace."

Fes tried to open himself to the sense of the mountains that had been bothering him. When he couldn't do it, he knew Alison was wrong about him. "That's why you wanted me?"

"That's why Talmund wanted you. When you stole the dragon bone from him, he saw it. A connection. When I learned what it was, I knew—*knew*—that was why you'd been used by Azithan."

"He hired me, not used me."

"It's the same. Just because you didn't know you were used doesn't mean you weren't. And now someone needs to retrieve the item."

"And by item, you mean the dragon heart."

She swore under her breath. "Micah should know better than to share things like that."

"He probably thought that I already knew." Fes smiled at her. "Aren't you going to tell me what it is?"

"It doesn't matter what it is. Not to you."

"It matters to me. It matters all the gold he promised to me."

"Nice, Fes. That's all this is to you?"

"This was a job, and you know it. Don't use the fact that I took the job to manipulate me into joining the rebellion. I think it's only fair that you tell me what exactly the dragon heart is."

"You already heard what it is."

"I heard that it's a dragon heart. I don't know what that means. I presume a relic of some kind, and since Carter has decided to risk herself coming north, it tells me the heart must be valuable, but I don't know what it is."

"It's so much more than a relic," she said.

Carter wouldn't send as many mercenaries out here if

it weren't. That still didn't tell him *what* it was. "Like a dragon pearl?"

"Imagine the largest dragon pearl that was ever found," she said.

Fes reached into his pocket, where the dragon pearl remained. It was warm, though not painfully so. Certainly not as warm as it had been when he had found it. "I'm imagining it."

Alison held her hands out, stretching them into the size of a small ball. "This is the largest dragon pearl that was ever found. It's larger than both our fists and that pearl had enough power to enable one fire mage to bring down a dragon on their own. They used the power stored within to destroy. Now, imagine what would happen if they find one ten times that size."

"That's the dragon heart?"

"That's the *power* of the dragon heart. Without that source, any hope that we have of restoring the dragons is gone."

Fes shook his head, laughing. "Not you too."

"What do you mean, not me too?"

"I'm just saying that you believe that the dragons will return?"

"I think it's possible. And considering how we are responsible for what happened to them, we need to do whatever we can to bring them back in the world."

"We've been through this before," he said, not bothering to hide his annoyance. "Haven't you ever stopped to think that there might be a reason the dragons are gone?"

"I know what that reason is. It's because people destroyed them."

"It's because people *feared* them. And likely for good reason." Fes looked over at the fire and noticed that it was crackling warmly. There was heat pressing on his back, and it pushed away the chill wind that gusted out of the northern mountains, carrying with it the promise of snow. "Think about that claw Talmund had. If that was a child, little more than a baby, what must a fully grown dragon have been like? How terrifying must they have been?"

"We don't have any reason to fear the dragons."

"I've seen the Issana Forest. I know how powerful the dragons once were. I don't need to reach the dragon plains to understand. If they could destroy a forest like that, what would happen if they turned on the cities of man?"

"Those are the stories the empire wants you to believe. The priests tell of a different truth. One where the dragons lived among man, not dangerously."

"What if you're wrong?" He motioned to the people camped. "What if they're all wrong?"

"That's a risk I'm willing to take. At least I feel like I am making a difference. Maybe if you took the time to listen and learn about what we are doing here, you might feel differently."

Fes frowned, shaking his head. "Why would I feel differently? You forced me here. You are the reason that I'm here."

"But you could be a part of this."

Fes stared at Alison, unable to respond. "You can't force me into your beliefs. I've seen the destruction of dragons, and I've seen the way the fire mages use their remains to defend the empire."

"Which is *why* you should side with the rebellion."

"I don't want any part of it."

"So you would rather just return to the city, return to what you know?"

"I would rather have the gold that was promised me. I'd rather the stability I know. You may think otherwise, but Azithan has been good to me, much more than Horus ever was. I'm doing this because of the money Horus promised, nothing more. When it's over, I'll return and continue working for Azithan."

"You didn't complete the job."

"I'm beginning to think I never was going to be able to complete the job," Fes said.

"That's not fair."

"That's not fair? I think it's not fair the way that you coerced me into coming here. So whether or not my comments are fair is not really applicable here."

"You could return. I doubt anyone would stop you. It would take you the better part of two weeks to return to the city anyway. Longer if they didn't allow you to bring a horse."

Fes shook his head. Turning around meant Carter got what she was after. And it might mean that she harmed Theole and Indra. More than anything, that was the reason he continued to be willing to go along with all of this. "And I'm sure that you would make certain that I didn't have access to a horse."

"I don't have any control over that, Fezarn."

"Stop calling me that."

"Fezarn. Fezarn. Fezarn."

Alison was as frustrating now as she ever had been. And, at the same time, seeing her here made so much sense, especially with everything that he had been through with her.

"Where did the men who rode out of here go?"

"You know that I can't answer that."

"I don't know anything about what you can or can't do, Alison. You made it clear that there isn't a whole lot about you that I'm aware of."

"And you haven't been the most forthcoming about yourself."

"Did they go off thinking that they could find Talmund?"

"There might be some word that we've had about where Carter might have taken him."

"Then let me be a part of it." If nothing else, he could finish this damned job so that he could get paid. "I know Carter and what she's like. I can help."

"There are others of us who have experience with Carter. Not just you, Fes."

There had to be, especially considering how many people Carter likely would have angered over the years. "There might be others, but I've dealt with her quite a bit the last year. She has connections. And I think I can get through to her. Besides, we both know I have some connection to dragon relics."

"I thought you didn't want to get involved with the rebellion."

"Who said anything about getting involved with the rebellion? I only want to finish my job."

"That's why you're pushing?"

He wasn't about to tell her the other reason. She wouldn't understand. She couldn't. It would make her question why he'd be concerned about the merchants and had been willing to leave her behind. "What else would it be about?"

She studied him, almost weighing him with her gaze. "I will see what I can do, but it's not a promise."

"I didn't expect a promise."

"This will be easier if you are willing to listen and accept that there's a reason for the rebellion."

"You haven't shown me anything to make me believe that I should. As far as I can tell, the rebellion wants the same things as the empire—only they want to fight for their power. How many will be harmed with what you're after? How many more would be harmed if the rebellion managed to do what you intend and raise a dragon?" He shook his head. "I'm here for the job. That's it. I'll help save Talmund, but don't try to make this about more for me."

Alison glared at him for a moment. "You may not like it, but I do know you, Fezarn. This *is* about more for you."

Fes could only watch as she departed. Micah approached, but Fes turned away, disappearing into the camp. He wasn't in the mood to talk to anyone, even someone who was as often welcoming as Micah had been. Fes didn't want to feel welcome, not here, and not when he wanted nothing to do with the rebellion.

CHAPTER FIFTEEN

The caravan paused about midday. The air had
grown cooler, almost cold, and Fes wondered how
long that would last. If the stories were real, the ground
near the dragon plains still steamed, though with as cold
as it had already gotten, he wasn't sure how they could. If
the dragon plains were anything like the Issana Forest, he
expected destruction. Maybe there would be the husks of
trees or other signs of devastation from the dragons. And
maybe Alison would finally understand that the dragons
were dangerous.

As Fes stared down from atop his horse, he realized
why they had paused. There was a small village, though
village didn't seem quite the right word. Whatever was
down there wasn't a village so much as it was a forti-
fication.

"What is that?" he asked Micah.

The other man looked over. "There are places like this scattered around the northern lands. Most of them are remnants from the time when the dragons were slaughtered."

"That's one of the ancient dragon bases?" Fes had heard of the dragon bases. Everyone had. They were where the empire had launched its attack, using dragon relics from the first dragons they had slaughtered to push back the dragons. Even the bases were said to have particular fortifications. He knew them to be scattered around the empire, though had never seen one.

"It's what remains of it. Most of those buildings are old, and what remains has been rebuilt many times over the years."

"They're abandoned and have been for years. Why would they need to be rebuilt?"

"Mostly because the people here want to remember."

"What is there to remember? We know what happened."

"Some want to remember the way the dragons were slaughtered. They want to remember what the empire did to the dragons."

Fes shook his head. He started to say something when movement in the dragon base caught his eye. A hushed murmur passed through the caravan, and he saw a pair of men riding quickly toward the commander.

"Stay here," Micah said.

He started off, heading toward the commander, and Fes ignored his request. What would be the point? Fes was determined to know what was taking place here, and if this was where they were going to find the priest—or more of Carter's men—he wanted to be a part of it.

When he approached, he saw a small group—no more than ten, much like the last time—circling the commander. Alison was one of them.

"If there is any empire presence, we need to know," one of the men said.

"We saw movement," another was saying.

"Movement doesn't necessarily mean empire presence," the commander said. He looked around and his gaze settled on Fes before continuing to look at the others. At least he hadn't told Fes he couldn't stay. He doubted he would have listened anyway.

"It could be Carter. She has a squad of mercenaries, along with Talmund. Maybe even a fire mage," Fes said.

The others glanced over at him but said nothing before turning their attention back to the commander.

"We can go and investigate. If there is anything..." Alison started.

"If there's anything, I want you to be ready and to send word back. Don't go into it on your own," the commander said. "Once we reach the pass, there won't be any way for them to escape."

One of the men nodded, and the commander made a motion with his hand, and they all started riding off. Fes kept pace, riding with them, and Micah glanced over at him, frowning and shaking his head. Fes ignored him and rode up to Alison. As he did, he noticed the rest of the rebellion had begun to move behind the nearby hillside, hiding from others who might realize they were here.

"I need be a part of this," he said. "This was my job too."

"I don't care if you're a part. I doubt the commander would either. But don't get in the way."

"When have you ever known me to get in the way?"

She glanced over. "I can think of a dozen or so times when you did."

"Most of those you weren't opposed to."

"Not now, Fes."

As they galloped toward the base, there was another flurry of movement near the base. Not mounted, but definitely activity. "Did you see that?"

Alison nodded. "I see where they went, but why into that building?"

It was one on the outskirts of the base, but it was larger than most of the others. It was also stouter. Some of the other buildings appeared to be crumbling, but the one that the people had disappeared into did not. Many of the windows had bars over them and looked to be generally defensible.

"These places are abandoned."

"Looks like this one is not," Alison said.

"Weren't you supposed to get help if it came to this?" Fes asked.

"There can't be too many people here," Alison said.

"If it's Carter, then we might have to deal with more than the mercenaries. If it's the empire—"

Fes didn't get the chance to finish. One of the men suddenly fell from his horse's back, an arrow jutting out of his chest.

The rest of them reacted quickly, splitting off, making a more difficult target—or possibly an easier one, depending on where the soldiers fired from.

Fes stayed close to Alison, and they raced toward the building. Alison jumped from her horse and Fes joined her, kneeling next to a window.

"We shouldn't enter at the same spot," he said. Alison glanced at him for a moment. "We don't know what's inside, and it would be better if we came at this from multiple angles."

"You know that you aren't the most trustworthy when it comes to planning."

"I'm trustworthy. You just don't want to trust me."

"I seem to remember what happened the last time I tried to trust you. You didn't finish the job. And then you left us."

"It's been a year, Alison."

"A year that—"

Fes shook his head. "We don't need to do this now. If we're going to go in together, then let's go in together. Otherwise, we should split up and see what we can learn."

While Alison stared at him, the sound of their horses thundered as they raced through the dragon base. There came another shout, though it was muted. Had someone else fallen?

"If this *is* Carter—" and the suddenness of the attack made him think it was. The empire wouldn't attack without any reason—"then we can find Talmund and get the dragon heart," Fes whispered. "It will go faster if we separate."

"Fine. We split up, but don't betray me," she said.

"If you're in any danger, shout. I'll come for you."

"I'd say the same to you, but I'm guessing that you won't ask for help. That's just not in you."

"I've asked for help before."

"Not any time recently," she said.

"You haven't known me recently." Alison looked behind her a moment, and Fes grabbed her arm to draw her attention back to him. "Give me the count of ten before you climb in."

After she nodded, Fes crept around the outside of the building. He kept the doorway in sight, wanting to avoid any surprises, but not knowing whether going through the window would allow him to sneak in quietly enough.

The window was split in two, and he forced one of the daggers in between the two windows and managed to pop it open. It swung open slowly, and he peeked inside, looking for any signs of movement.

The room was quiet.

Silence like that made him uncomfortable. He had enough experience with sneaking in to know that there should be some sounds within buildings like this. It was part of his job working on behalf of Azithan, occasionally turning him into a glorified thief.

There was no way around it. He would just have to throw himself inside.

He climbed over the window ledge and landed with soft feet inside the room. It was a bedroom. There was a wide bed along one wall. A weathered wardrobe lined another wall. A chest, the stain fading, occupied the space at the end of the bed. There was no light in the room other than the moonlight that spilled in through the open window. A musty odor hung over everything.

Fes padded forward slowly.

A scraping sound caused him to freeze.

Fes spun and faced a man with a club.

He jumped, rolling to the side. The club whizzed through the air, narrowly missing him, whipping through the air where he had just been. Had he waited even a fraction longer, it would've been too late. Fes threw one of his daggers. It flipped end over end and sank into the man's shoulder.

Fes jumped, kicking the man in the side, knocking the wind out of him, and then rammed the hilt of his other dagger into the side of the man's head. He collapsed.

After retrieving his dagger and wiping it on the man's shirt, he kept them unsheathed. Without knowing what he might face, it would be better to be prepared, and there was a distinct possibility that there would be others waiting just outside the door. They obviously had expected the possibility of a break-in here, but why like this?

The man should have made more noise. Had he been concerned about preventing Fes from getting very far, he should have cried out.

Fes crawled back over to the man and examined him. Was there some reason that he hadn't cried out?

He was dressed differently than the other men Carter had with him. There weren't the same dark leathers. The club was too blunt a weapon for her, too. She preferred swordsman and archers, not brutish soldiers.

Maybe Carter wasn't the one to have taken up in the dragon base.

This man wasn't an empire soldier, but could he have been hired by the empire?

Fes glanced at the man's face. He was unremarkable,

with freckled cheeks and a crooked nose, looking like most fighters Fes had ever encountered.

He didn't want to wait here too long. Waiting only put Alison in danger. He had promised. He wouldn't let her down this time.

He tested the door and found it locked.

That was odd.

Why would they have needed to lock the man in the room? He glanced back over at the man but saw nothing that would explain it.

Something was off. If this *was* Carter, he knew to be careful, especially as she likely had planned for multiple possibilities.

He twisted his dagger into the side of the door until it popped open. When it did, he pulled the door open slowly and peeked out into the hallway.

There wasn't anyone moving.

He half expected to find a dozen other of Carter's men, but there weren't any.

That gave him a moment's pause.

Carter would have had other people here, and the fact that there weren't left him wondering if he had been wrong. Fes crept slowly along the hallway and reached another door. He rested his head against the door, listening for sounds on the other side. There was nothing there, nothing that was obvious.

Where was Alison?

She should have circled around the building by now and come in a different way.

Fes decided to test this door. Like the one he had come from, it was locked, only the lock faced outward, into the hallway, and he was able to twist it and sneak inside. Why would they have secured the doors from the outside? Why would the locks be facing this way?

What if these weren't what he thought? What if they were cells?

He glanced over his shoulder toward the room where the man had attacked him and frowned. What was Carter up to?

He stepped into the room. An elderly man sat at a table, hunched over, with a lantern resting on the table beside him. A spherical sculpture rested next to him, and he studied it, then turned his attention to the work in front of him.

"I should be done soon," the man said.

"What are you working on?" Fes asked. He pulled the door closed behind him, not wanting Carter—or whoever was in the base—to surprise him.

The man glanced up over his shoulder. "I'm working on the same thing you asked me to." He frowned and his eyes widened slightly. "You're new here."

Fes nodded. "I came to check on your progress," he said. It seemed reasonable to pretend that he was somehow checking on this man, though he wasn't sure whether the man would believe him. If he did, would he be able to figure out what was that Carter was doing here?

"And I told you. I'm almost done."

Fes approached the table and looked down. His breath caught. The man had what appeared to be a dragon pearl resting on the table, and next to it was a similar item, though only halfway completed. A replica. A forgery.

That couldn't be what Carter was after. She wanted the dragon heart—the same as Talmund and the rebellion. Why the forger, then?

He picked up the dragon pearl and noticed that it had a slight warmth to it and was different than the one in his pocket. That one, while inert, was always slightly warm. The colors within it seemed to shimmer at times, enough that Fes wasn't certain whether the shimmering came from something within the pearl or whether it was only his imagination.

He moved on to examine the forgery. There was no warmth to it, though that would seem impossible to forge, but it had the same heft and the same smoothness.

"What other items have you made?"

The man frowned. "Who are you?"

"I told you—"

The man shook his head. "You're not with them. If you were, you wouldn't be asking that question. Who are you?"

Fes shrugged. "I'm looking for a priest."

"This isn't the best place to find a priest. If you have questions for your god—"

Fes grunted and set the replica down. "I don't have any questions for my god. That's not the kind of priest I'm looking for."

"A dragon priest," the old man said.

"Have you seen one?"

"If I have, what does that mean for me?"

"It means that he's here and I would try to help him."

"Help? Is there any help for him? I think not."

"Why not?"

"That one has become embroiled in something beyond him. He knows too much, and he has done too much."

"What exactly has he done?"

"He has made the mistake of challenging the empire."

Fes chuckled and turned back to the door. "I doubt he'd be so foolish as to do something like that," he said. Could the priest have been so vocal about what he was after that others knew? It would be a mistake, especially mentioning anything to do with the rebellion.

The man watched Fes, saying nothing.

"You can resume your work," Fes said. He pocketed the dragon pearl—or whatever it was. He wasn't wholly convinced that it was an actual dragon pearl, but it was near enough that he thought it was worthwhile for him to keep. And if it was a pearl, and if there was anything to it, then he would rather be in possession of it than Carter.

"I need that," the man said.

"Not for what you're doing."

"You can't—"

Fes turned to him. "And why can't I? Do you think that I care whether this stays with you? You can do your work—and from what I can see it is skilled work—without it. You are already far enough along that you no longer need it."

The man smiled at Fes. "A thief? You have come here to steal from them? I'm not certain that is wise."

"I'm not certain that many things I do are wise. Doesn't change that I'm going to do them. Now. What other items do you have here?"

The man shook his head, but Fes ignored him and started searching, looking for whatever else he might be holding onto. If there were other relics here, they would be valuable. Other than the pearl, he came across what appeared to be a claw, much like what the priest had. It took him a moment, but he realized that it was probably the same one.

That meant Carter *was* here.

He grabbed it and stuffed it into his pocket along with the pearl. What else could he find here? He searched the drawers. Inside one was a short length of bone that he stuffed into his pocket. He looked around again but found nothing else that pulled on him.

The old man watched him for a while before turning back to the table and resuming his carving of the sphere.

Fes stepped out into the hallway and made his way along the hallway. There was still no sign of Alison. Had she gotten hung up somewhere?

At the next door, Fes unlocked it and peeked inside but found the room empty. There was a wall of shelves, and on those shelves were items that appeared to be dragon relics. Fes approached slowly and ran his hands over them, looking for signs of warmth, but there was none.

Either these weren't actual dragon relics, or they were inert.

He ran his hands along one of them and didn't feel the same striations as he felt on other dragon relics. None of them had the same shimmery color. Either that was difficult to forge, or not all dragon artifacts had that same shimmery color to them.

Fes turned away from the shelves. There wasn't anything else in the room. It must be a storeroom for dragon replicas.

When he went into the hallway, he hurried to the next door. This one wasn't locked. When he pushed it open, he was facing a small kitchen, little more than an oven with pots hanging over it. Three men sat on stools, chatting softly. When they saw Fes, they jumped from their seats and lunged toward him.

Fes reacted, jamming his dagger into the chest of one, spinning and cutting into the shoulder of the next, and slamming the hilt of one dagger into the man's forehead. All men fell before making a sound.

These men were dressed differently than the man he'd seen in the first room. They wore dark leathers of the mercenaries and were armed with swords. Carter's men.

The kitchen was sparse. There were cabinets, and when Fez sorted through them, he saw nothing but a few bags of grain. A counter had dried bread stacked on top of it. Coals glowed in the hearth along one wall. The air smelled of flour and that of roasted meat, so he suspected there had been some baking and cooking done here recently, though when?

Fes gathered the swords and brought them over to the hearth. He dumped the swords into it and kicked the coals, sending them glowing a little more brightly. If the men came around, he didn't want to run the risk of them grabbing the swords and coming after him.

Back in the hallway, he paused, listening for the sounds of anyone else who might be out here. Where was Alison? By now, she should have found a way of following him, and the fact that she hadn't troubled him. Could Carter have come across her?

No. He wasn't even certain that Carter was here.

Whatever this was seemed to be something other than the plan that Carter had for the priest.

Fes tried another door and found it empty like the others.

How many rooms were in this building? How many places would he have to check before finding where they had brought the priest?

If he was even here.

When he pushed open the next door, he hesitated.

It was a vast, open room that reminded him of the common room of a tavern. A dozen men were inside, and they looked up the moment that Fes pushed open the door.

He swore under his breath.

A dozen. Could he really manage a dozen?

He didn't have much choice. The alternative was backing up, and the door hadn't been locked, which meant that he would be unlikely to lock it from the other side.

He lunged forward.

Fes's mind went blank, but the anger didn't boil up within him—not as he needed it to. He kicked, striking one man in the knee, dropping him, and he spun around, ramming the hilt of his dagger into his temple. Another came toward him, and Fes pushed on a chair, sliding it underneath his legs, knocking him down. He kicked him as he fell, connecting with the side of his head.

That was two.

Something slammed into him, and he staggered forward, struggling to catch his breath. When he spun around, he faced three attackers, though they were more cautious than the first two had been.

Getting hit sent his anger boiling within him. He would use that. He *had* to use that.

Fes dropped and rolled, kicking out as he did, and caught one man in the ankle. He brought his hand around, jabbing his knife into the next man's thigh before slicing with the back of the other blade along another man's leg, cutting his tendon. He fell with a scream.

Five down.

Seven left. Seven men and they converged on him all at one time.

It was more than he could manage.

The door crashed open, and Fes used that distraction to lunge at the nearest man. He stabbed, catching the man in the gut, before spinning and crashing into the next. Someone grabbed his arm, and he threw them off, shaking and thrusting with his dagger. He kicked out, lashing at attacker after attacker, and then the attack was done.

Fes looked around. The dozen men were all lying on the ground, most unconscious, though a few of them were bleeding heavily and probably wouldn't survive. He pushed back irritation tinged with anger and swallowed the lump in his throat.

Why did it have to be like this? How could he attack like this?

"That was… impressive."

Fes spun around, half expecting to see Carter or one of her men, but Alison stood with her sword unsheathed, watching him with amusement glittering in her eyes.

"Where have you been?"

"I've been trying to get through this place. It's like a maze. I broke into a room and got jumped, and barely made it here when I started to hear the sound of your fighting."

Fes sighed. "It is a maze. They're making dragon relics."

"Replicas?"

Fes nodded.

"Why would they be making replicas here? We're so close to the dragon fields."

Fes shook his head. "It has something to do with Carter, I'm sure of it, but I'm not entirely certain what."

"You think it has anything to do with who she's working for?"

"I don't know. I think fire mages would know if they were given a forgery, but others might not. There are enough who want dragon relics, even if they're inert, that replicas could be valuable."

"I didn't find any evidence of Talmund," she said.

"I found a man who I think had seen him, but I can't be certain."

Alison looked at him. "If there's a man who might be helpful, then we need to go question him."

Fes looked at the fallen men once more. Killing had always been so easy for him, but why? Maybe it was what Alison and Talmund said about him, and maybe it did have to do with his heritage, but what was it?

"I'll show you to him," he said.

Fes led her back to the room where he'd come across the priest. When he checked the door, he found that it was cracked open and the man who had been inside working on the forgeries was gone.

"He was here," he said to Alison.

Alison made her way into the room and looked around. "Where's he gone?"

Fes leaned over the table, looking at the contents. There were the replicas that had been crafted by the man, but nothing else. He peeked out the window. In the distance, he noted movement.

Alison joined him at the window. "You let him get away?"

"I didn't *let* him do anything. He happened to climb out. How was I to know?"

"What was he working on here?"

Fes patted his pocket where he had put the dragon

pearl, along with the claw. He was reluctant to reveal that he had taken them from the man, not sure what Alison might do.

"Fes?" she asked, turning to him.

He shot her a hard look. "They had him making replicas."

"There's something you're not telling me."

Fes reached into his pocket and pulled out the dragon pearl, showing it to her. He held on to it, not willing to release it to her.

"Is that—"

"Yes. It's real."

"That's what they've been working on?"

"At least here."

"If they have authentic pearls, we need to get them back to the others."

Fes didn't know what they would do with the pearl, but he knew how valuable it would be to Azithan. "I'm going to hold onto it for now."

"You can't think to give it to *him*."

"And why not?"

"You give him too much power. And you fail to recognize how dangerous he is. You got caught up taking his jobs, and I don't think you paid any attention to the consequences."

Fes turned his attention back to the window. It was

time for them to get out of there, not continue to argue. "Let's get going."

"You don't want to evaluate anything more in here?" she asked.

"What else do you think there is here? I can tell there's nothing of value." He didn't go into *how* he could tell. "We don't have any use for replicas, and I'd like to catch up to the forger," he said.

"And how does that help us with Talmund?"

"It gets us more information."

She stared at him for a long moment before letting out a long sigh. "Fine, Fezarn. I'll do what you suggest this time, but more is at stake than you realize." Her gaze lingered on the pocket where he kept the dragon pearl. Would they have issues about that?

They chased the man out of the dragon base. When they finally caught up to him, he looked at Fes with a mixture of resignation and disgust. "What do you want from me?"

"Answers," Fes said, grabbing him and dragging the man with him.

CHAPTER SIXTEEN

"Where did the priest go?" he asked the old man. They were at the edge of the dragon base with the buildings rising nearby. Fes wasn't comfortable remaining there too long, but he needed to decide what to do with the forger. Where were the others? They had gone deeper into the dragon base but then had disappeared.

Alison had gathered the horses and now paced nearby, making a steady circle around them. Every so often, she would pause and glare at the old man, almost as if believing that the irritation in her gaze could convince him to say something more than he already had.

"I wasn't there for what happened with the priest," the man said.

"But you were there for the rest of it," Fes said.

"I was hired for a task."

"Making replicas."

The man nodded.

"Who hired you?"

"Does it really matter?"

"It matters," Fes said.

"I didn't get his name. He was a hard man, and he had angry features, so I knew to be cautious with him."

Fes glanced over at Alison. That wasn't Carter, but who could it have been? Someone working on her behalf? Someone else? Maybe it was even Carter's employer. That would be valuable to learn, especially if it meant he didn't have to worry about her beating him to assignments in Anuhr. "What else can you tell me about him?"

"I'm afraid nothing that will be of much use to you. All I know is that he asked me to make copies of a few items that he had in his possession."

"Like the pearl."

"Like the pearl. And the claw. And…"

"And what?" Fes asked when the man didn't elaborate.

"He said there would be other items, but he wanted to test me first. He wanted to see how capable I was at making replicas. As if he needed to test me. I am the best north of Anuhr."

"North of Anuhr?"

"There are a few within the city with some skill. Fools

will pay far too much for what they believe to be authentic replicas. I'm happy to oblige them."

"How did you learn to make them?" Alison asked.

Fes frowned at her for a moment but realized that he was curious too. Maybe if he understood the key to making dragon replicas, he might be better equipped to identify them. Knowing when something was a forgery would be beneficial.

"The key is getting the striations just right," the old man said. "When you're dealing with a dragon bone, you have to look closely. Sometimes you need a magnifying glass, though not always. Most of the time, you need to go by feel. Sometimes you can even add a touch of heat. Certain metals hold heat, but you have to be careful encasing the bone around them."

"How do you make the colors?"

The man frowned at him. "The colors?"

Fes nodded. "When you have a true dragon artifact. How do you replicate the colors?"

"There are no colors when it comes to dragon relics. The bone is ivory, and the claws are a deep brown that's almost black. Even the pearls have no color to them."

Fes frowned, thinking about the dragon pearl that he'd taken from the forger, as well as the one that he had seen in the merchant tent. Both of them had colors shimmering around them. Fes was confident that they did and was sure those colors weren't imagined.

The man shook his head and smiled. "As I was saying, the key is matching the striations. Someone skilled at identifying an artifact will know whether the striations are accurate or not."

"How do you make the striations as accurate as possible?" Alison asked.

"It is a delicate touch. It's like making art." The man held up his hands. They were twisted, but he tapped them together quickly. "I have been at this a long time. In all that time, I've learned to trust what I can feel. Even if my eyes were going to fade—which they haven't—I can still feel where the striations on the relics can be found. If I can feel them, I can copy them."

"What's the key to copying a pearl?" Fes asked. "That's what you were doing when I found you."

"A pearl is a very different trick to master. Each pearl has a different texture to it, a smoothness, and most have swirls of darker bone mixed within them. It makes them incredibly difficult to replicate, but I can do it. I might be the only one who can fool the emperor himself when it comes to replicating a dragon pearl."

Fes doubted that, especially if the emperor was a fire mage, as it was rumored. In all the time he'd worked for Azithan, Fes had never met the emperor. He looked over at Alison. "We should bring him with us."

"We don't need a forger."

"Forgery?" His mouth twisted as he said it. "Not a forgery. I make replicas."

"Fine. You make replicas." She turned to Fes, lowering her voice as she stepped closer to him. "Whatever he is doesn't change the fact that he is going to stay here."

"And if Carter comes and realizes that we've talked to him?"

"There's too much risk in him coming with us."

"Think about what he can teach you. This is a man who claims to be one of the best at this skill. Don't you think that there is value in having someone like that with you? Your rebellion could make replicas, pass them off as the real thing and—"

"We aren't after replicas. We are looking for actual relics."

Why was he even arguing with her? He didn't care whether the rebellion had the necessary funds to continue with their war on the empire. "Maybe having someone like him who can help you identify when a relic is a forgery or not would be beneficial."

"We have someone."

"You *had* someone. The priest is gone."

Alison frowned. Finally, she stepped away from Fes and waved at the man as she raised her voice. "Come on then."

"Where are you taking me?"

She glared at Fes a moment. "You can't stay here, not with what happened."

"But I haven't been paid!"

"I doubt that you will be paid now," Fes said. "We left a dozen or so bodies in there, and you would be welcome to stay with them if you want, but I thought that you might prefer to come with us rather than remain with the dead."

The man's eyes widened. "A dozen? You killed a dozen between the two of you?"

"He did most of the killing," Alison said. "He doesn't need much help, at least, if you listen to him tell it."

Fes groaned and shook his head. "Don't get her started. She's still angry that I was more interested in money and stability than I was in her."

The man looked at Alison, looking her up and down for a moment. "Then you're a fool."

Alison laughed. "I think I might like this man."

"I wouldn't send you away. I'm old enough and have enough money that I'm not after more."

Alison smiled. "I definitely like this man."

Fes could only shake his head as he climbed into the saddle and waited. Alison shot him an angry expression and pushed the old man toward Fes. The man looked up at Fes expectantly until he reached a hand down to pull him up.

They rode out of the dragon base and up the hillside

that was concealing the caravan. When they reached the top of the hill and crested it, the rebellion waited.

The man gasped. "What is this?"

"This is your support."

The man stared at the people before turning his attention back to Fes. "The rebellion? Oh, I want nothing to do with this."

"Neither do I," Fes muttered.

"But you're with them!"

"Only because I have no other choice."

They rode into the encampment and Fes looked around, searching for signs of the others who had gone with them. How many had returned? No one else had waited in the dragon base while they had finished, and he didn't know whether that meant that they had found trouble or if they simply chose not to remain behind.

"Where are the others?" he asked Alison, pitching his voice low.

"They should be here."

"What if they came across the same sort of trouble that we did?"

"Then we should have heard or seen signs of them," Alison said.

Fes wasn't certain that they would. He turned around, looking back toward the dragon base. There was something there that troubled him. They had found a dozen men and survived the attack, but would others have survived?

It depended on how skilled a fighter they were. Fes didn't know enough about any of the rebels, other than that Micah had a confidence about him.

He lowered the forger to the ground. "Wait here," he said and peeled off, kicking his horse as he headed back toward the dragon base. At the top of the hill, he paused. The base was more extensive than he remembered, and they had only investigated part of it. Beyond the first rise where they had come to the building with the forger, there was another section that was almost as large as where they had gone in. The rest of the rebellion must have gone deeper into the base, but where were they?

"Fes!"

He glanced back at Alison. "The others haven't returned, which means they are still down in the dragon base. With as many as we faced, they would likely have found the same that we did."

Fes raced back down the hillside, not waiting on Alison. When he reached the building where he and Alison had gone in, he rode around it, released the horse's reins, and grabbed for his daggers.

He found a body. For a moment, he feared that it might be Micah. Fes didn't want to see Micah dead, if only because the man had been kind to him. Thankfully, it wasn't, but it *was* one of the rebels, and when he continued forward, he found another fallen, an arrow sticking out of his neck. Two more lay on the ground, unmoving. Blood pooled around them and flies had already begun to descend.

They hadn't been like that when they had left, had they?

Fes jumped out of the saddle. As he did, something whizzed through the air, barely missing him. It sunk into the stone of one of the neighboring buildings.

Fes looked across, searching for where it would've come from, and spied an open window in a small building. The building was crumbling, little more than the remains of something greater, and not nearly as well-maintained as the one he and Alison had broken into.

He raced forward and jumped to the side as the top of what might be a bow came into view. He hurried forward so that he could get to the building.

When he got there, he saw no way in.

What was this? How could he find the archer? He circled the building, but there was no entrance other than a small window on each side of the building, archer slits that were designed to allow an archer to look out but prevented anyone else from getting in.

Fes crept along the side of the building before stopping. Grabbing a stone from the ground, he threw it across the clearing. He waited, dagger in hand, for the bow to reach the window.

Fes spun, slamming the dagger through the opening and jamming it into flesh.

The person screamed.

The sound gave him a twisted sort of satisfaction. He hated that he enjoyed it, but he would've hated even more had he been shot. Fes waited, keeping his back against the building. He still hadn't seen Micah or the other rebels who had left the caravan.

When no other sounds came, Fes made his way from hiding and crept toward the next building. This one had a door that barely hung on the hinges. He pulled it open and paused, letting his eyes adjust to the darkness. When he stepped inside, a musty smell greeted him, clogging his nostrils. It was a mixture of dust and time and mold, all odors that nearly overwhelmed him.

He made his way along the hallway, moving carefully. On the inside of the building, the stone had begun to decay and crumble. Some sections had massive cracks occupying the entirety of the wall. One wrong move and he feared that he would crash into the wall, making it collapse onto him.

There were three doors along the hallway. Fes glanced behind the first one and saw nothing. It was a small room, empty other than fragments of stone and a few piles of bones that appeared to have been left by some creature that had dragged its prey here. The next door led into a larger room, but this one was still not very big.

There was more in the room. The remains of a table that had long ago lost one of its legs and teetered forward filled the center of the room. The broken chairs that once had surrounded the table lay scattered along the back wall. Fragments of glass and ceramic littered the floor.

Fes moved on. At the end of the hall, was the third door. This one appeared to be newer, and it was solid. Fes checked the handle and, surprisingly, it was locked.

Why would there be a locked door inside abandoned buildings? This wasn't like the other, and it wasn't like where he and Alison had found the old forger. Why should this be where they came across a locked door?

Then again, the doors in had been locked, though most of them from the outside.

Fes jammed his dagger in the doorframe, trying to pry it open. The wood screamed as he forced it open, and he worried that he might have been too loud. Someone had to be here. There was no other reason to explain why this door would be locked.

He jiggled the handle, and it finally popped open.

Something shot out of the room, clattering into the wall behind him.

Fes ducked back, looking around. It was a piece of rock. Had it hit his head, it might have been enough to do some damage.

He stepped around the corner and rolled into the room, prepared for whatever might come his way. He wasn't sure what sort of attack he might face and heard a soft yelp, little more than a child's voice.

"I'm not here to hurt you," he said.

"You hurt my father."

There was something about the voice that was familiar. "Indra?"

He heard a strangled cry and then saw a movement in the shadows.

"It's Fes. I was the one who spent the night with you camping. I was the one your father gave the totem to."

"Fes?"

The girl crawled forward, and anger bubbled within him. Her face was bloodied and bruised, and her clothing was tattered.

"What happened?" he asked.

"They came across us while we were traveling. There were too many of them. Too many for the…" She shook her head. "It doesn't matter. There were too many. Father tried to stop them, but…"

"What happened to your father?"

"I don't know where they took him."

Fes glanced at the door. "How long have you been here?"

"I don't know. They brought me here, locked me in…"

"Come with me. I can protect you."

"There were too many, even for you."

"I'm not alone."

"You were alone when you came across us. You said you were doing a job."

"Apparently there are others who are helping me with this job. Come with me, and I'll make sure that you are safe."

"What about my father?"

Could Theole be here somewhere?

They had found the forger, and he imagined that Theole's skills would be appealing to Carter—or whoever had captured them—especially if he was having someone make forgeries of dragon relics.

"I don't know where your father is, but I'll look for him."

"You can't leave me."

Fes squeezed his eyes shut. She was right. He couldn't leave her. He didn't know what had happened to her, but he knew that whatever it was put her in danger. If Carter was responsible for capturing her and her father, given the strangeness of the totems they made, he wouldn't put it past her to have some interest in them.

"Come on," he said.

He crept from the room, and when they reached the door leading out of the building, he paused, holding his hand up. He peered around. Five men waited in the center of the collection of buildings. None of them were rebels, which meant that they must have come out of some of the nearby buildings.

He would have to get her out of here and to safety, but could they wait until these men departed?

They started coming toward them.

"Go back to that room," Fes said.

"I thought you said you were going to protect me."

"I intend to protect you. That's why you need to go back to that room."

She looked up at him, her eyes wide. She paused for a moment, then her hand darted into her pocket. She pulled out one of her totems and handed it to Fes.

"I doubt that will help."

"Take it," she said.

He shrugged and took it, stuffing it into his pocket with the others.

She scurried off to the end of the hall, and when she had disappeared behind the door, pushing it closed, Fes turned his attention back to the doorway.

Five men. What approach could he take that would handle five men? But then, if he let the anger fill him, he could easily handle five men. If only there were some way to have control over it.

He had an advantage in that he was here and they didn't know it—at least, he didn't think that they knew it. Unless they'd heard him. He'd made plenty of noise freeing Indra.

Fes positioned himself so that he could keep watch

outside the door, and as he did, he realized that his count was wrong—or more had joined them.

Now there were eight.

Eight men coming toward this building. All were heavily armed, and all appeared solid, as if they could handle themselves. They would be more than Fes could take on, especially in small quarters like this. They could swarm over him, and if they did, they would reach Indra.

Fes was not about to let them reach Indra.

He glanced at the wall, and an idea came to him. When he'd first come in, he'd noticed the stone crumbling. There were sections of the wall that were unsound and wouldn't take much to collapse onto the attackers.

It was risky, but against this many, it might be the only way he could get out. Fes stepped out into the doorway, revealing himself.

The men gathered themselves, and Fes darted deeper into the building, backing up.

He waited. The men followed him in, three of them at first, and then two more. That would have to be enough.

He took one of his daggers and jabbed it into the wall, shoving it into a crack. He twisted the dagger and jammed it forward before pulling back.

The men continued to swarm toward him.

That hadn't worked as he had hoped.

He jammed his shoulder into the wall and then scampered back.

At first, he heard the sound of stone falling from the roof. Then it increased, growing louder and louder until he realized that the collapse was going to be greater than what he had intended.

He slammed his shoulder into the door Indra was hiding behind and ducked inside, pushing against it from the other side.

"What happened?" Indra asked.

"Watch your head."

"What?"

When the building collapsed, it did so with a thunderous explosion. The door shook, and the walls adjacent to the door trembled before they collapsed. A section crashed onto his shoulder, and he bit back a scream. Pain shot through his arm.

How badly was he hurt?

When the dust cleared, he looked around. Dust hung over everything, a haze glowing around them, but daylight shone overhead.

If his plan had worked, the others would be dead, but he wasn't certain that they were. And only five of them had entered the building, which meant that three others were still on the other side.

Fes pointed to the far wall, and they hurried up it. When they climbed up the wall and over, he was met by four soldiers.

Two of the men went for Indra.

Fes jumped at one of them, kicking out. His arm screamed in pain, and he ignored it. Using his good arm, he struck the man in the chest and spun around. He slashed at the next man, his dagger slicing across the man's chest.

Anger boiled within him. "You aren't going to take her," he growled at one of the attackers.

He jumped, and his jump carried him up and over one of the next men. As he landed, pain jolted through him, but he jammed his dagger into the attacker's back until his victim staggered forward, falling to the ground.

That left one man.

Fes turned around and saw that he had one arm wrapped around Indra's neck. An angry gleam crossed his eyes. "Lower your daggers."

Indra trembled.

He wasn't about to let this man harm her. His injured arm hurt too much, and he didn't think he could be fast enough to get to her.

There was something he could try.

He brought his hands up, as if to drop the daggers, and then flicked one.

It sailed true and pierced the man's eye. He collapsed, releasing Indra as he did.

Fes ran over to her. "Are you okay?"

She nodded, eyeing the man with the dagger sticking out of his eye. There was a curiosity in the way that she looked at him, nothing more. It should disturb him, but at her age, he had already killed more times than he could count and had been used for that ability.

Fes withdrew the dagger from the man's eye and wiped it on his shirt before slipping it into his sheath. "We need to get you out of here."

"What about my father?"

"We can return when I have others with me. There are some of their people who are missing, too."

Fes scooped her up in his good arm, and they raced out of the clearing, away from the dragon base, and up the hillside on foot. He wasn't sure where his horse had gone, and in the noise from the explosion, he probably had scared it off. He didn't want to wait behind any longer, and a part of him was hopeful that Alison and the other rebels had heard what had happened and would come for him.

He was about halfway up the hillside when the sound of pursuit behind him forced him to turn.

Two dozen men chased him up the hill.

Where had they been?

He glanced behind them and saw more streaming from within a building on the far side of the dragon base clearing.

Between the dozen that he and Alison had taken down and the eight more that he'd faced, they would have had to have been a group of nearly fifty stationed here. All mercenaries. Enough that he should have seen Carter, but hadn't.

"Alison!" Fes screamed as he raced up the hill.

He wouldn't be fast enough, not on foot. The men were storming up behind them, moving more quickly than he could manage while carrying Indra. He put himself between Indra and the oncoming men. If nothing else, he would protect her from the initial attack. Maybe buy her time.

And then the rebels appeared over the hillside.

A dozen had bows out, and a dozen more had crossbows, and arrows arced over his head and dropped the on comers. The few that remained turned, as if to run off, but they were chased down.

When Alison saw him, and when she saw Indra, a puzzled expression came to her face. "I don't know where Micah is or her father, but we need to go back and see," he said.

"Where did these men come from?"

Fes turned back to the dragon base. The buildings he'd explored hadn't been large enough to house this many soldiers. It meant there was someplace else, and likely underground.

And he would find it.

CHAPTER SEVENTEEN

Returning to the larger building with others gave Fes and Alison a chance to examine it more closely. They made their way through the building slowly, patiently, and explored room by room until they found what Fes expected to find—a stair leading down.

He glanced over at Alison. Indra remained near Fes, unwilling to leave his side. He didn't blame her. After everything that she'd been through, she only knew Fes, and even he wasn't someone she knew well. Then again, she knew that he wouldn't leave her, and she knew that he had fought on her behalf.

"Where do you think this goes?" Alison asked.

"It seems as if it goes down," he said.

"I can see that it goes down, but why?"

Fes looked into the darkness, not sure. Whatever was beneath here would be where the other men had come from. Maybe there were more like that. Maybe Micah and the others had been dragged here. If so, he needed to see why and if there was any way that he could get to Theole. Indra deserved to have her father with her.

"I'm going to go down and see."

"Do you think that's wise?" Alison asked. "The last time you ran off on your own, you nearly died."

Fes looked over at Indra. "I nearly died, but I found someone who needed my help."

Alison frowned at him. "Yeah. Because that's exactly what you do. You help others."

He bit back a response. Alison wouldn't understand. Indra and her father had been kind to him while he had been traveling, and that was valuable, even to him. It was not something he was going to easily overlook, especially as he feared what Carter might have done with her father.

"We need a lantern."

Alison chuckled. "A lantern? We might be able to find a torch, but there aren't any lanterns here."

"Fine. Find me a torch."

"I've got something that might work," Indra said.

Alison and Fes watched as Indra pulled one of her figurines out of her pocket. This was different than some of the others and had less detail. She ran her finger along the side, and it began to glow softly at first and then with increasing brightness. Soon it put off enough light to push back the shadows leading down the stairs.

"How did you do that?"

"It's something that my father taught me to do," Indra said.

Fes had more questions, but now wasn't the time to ask them. Was the same magic used in making the totems? If so, did that mean that the totems he carried had that same magic?

Indra handed the glowing totem to Fes, and he took it, wondering whether it would be hot, but it wasn't. The carving remained cool despite the steady glowing.

He started down the stairs, unsheathing one of his daggers as he did.

The stairs led down deep beneath the building. They weren't very wide and had been cut into the stone. The walls had a slight dampness to them. A chill came to the air as they descended that wasn't present up above.

Fes glanced back at Alison. She followed him, along with a dozen rebels. Fes was thankful that they had come along. They claimed not to have known about the attack, and from where they were situated behind the hillside, that was possible. But if there was another attack, if there were more of Carter's men, Fes didn't want to be stuck facing them alone.

Indra stayed close behind him.

"Are you sure you want to do this?" he whispered.

"I'm not being left up there."

"I'm not sure that you should come down here," Fes said.

Indra shook her head.

Fes turned his attention back down the hallway. It was narrow, and there were no outlets off it. He followed it until it reached a branching point, where he paused.

"What is it?" Alison asked.

"I think these tunnels connect to the buildings."

"What makes you think that?"

"Because this branching point would be where we would come across the building that collapsed."

"That you collapsed."

"Fine, that I collapsed. I suspect that one would lead us to the building where the archer had hidden."

"I don't see any signs of anyone else here."

"I don't either," Fes said.

"Where would they have taken Micah?"

That wasn't even Fes's biggest concern. Micah, as one of the rebellion, had known what he was getting into. Anything that happened to him would be considered part of what he had gotten himself into. Theole, on the other hand, had done nothing wrong. He was a merchant who had been trying to reach his family, nothing more.

"I am going toward that one," Fes said, motioning toward the tunnel on the right.

"Why that one?"

"Because the other one likely leads to the building that was destroyed, and I couldn't find a way into the building with the archer."

He made his way down the hall. The tunnel was barely wider than his shoulders, and it forced him to stoop. He was tall, but not so tall as to typically need to hunch over when passing through doorways. The farther they went, the more Fes worried that perhaps he had been wrong.

And then they reached another branching point.

In one direction, the tunnel veered off, likely heading toward another building. In the other, Fes suspected there would be stairs. He motioned to Alison and Indra and started down the tunnel until he found the stairs he expected.

"I don't think we could've found this without your help," he said to Indra.

"My help?"

"Your light. Without it…"

He almost shivered. Without the light, they would have been wandering in the dark, and though Fes wasn't necessarily afraid of the dark, coming into unknown tunnels that led deep beneath a thousand-year-old dragon base left him uneasy.

When he climbed the stairs, he found a door. The door was newer, and the lock was solid. Fes twisted it and finally was forced to jam his dagger into it, prying at it.

The door popped open.

He stepped inside. It was a small room, and the building was small to match. He found the fallen archer near one of the archer slits, but there was no one else here. Whether or not they had been here at one point or not, Fes didn't know.

Indra's breath caught when she saw the fallen archer.

"Is he..."

Fes nodded and placed himself between her and the body. "He was shooting from here. He took down several of Alison's people."

Alison looked at the archer, noting the wound, and turned her attention to Fes for a moment. "We shouldn't have gone into that building."

"If we wouldn't have gone in, more might have died. Think about what would've happened had all of them come after the rebel caravan."

Alison frowned, but she didn't say anything.

Fes looked around the room. Something about it left him unsettled. There had to be more. What was it that he was overlooking?

"They have to be somewhere," Fes said. "We couldn't have missed them, and we've searched most of the buildings."

"Maybe there's some other place down here," Indra said.

Fes looked back down the stairs, behind him. Where else could there have been something? He hadn't seen any sign of anything in the tunnels below, but what of the others he hadn't looked through?

Then again, these buildings were a thousand years old. Old enough that they were lucky to have survived. In some of them, it was evident that people had rebuilt the buildings over the years, but in others—those like the building he had destroyed— the decay had taken hold. Fes had a hard time believing that these buildings had once been strong enough to withstand an attack from dragons.

Maybe there was something deeper in the earth.

Fes started back down the stairs, Alison and the other rebels following him. Once again, Indra stayed close, not wanting to let him get too far in front of her. Fes didn't want to get away from her, either. He owed it to her to protect her if he could after everything that she'd been through, losing her father and getting attacked in the way that she had.

He glanced back at her, forcing a smile. "Do you have any other figurines that might be helpful?"

Indra shook her head. "Nothing that will help us now. I haven't had the chance to spend enough time on them."

"Maybe when this is all over, you can explain to me exactly what it is you do with these figurines and help me understand the magic that you use on them."

Indra studied him for a moment before nodding.

They reached the central part of the tunnels and Fes halted after going about a dozen steps. Another sound indicated the presence of something or someone.

Fes handed the light over to Indra and reached for his other dagger. With both daggers in hand, he continued forward.

He paused at the intersection and looked down the hallway, searching for movement. He didn't see anything obvious and turned back, motioning to the others with him to follow.

When Fes turned the corner, the shadows flickered.

He raised his hand gently pushed Indra back. Thankfully, she didn't argue, and took a step back around the corner, moving out of the main part of the tunnel.

Fes slipped forward, clutching the daggers tightly. There was a sense of irritation that washed through him. How many men had Carter stationed here? What exactly would they do?

He stepped forward, aware that the light he'd left with Indra had made him vulnerable. If there were others in the room—and he was certain that there were—he exposed himself by coming this way so openly.

Alison accompanied him, and Fes glanced over, thankful for her presence. They fought well together, regardless of whether they wanted to acknowledge that. She had a quick sort of brutality, and he had his daggers, along with the strength that he managed to summon when the anger boiled within him.

"What did you see?" Alison whispered. Her voice was soft, barely more than a hint of the wind, and it reached his ears and hopefully no further.

"I don't know what it was I saw, but there was movement."

"Movement?"

Fes stared at the end of the tunnel, and that movement came again. He motioned toward it and darted forward.

When he reached the end of the tunnel, he didn't find another person as he had expected. Instead, there was a curtain hanging in front of an opening in the wall. A strange breeze blew through it, causing the movement that he'd seen.

Fes pulled the curtain off to the side and Alison stared at it, as if expecting a curtain would provide answers. "What do you think this is for?"

"I don't know. Whatever is back there is meant to be hidden, even here."

"But it's not hidden that well," Alison said.

"I don't know that I would've seen it were it not for the fact that we were at the opposite end of the hall, and for the fact that we were looking for something else." He nodded to the curtain. "It looks like we found something else."

He used his dagger to push the curtains open, and he carefully stepped inside.

The air was different here. There was heat, but it was unnatural and burned in his nostrils.

"What is this?" Alison asked.

"Get the others," he said.

He waited while she hurried off and grabbed the other rebels along with Indra, and when they joined him, Fes had taken a few steps into the room, barely more than that. The heat continued to build, rising around him. It was unpleasant but tolerable.

One of the rebels coughed when he stepped inside the tunnel." What is this, Alison?" the man asked.

"I don't know. Fes saw it."

"We should return for the others," another of the rebels said.

"If we return, we will lose the opportunity to see what they did with our people."

"And her father," Fes said, looking at Indra. She gave him a nod of thanks. Fes wanted to find Theole almost as much for himself as he did for Indra. What had happened with him? There had to have been something, and he hadn't seen anybody, which meant that wherever the others had gone, it wasn't above ground. The only other possibility was for them to go deeper. Which meant going deeper into the dragon base.

They made their way through the narrow tunnel. As they did, Alison leaned toward him. "I think this has been here from the time of the dragon wars," she said.

"Probably."

"That doesn't impress you?" she asked.

Fes glanced over. In the light from Indra's figurine, he was able to make out the walls of the tunnel. They were more irregular than the walls elsewhere, and the ceiling seemed even lower, though it was difficult for Fes to determine. Everywhere that he'd been in these tunnels had been too low for him.

"Why should it? I don't know what it was like a thousand years ago when the empire was slaughtering the dragons. All I know is that I don't have to worry about fire raining down on me from the sky. I don't have to worry about entire cities destroyed by those creatures. I don't have to worry because the empire took care of that."

"And at what cost? All stories speak of the dragons having a connection to some men. A desire to protect. Was it worth losing that?"

Fes shook his head. The price had been the dragons, but for the safety the dragon relics offered, wasn't that a worthwhile price?

He turned away and continued deeper into the tunnel. The farther he went, the more he began to feel that there was something to what Alison said. These tunnels were old, and there was something impressive about that. The age of the tunnels amazed him. These had been here when man had last faced the might of the dragons. What magic did those men know? What power did those armies have to enable them to defeat the dragons?

"Why is it so hot in here?" somebody asked from the back of the line.

"Probably some ancient dragon relic down here," another person muttered.

If there was a dragon relic here, it would have to be enormous for it to put off this much heat. Most of the relics that he had encountered had put off some heat, though none with much significance.

The tunnel turned and began to descend.

Fes was forced to duck his head, more and more needing to keep from scraping his skull on the stone above. Every so often, he would crack his head on the rock, and he winced, dropping back down, ducking his head to keep from doing it again. None of the others seem to be having the same difficulty.

"I'm not sure that we should be going this deep into the tunnels," Alison said.

"We need to know what happened to your people."

"That's the only reason you want to come here?" she asked.

"I'm curious."

"About what?"

Fes looked around at everything. "About the tunnel. About everything. I have no idea what these tunnels are for or where they might lead."

Now that they were descending downward, Fes had even less of an idea of where they were going. How deep into the earth would they go?

The heat didn't change. It remained a constant presence, a persistent, dry heat that sucked the moisture out of his mouth and dried the sweat off his brow. The strange breeze that gusted the curtain remained and whispered along his skin. Fes could almost imagine voices within that wind, though he shook away that thought.

In the distance, he saw a glowing light. He motioned to it, pointing at Alison. "What do you think that is?"

"Whatever it is seems to be where we're heading."

Fes continued to hold onto his two daggers. He glanced over at Indra, who tightly clutched the figurine that glowed. She was brave—possibly braver than he would have been were their situations reversed. Then again, Indra had traveled extensively, and she likely wouldn't be as concerned about meeting new people, not the way that Fes might be.

When he reached the light, he hesitated. It was bright, and though it might only be his imagination, it seemed to shimmer, reminding him of the glow of dragon relics.

This seemed to be the source of the heat. Whatever was causing it came from there, and it gave Fes a moment of pause. He didn't want to enter too quickly, especially as he had no idea what he might encounter. He glanced back at the others with him, counting the rebels, and his gaze drifted to Indra before he turned his attention back to the room.

What choice did he have but to enter?

As Fes looked at Indra, it motivated him to step inside.

Three men were bound to chairs, one of them with his neck split, his head hanging forward. Blood pooled around him.

Micah was one of the men, and he looked at them with a wild-eyed intensity.

Fes darted forward and slipped Micah's bindings, releasing him. "You've got to get out of here. You've got to—"

Micah's eyes widened. He looked over Fes's shoulder, and Fes followed the direction of his gaze, realizing that they weren't alone.

He turned to see what he could only consider an altar. It was a long table that glowed, filling the room with the light. Behind the altar was a woman dressed in all maroon leather. Her dark hair hung to her shoulders, and in the flames that flickered along the table, giving light to the room, her hair seemed to burn.

She turned to him and pointed.

As she did, she said something, though the word was not one that Fes knew. A finger of flame leaped from her hand.

A fire mage.

Fes did the only thing he could think of, and he swiped at it with his daggers.

The flame disappeared.

The woman stared at him and turned entirely to him. "Who are you?"

"What are you doing with this man?" Fes hazarded a glance at the others and was both relieved and worried that he didn't see Theole. Where was he?

"Where did you get those daggers?" the woman asked.

Fes took a step toward her, and as he did, heat pushed him back. He slashed at it and managed to take another step before he was thrown back once more.

The woman studied him, almost as if he were a puzzle that she needed to solve. "Interesting. Perhaps I have misdirected my attention."

"Who are you?" Fes asked again.

"I am Reina," she said and as flames began to flicker around her, Fes understood.

This was the person responsible for the destruction of the Bayars' caravan. This was either the fire mage Carter had hired—or the person she worked for.

CHAPTER EIGHTEEN

F es attempted to take another step forward and was
once more thrown back. Only then did he think to
look over at Alison and the other rebels waiting at the
door. None of them moved. They seemed frozen in place
—or more likely, burned in place.

"What happened?" Fes hissed at Micah.

"I don't know. We were captured and then we were
brought down here. She's using us in some—"

Fes didn't need him to finish. He could see that whatever Reina was doing involved using them in a ceremony
of sorts, almost as if she intended to sacrifice them.

Even those who worshipped the ancient dragons
didn't believe in such sacrifice.

They had to get past this Reina. In order to figure out

what was going on here, he would have to somehow stop her.

She continued to hold her hands up, what looked like fire glowing between them in a ball that formed between her palms. She held them out toward him, directing the ball of fire as it floated in the air. As it neared, heat continued to build, growing hotter and hotter, to the point where Fes was forced to take a step back.

When he did, he slashed a dagger at the ball of fire. He already knew his daggers could withstand heat and flame, but he was surprised at the way they seemed to force the fire to evaporate, almost as if it wasn't there.

He continued to push forward, but it did no good. He couldn't get past where he was.

"Help the others," Fes said.

"With what?"

Fes thought about handing him one of the daggers, but the daggers seemed to have some resistance to whatever magic Reina used. He didn't dare give up the dragonglass daggers.

He had the dagger Tracen made for him, and he fished it out of his pocket and handed it to Micah. The other man began to work quickly and cut the others free. When they were freed, they joined Fes and Micah and stared at the woman.

"It was a mistake for you to come here, Deshazl."

Fes frowned. Something about that word that was

familiar, though he didn't know why. Had he heard it somewhere?

"All I want is to get these people to freedom. Then I'll leave you."

"Leave me? No, I don't think that you will be leaving me, certainly no time soon. The fact that a Deshazl still exists..."

"You can go ahead and try and stop me, but—"

Reina pressed her palms toward Fes. She made a sharp movement, much quicker than any she had made before, and when she did, heat and fire erupted from her palms.

Fes dropped to the ground, pulling the others with him, ducking beneath the flames. They streaked over his head, and he smelled burnt flesh and realized that one of the men who had been with Micah hadn't managed to move in time. Fes looked over to see the man's face scalded, a chunk of flesh burned off his cheek. The stench of it was incredible and almost unbearable.

How were they supposed to get out of here?

Fes started crawling, pushing Micah and the others in front of him, bringing up the rear as they worked to escape.

The woman began to make a swirling motion with her hands, and Fes jumped to his feet, sweeping the daggers out in front of him. With them, he somehow cut through the heat in the air, and Micah and the others reached the doorway where Alison, Indra, and the rest of the rebels waited.

"Go. I'll meet you."

"Fes—"

Fes shook his head, keeping his focus on Reina. "Get going, Alison. Don't be stupid with this."

He swept toward Reina with his daggers, trying to cut through the heat. He needed to give them time, and then he could make an attempt at escape. Not before then. If he couldn't provide them with enough time, he wasn't about to sacrifice himself, but it might not matter. From what he had seen of Reina, she was powerful.

"What kind of fire mage are you?"

She took a step toward him, moving with a strange, fluid sort of grace. Each step seemed to shimmer, much the way that flame might dance and shimmer. "One of the Deshazl must ask that question?"

"Considering I don't know what you mean by that, I guess that he does."

"You made a mistake in coming here. And I will make certain that none with you escape."

"I'm sorry to hear you say that. Because I have every intention of getting myself—and the people with me— out of here."

She grinned at him. Heat continued to build.

He swiped at the air. Each time he did, he managed to part the heat a little bit more. It was subtle, but it was noticeable. And from the look on her face—the tension at the corners of her eyes—and the strange way that she watched him, he could tell that she knew it and was troubled by that fact.

The air became almost unbearably hot.

He tried to ignore that, but doing so was difficult, especially the longer that he was exposed to the heat. Each breath became a struggle, almost as if he were fighting with himself, straining against his body as he struggled to breathe. His throat and lungs became raw, and it was all he could do to ignore that sensation.

The woman watched him, though she said nothing.

Could the sensation even be real?

The heat on his skin didn't seem any worse than it had been.

Maybe it was only in his mind. Maybe this was some way that she had of trying to manipulate him into believing that something was going on with his breathing.

He brought the daggers around, cutting through the air near his mouth and throat.

As he did, the horrible sensation that had been nearly overwhelming him subsided.

How much longer would he be able to keep this up? The daggers seemed to mitigate her magic, but he expected there would come a time when even that wouldn't be enough.

That meant that anything he would do would have to be quick.

Fes made a sweeping motion with his daggers. He brought them around in a circle, cutting through the air in an arc. He continued to swirl with the daggers, slicing at the heat and whatever magic she used.

Fes exploded at the barrier her magic created and lunged at her.

There was a flash of smoke and flame. When it cleared, she was gone.

Fes took a few breaths, and the air began to cool. The room was dark other than the flickering flames across the tabletop.

He turned his attention to whatever it was that she had been doing, trying to understand her intentions. There was a small length of ivory bone on the table, and Fes pushed at it with his dagger, moving it away from the fire. He wouldn't reach for it, not until he knew how hot it had gotten, but when he stared at it, he saw the same shimmering colors to it that he saw from most dragon relics.

Fes looked over at the doorway. None of the others remained, which gave him hope that they had managed to escape.

He made a quick survey of the room. Other than the fallen man, there was nothing else on that side. On the altar, he found a chalice that seemed to contain blood, but nothing else. There was the bone and the chalice.

Fes returned to the tunnel, hurrying through it. When he began to ascend, he sprinted forward, wanting to reach Alison and the others as quickly as possible. It was time for him to be anywhere else.

The others were gone by the time he reached the main tunnels, passing through the curtain and out into the section of tunnels that they had first discovered. Fes hurried through them and raced up the stairs and into the building, and then back outside.

Once there, he looked around frantically until he saw Alison and the other rebels on the far side of the clearing and heading back toward the rebel camp.

He breathed heavily, taking deep breaths of the fresh air. Day had changed over, leaving the sun falling beneath the horizon. Darkness would soon greet them, and Fes wanted to be somewhere away from here, especially if Reina might still be here.

"What happened?" Alison asked when he hurried over.

"I don't know."

"How did you manage to get away?"

Fes shook his head.

Alison watched him, arching a brow at him. "I wasn't able to even get into that room. She was... Doing something."

"I'm aware," Fes said.

"Yet you were able to resist whatever it was that she was doing. How was that?"

Fes looked around. "I don't know what I was able to do, and I don't know what she was doing. All I know is that she was controlling fire and flames and making the air so hot in my throat, it burned and..."

"What happened to her?"

"She disappeared."

"Disappeared?"

Fes nodded.

"That doesn't make any sense. Micah told me what happened. The others were captured, and she chose Victorn for sacrifice."

"We need to get moving. Let's get out of here," he said.

"What about my father?" Indra asked.

Fes licked his lips, looking over at the young girl. Her dark eyes looked up at him, begging. How could Fes refuse that? And yet how could he do what she needed? There wasn't any way to find her father, especially as he wasn't confident that he was even still around here.

He turned to Alison. "Did you find any other survivors?"

"Some," she said.

"I think it's time that we interrogate them."

"They probably don't know anything, Fes. If Carter is

running them, it's unlikely that she would have shared anything with them about her plans."

"They'll know something. They have to." He looked at Indra. Somehow, this was connected. He wasn't sure how, and he wasn't sure what it meant, but there was a connection between what had happened. He would find out whatever purpose they had in capturing her father. And then he would save him.

Fes crouched down in front of Indra. "I have to do a few things that you shouldn't see."

"What sort of things?" she asked.

"Things that I won't be very proud of when they're done."

"Why not?"

"For me to learn what might've happened with your father, I'm going to have to ask these men some questions. Doing so will require that I force them to share what they have no intention of sharing."

"If my father is involved—"

"You can't be there for this," he said.

He worried that she would argue with him and was thankful she did not. If she had argued, what would he have said? Would he have been able to tell her that there was no way for her to learn what he was going to do? Would he have told her that he needed her to stay away while he tortured at least one man, and possibly many more?

"Please find out what they did with him," she said.

Fes looked up at Alison, tearing his gaze away from Indra, not able to meet her eyes. "Is there anyone who can stay with her?"

"I think I can find someone," she said.

"Are you going to try and prevent me from doing this?"

Alison shook her head. "Even if I could, I would not."

They made their way behind the hillside and into the caravan. It seemed as if it had been days since he had traveled with them rather than only hours. So much time had gone by and so much had happened that he felt uncertain about.

Alison led him to a wagon near the center of the caravan. Two men stood outside the back, and Fes noticed that bars were set on the windows. A massive lock prevented access to it.

"Let us in," Alison said.

The nearest guard shook his head. "You know what the commander said."

"I know what he said, but we have to find out what happened."

"Not without getting his permission."

Fes stepped forward and quickly unsheathed his daggers. He flipped them, jabbing them up at each man until the tip pressed into the underside of their necks. "Don't make me do anything that will get me kicked out of the caravan. I'm already not all that thrilled about being here."

The men glared at him, but the first man tipped his head back, away from the dagger. "The key is in my pocket."

Fes fished into the man's pocket and pulled the key out. He tossed it to Alison, who reached past him, unlocking the wagon.

"I won't be long," Fes said, pulling the door open and jumping inside.

It was dark, the only light inside coming through the barred windows. The man inside was shackled. He looked up when Fes stepped into the wagon, and then looked back down at his shackles.

"I'm not going to say anything. I know that you want me to talk—"

Fes took a dagger and jammed it into the meaty part of the man's thigh.

He screamed, and Fes slipped forward, clasping his hand over his mouth, silencing him. He left the knife in the man's thigh and kept his face only a few inches away from the other man. "I need you to be quiet, or I'm going to continue to jab this dagger into your leg. Do you understand?"

The man met his gaze with a wide-eyed stare before nodding.

Fes carefully brought his hand away, and the man

sucked his breath, trying to control his breathing while the dagger remained in his flesh.

"Good. Now that I have your attention, I have a few questions for you."

"I already told you I don't know anything."

Fes twisted the dagger slightly. The man's eyes widened even more. "I'm thinking you know more than you let on. Tell me about the terms of your employment."

The man shook his head. "We took a job. It was a simple mercenary job. We've taken many of them over the years, and this one was only meant to bring us to the north."

"You didn't know that you would be asked to attack a merchant caravan?"

The man hesitated too long, and Fes twisted his knife.

"So you did know. Interesting. Was that part of the term of the employment?"

"We were told that we might need to be involved in something that required a certain level of aggression."

"Such as slaughtering an entire family of merchants."

"There wasn't a family. There weren't even that many merchants there."

"Did you bother to look in the wagons?"

"We looked, but most were gone."

Fes frowned. That wasn't what he'd seen, was it? Could they have abducted some of the Bayars? What purpose would that serve?

"And you didn't have any trouble with the fact that you would be asked to destroy so many people?"

"I've seen the way you fight. I know that you understand that sometimes the job requires difficult decisions."

Fes sighed. "Difficult decisions. I have never made a difficult decision to destroy an entire family."

"You would if the price was high enough."

"And how much have you been promised?"

"A gold a day."

Fes's breath caught. He had thought that he was getting paid well, but if these mercenaries were offered that much...

It meant that whoever Carter worked for had *real* wealth.

He already knew that whatever they were after was incredibly valuable. It might be more valuable than anything that he'd ever been asked to collect. This confirmed that for him.

"How many days have you been out here?"

"We followed the caravan when it left the city."

Fes had lost track of time and no longer knew how long he had been out of the city. Had it been two weeks? Three? Maybe it was even longer than that.

"What was the purpose in staying here?"

"We were asked to guard."

"Guard what?" When the man didn't answer quickly enough, Fes twisted the dagger again. He had pressed it down this time, digging into the bone. Each time that he twisted would be incredibly painful, and he was more than a little surprised the man was still coherent through the pain.

"We were asked to guard the dragon base."

"Did you know that there was a fire mage there?"

The man's eyes widened. "There was no fire mage. We were supposed to meet up with the rest of our party, and from there we would continue our journey."

"The rest of your party? How many more were you expecting?"

"I don't know. A couple dozen? Maybe more."

Maybe that was the second wave of soldiers that they had encountered. They hadn't hidden at all; they had been sent here, coming to meet the rest of the mercenaries.

"Why here?"

"I don't know. That's not part of the job that I'm given. I'm given information that I need, and I fight when I'm asked. You know how that goes."

"Why do you keep saying that?"

"Because you have the look of a mercenary about you. And I've seen the way that you fight with those daggers. In the way that you're torturing me."

"Be glad that it's me who's torturing you and not any of the others. There's a woman who's with me who is even more eager to extract information from you."

"What are you going to do with me?"

Fes shrugged and gently wiggled the dagger in the man's thigh. "That really depends on what you do. If you cooperate with us, if you can be counted on to provide information, it's possible that you'll be allowed to live."

"Even after I've seen the rebellion?"

Fes smiled. "Rebellion? What makes you think that this is any sort of rebellion?"

"Because I have eyes."

Fes smiled. "Then if you have eyes, you should recognize that you need to cooperate. If you're willing to cooperate, they will allow you to leave."

"The way that you're cooperating?"

"What's that supposed to mean?"

"I never saw you anywhere with them. You aren't one of them. You were hired, or brought in, but you're not the same as them. What happens to you when whatever cooperation you have been providing begins to end?"

Fes resisted the urge to jam the dagger deeper into his thigh. Instead, he yanked it free and wiped it on the man's pants. "Like I said, you would do well to cooperate with them. There is a woman with me who is more than willing to show you just how far she'll go to get the information she wants."

He crept back out of the wagon and jumped down, slipping the lock back on the door. He looked over to see Alison standing with the commander. He recognized the expression on her face, a mixture of annoyance and disappointment. He had seen it from her often enough during the time they were together, and he knew it well.

"Come with me," the commander said.

Fes shrugged at the two guards before following the commander and Alison. They reached the edge of the caravan and then went beyond it, heading to the ridgeline that looked out over the dragon base.

"What do you think you're doing?" the commander asked Fes.

"I'm trying to find information. I understand that I'm not one of you, but that doesn't change the fact that there are things that I can do that can help."

The commander looked from Alison to Fes before. "What kind of information do you think that man will be able to provide you, Fezarn? What kind of information do you think that a low-level mercenary will know about whatever is planned?"

"For starters, I learned that they were hired with the intent of attacking the merchant caravan. He knew what he was getting into when he took the job. And he claims that there weren't that many people in the caravan when they came through. I don't know whether that's true or not, but if it is, it raises the question of what would they have done with the rest of the Bayars family?"

The commander sighed. "Even if that were true, that's

not what we're here for. What we're after is more important than one family."

Fes shrugged. "It might not be what you're here for,
but it's a question that I need to be answered. If I am to
understand what is taking place and what Carter is after,
I need to—"

The commander stepped forward and got close to
Fes, looking up at him. "You need nothing. You are here
because you were hired for a job."

The commander started to turn away, and Fes called
after him, "What are the Deshazl?"

The commander froze. He turned back to Fes. The
color had leached out of his face. "Where did you hear
that term?"

"You first."

"No. This isn't a negotiation."

"Maybe not to you, but I'm the one who faced a fire
mage beneath the dragon base. There was a woman
there. We found an altar and she had sacrificed one of
your men—"

"Victorn," Alison said.

The commander squeezed his eyes shut and nodded.

"Now, what does all of that mean?" Fes asked.

The commander took a deep breath. "What all that
means is that you came face to face with someone who
could succeed at getting across the plains before us."

"She wasn't terribly interested in harming me so

much as she was interested in keeping me from going anywhere else."

The commander sighed and turned back to Fes. "And what did she say to you?"

"She used the term Deshazl."

"Are you certain that you heard that?"

Fes frowned at him. "I'm pretty certain. That's what she used to refer to me, whatever that is."

The commander regarded Fes with a different sort of interest than he had before. He stepped to the side, cocking his head, and he frowned. "Deshazl. That can't be right, can it? There can't be any of the Deshazl remaining."

"What are you talking about? What are the Deshazl?"

"You are aware that we are trying to head north, and that we intend to find a powerful dragon relic."

"How can I not be? That's what I was hired to do."

"This relic is considered nothing more than a myth. After a thousand years, how could it be anything other than myth? Yet we have some among us who believe, who feel that the dragon heart must be real, especially considering what has been observed in the dragon fields of late."

"And what has been observed there?"

"Life."

"I don't understand."

The commander watched Fes for a moment. "The dragon fields have been barren for the last thousand years. In all that time, there has rarely been anything other than steam rising over the rocks, a reminder of the battle that waged centuries ago. The remains of the dragons have long since been picked over, the dragonwalkers having claimed anything of real value, but there has always been a hope that there might be something else."

"The dragon heart?"

"What has been seen is activity, life, where none has been for many years. A single flower, and within it draws the power of those lands."

Fes started laughing. "This is about a flower?" He looked at Alison. "You brought me here to help you find a flower?"

"Don't laugh, Fes."

"How can I not laugh? If this is all been about a flower, then you could have chosen any along the way. There are plenty of flowers that grow in the forest that we passed, or even along the planes here. Some of them are pretty enough."

"It is not necessarily the beauty of the flower that will be impressive. For that matter, I suspect that few will find this particular flower to be of much beauty, but what it is, and what it has, is the fact that it has grown in lands that have not supported life in centuries. And it has grown and drawn life from the dragon fields."

"Why is that important?"

"It's important because the dragon fields carry with them the blood of the fallen dragons. They were the killing fields, the place where the dragons were slaughtered, or where they retreated when they were dying. Their blood seeped into the rock and seeped into the land, and for centuries, nothing has lived there."

"What happens when you take this flower?"

"We don't know. Possibly nothing. But the Bayars found it when they were searching the plains, and they were the ones to have reported it exists."

"If they saw it, why would they not have claimed it?"

"For many reasons, but the simplest is that they weren't certain what it meant."

Alison watched him, almost as if knowing what he was thinking about. And maybe she did. Alison had always seemed to know him too well.

"It's not the flower that you're after though," Fes said.

The commander shook his head. "The flower is the proof that the dragon heart exists. There have been others, but they are incredibly rare. Beneath the flower, far beneath the earth, there will be an item of great power. If we dig it out, if we can bring out the dragon heart, then we will be the ones who can use that power. It's a marker, a symbol of the fact that the dragons are ready to return. With a dragon heart, we might finally have the power necessary to resurrect the dragons."

CHAPTER NINETEEN

The horse seemed to hate the fact that there were now two riding on its back, even though Indra was not particularly heavy. Every so often, Indra would look back at Fes and study him, as if trying to decide whether he was deceiving her or not. Fes would smile reassuringly and nod. What else was there for him to do?

In the distance, the mountains continued to loom, their whitecapped peaks growing ever closer. The chill that had come to the air was more pronounced, and with every passing day, he realized he was underdressed for the cold. He had known they were traveling north but hadn't expected the bitterness to the air. Indra wasn't much better, which was why has stayed close to her, wanting to at least allow her to take advantage of his body warmth, and she didn't seem to resist.

Alison remained close—much closer than she had before he had decided to stay with Indra. They were making good time and had seen no further evidence of the mercenaries—or of Carter. With each passing day, Indra grew more and more restless. There was nothing that Fes could say that would reassure her, especially as he didn't know whether they would come across her father again.

When they camped for the night, Fes worked with Indra and one of the other rebels to help set up a tent they had been offered. Indra refused to go with anyone other than Fes, and so there was a tent that he considered his and hers, and when it was erected, she began to place totems around the inside, stationing one in each corner.

A group of the rebels had taken the old man—the forger—away, bringing him to one of the villages along the western border. With his skill, they intended to use him to create relics they could sell. Fes wondered how many of the replicas were forged by the rebellion.

He glanced over at Indra, pushing those thoughts away. "You still haven't told me anything about the totem magic."

Indra glanced up. She was crouched in the far corner of the tent, placing a strange totem with arms spread over its head. "We don't call it magic in Toulen."

"Then what would you call it? Especially as it seems to allow you to create light."

"That one did, but there are others that don't."

"What do you call it?"

"The dragon's blessing," she said softly.

Fes watched her. Everything had to do with dragons. "What about those?" He pointed to the totem that she placed along with the others.

"This one is the Watcher. It will alert us if there is any threat."

"How will it do that?"

"It just will."

"What about that one," Fes said, motioning to another totem. This one was squatting, almost mimicking the posture Indra was in.

"That is a Protector."

"And what does it do?"

"It protects, Fes."

Fes snorted and shook his head. "And the other two?"

"They are both protectors, though they have a different way of offering their protection than that one does."

"And how is that?"

Indra stood and wiped her hands on her pants. "It's hard to explain. I've grown up with them, and I recognize there is power in them, though it's probably different than the kind of power you are accustomed to."

"What kind of power is that?"

"I don't know. From what I heard, you managed to defeat a fire mage."

"I didn't defeat her so much as I kept her from attacking." And even that didn't feel completely right. Fes still didn't know what had happened that day, or what she meant by calling him Deshazl.

"Sometimes that is enough."

"I will help you find your father."

"What happens if we don't?" It was the first time that Indra had raised that question. It was the same question that burned within him. He didn't know what would happen to her if they couldn't find her father. Would she stay with the rebellion? Would she somehow make it across the mountains and back to her homeland? Fes didn't think it would be safe for her to go alone, which meant that he would have to see her back to her homeland. After the promise he'd made to her father, he had to.

"I don't know," he said.

Indra watched him. "And here I thought you might lie to me."

"It wouldn't do any good to lie to you," Fes said.

"Too often, people think to deceive those who are younger."

"I don't know everything that you've been through, but I do know that I will offer whatever protection I can while we are with the rebellion."

"And what happens if you aren't able to offer that protection any more?"

"Then I hope your protectors are able to keep tabs on you."

Indra looked around the tent, her gaze darting from protector to protector before looking back at Fes. "It's okay if you tell me that you don't believe."

"What's there not to believe? I've seen what you can do with your strange lantern. Why couldn't these figurines do something similar?"

"Because they aren't figurines. I already told you. These are totems."

Fes smiled. "Get some rest. I'm going to see what else I can learn."

She made a small bed in the corner of the tent, the same corner that she had preferred the last few nights. When she was settled, she looked up at him. "You're more than you let on, Fes."

"Don't tell them that."

She smiled. "I think your friend already knows."

Fes sighed and ducked out of the tent, looking around the campsite. Much like each night, it was an orderly arrangement of tents. He had found a way to ensure that his tent was set near the center, more for Indra than for him. Where it up to Fes, he'd prefer to be on the periphery, so that he could escape if it came to it. With Indra, he wanted to ensure that she was as safe as possible, which meant that he wanted to have her surrounded by as many people as possible.

He found Micah near the campfire. The other man looked up and coughed. In the days since the attack, Micah's voice had begun to return, but it was raspy, and he wasn't able to speak clearly.

"Does it still hurt?" Fes asked.

"About as much as it had before."

"Has anything changed?"

Micah shook his head. "Not so that I worry about it. I'll recover. That's enough."

"How much farther do we have before we reach the dragon plains?" Fes asked.

"A couple of days," Micah said.

"And where do we go from there?"

"From what I understand, you spoke with the commander. We're going, and if it works, then…"

If it worked, the rebellion would have access to some item of great power. Was that what he wanted? He didn't understand the reason for the rebellion, not really. They opposed the oppression they believed the empire caused, but Fes didn't have any experience with that oppression.

"Why?" Fes asked.

"Why the rebellion?" When Fes nodded, Micah turned to stare into the fire. "You know Anuhr, but you haven't spent much time outside of the city, have you?"

"Not much. Why?"

"You'd see the price paid by the villages."

"What price?"

Micah grunted. "The empire imposes a price for protection. Men are commissioned into the army and too few return."

Fes had avoided it but knew others didn't. "That's their choice."

"Is it? How many are lost fighting for the empire?"

"The empire hasn't been involved in any fighting for a long time."

Micah shook his head. "That's what they want you to believe."

They sat in silence for a while before Fes got up and started making his way through the rows of tents. Alison found him. "You need to come with me."

"Where?"

"We think we have found where they're keeping Talmund."

Fes looked over at his tent.

"I'll have someone keep an eye on her."

"That's not what it was."

Alison shook her head. "That is what it is, and while I am happy that you have finally found it in you to care about someone other than yourself, it's strange that it's for someone you barely know."

Fes glared at her. "I made a promise to her father."

"You and promises."

"You're only mad that I didn't make a promise to you."

"You're right. I am mad about that. You knew that you wouldn't be able to keep it."

"I knew, which was why I never made any sort of promise to you."

They reached the edge of the encampment, smoke from the cookfire hanging in the night air, and Alison led them to a pair of horses. They were already saddled, as if they were waiting for her and Fes. "Just us two?"

"This is going to be a quiet mission."

"And by quiet, you mean your commander doesn't know you're doing this."

Alison looked over at him and shook her head. "He doesn't know."

Fes glared at her. "What is this about?"

"Without the priest, everything that we do will fail. It will be my fault. I was tasked with getting the necessary help, and I thought that you..." She shook her head. "It doesn't matter. Talmund wanted you along, so we brought you alone."

Fes considered Alison for a moment. Was she doing this because she worried that he would betray them? He wouldn't put it past her to do that, especially as he *had* betrayed her before, and the fact that he had never made a promise to her that he wouldn't betray her again this time.

"Do you even know where Talmund might be found?"

"Scouts report movement to the northwest."

"What kind of movement?"

"The kind of movement that indicates that Carter and her mercenaries might be there."

Fes breathed out heavily. If Carter were there, maybe they *would* find the priest. Maybe they would find Theole. It wasn't the kind of mission that only two of them would be able to do. "You've cautioned me about going off on my own, but that's what you're talking about. Don't play me."

"I would ask the same of you, but I wouldn't have any guarantees, would I? Not without a promise."

"I promise not to play you tonight," Fes said.

Alison glared at him. "Fine. I won't play you either. The commander was going to continue moving north, which means that he intends to leave Talmund with Carter. He intended to have scouts continue to follow, but I don't think he intends to go after him. There is no plan to rescue him."

"Why not? I thought that Talmund was the only one who could find this flower?"

She glanced back toward the camp before meeting his eyes. "The commander thinks he now has another way of finding the flower and the dragon heart."

Fes found that surprising. Everything he had heard so far had led them to believe that the priest was important for this.

"What changed?" When Alison didn't answer, Fes looked over at her, holding the reins for the horse in hand but making no movement toward it. He wasn't about to climb into the saddle until he understood what was going on. What was Alison getting at? "Alison?"

"You changed, Fes. When you came across that fire mage, and she called you Deshazl, the commander no longer thinks he needs to have the priest to find the dragon heart."

"And why is that?"

"Because he's got it in his head that *you* will be able to find it."

Fes started to laugh but cut off when he realized that Alison wasn't laughing along with him. "How would I be able to find it? I haven't seen the flower, and I wouldn't have any idea of how to find it so there wouldn't be any way for me to help discover this dragon heart."

"You haven't, but if you *are* Deshazl, you would be drawn to it. And considering that you have this connection to relics, I believe it."

"Why?"

"The Deshazl are descended from the dragon lands."

"Like the Settlers?"

He'd seen what he had been able to do against a fire mage. That was power he shouldn't have, but either his daggers did... or *he* did. And there was the way he could use his anger—his rage—to do things he didn't think should be possible.

"This is different than the Settlers. This is about those who lived in the dragon lands, lived on the dragon fields, before the dragons retreated and perished. From what the commander says, the Deshazl had a special bond to the dragons, one that was even greater than the Settlers."

"And how is this different than what the priest was describing to me?"

"Because this is more than a sensitivity to dragon relics. This is more than the ability to identify those ancient artifacts. This is about power that burns within the Deshazl."

When she mentioned burning, Fes frowned. "I don't have anything burning within me," he said.

"Probably not. The Deshazl are supposed to be long extinct. More likely than not, the fire mage had it wrong. It's probably about those daggers that you carry, especially since they're dragonglass. What matters now is that the commander believes that you can help find the dragon heart."

"And that means he will abandon the priest." Alison nodded. "And the priest is important to you?"

"He's important to Horus, Fezarn. Is that what you want me to say? If we fail…" Fes didn't need her to explain. If they failed—if *she* failed—there would be no returning to Anuhr, nor to working with Horus. "Do you want me to tell you the commander is willing to leave him to Carter to get ahead of the mercenaries and find the dragon heart first?"

What should he do?

He'd abandoned her once before. Would he do it again?

As he looked at her, the expectant expression in her eyes, he knew he couldn't. "I'll help you find him." It was growing darker by the moment, and within a short period of time, he suspected that it would become too dark for them to navigate. What was Alison thinking, having them head out like this? "Will you really make sure that somebody watches after Indra?"

Alison nodded. "I have connections here, Fes. I'll make sure she's looked after."

That was all that he could ask for, and if she really would help, then he would do this for her. Alison deserved that much from him. "It seems that you want to go now."

"I need to go now. If we wait too much longer, any rumor that we have of where to find him will be lost."

Fes took a deep breath. He didn't like the idea of heading out into the night, especially not if it meant that he was going into the dragon plains. "How much do you know of the dragon plains?"

"Enough to get us across. And if you're with us—and have some way of crossing..."

Fes stared at her for a moment. It would have to be enough, wouldn't it?

He saw the beseeching look that Alison gave him, the expression that practically begged that he help. It was the same way that Theole had looked at him, demanding that Fes offer a promise. As with Theole, it was a promise Fes was determined to keep.

CHAPTER TWENTY

The edge of the dragon plains appeared as little more than a haze in the night. It was different than the surrounding landscape. Whereas everything else around them had been tall grasses spotted with the occasional tree, the dragon plains were bleak, barren rock, and a strange and surprising heat emanated from it. The air held a bitter stench, and he resisted the urge to shiver.

"From what Talmund told me, everyone is uncomfortable the first time they come here," Alison said.

"And how many people come here for the first time at night?"

Alison glanced over and smiled. "I doubt many are foolish enough to do that."

"What's the commander planning?"

"I don't really know. He thinks he can get ahead of Carter."

"And what will that serve?"

"If he does, there's a place where he thinks to pinch Carter's mercenaries. We have numbers, and hearing him talk about it, this place *should* let our numbers make the difference."

"Even with a fire mage?"

She sighed. "I don't know."

Carter moved quickly, and if she had the priest, she'd know *where* she was heading. "Wouldn't it be better if we found the dragon heart first? We know where Carter will be. If Talmund is guiding them toward the dragon heart—"

"Do you think you're Deshazl?"

Fes blinked. "What?"

"Do you think you're Deshazl?" she repeated.

"You know that I don't."

"Then how do you think you'll find the dragon heart? That's what the commander counts on, but if you're *not* Deshazl, there doesn't seem to be any way for you to actually find the heart."

That was the challenge.

Then again, from what Carter had said, they should need a fire mage to even be able to cross the dragon plains, but they had been able to do it without one so far. Would there come a time when that would change?

"Let's hurry," he said.

She nodded and guided them onto the dragon plains. The horses' hooves sounded incredibly loud across the stone, clattering strangely. The longer they went, the more the sound began to fade, becoming almost muted. It was an odd noise, and he looked over at Alison, thinking that she would notice it, but she didn't seem to.

He focused on the ground beneath them and saw the dragon fields spreading out around them in the faint moonlight. Something like a haze hovered over the ground, making it difficult for him to see clearly. Then again, if it was difficult for him, then it might be difficult for others to see clearly. It might be the perfect night to attempt a rescue of Talmund. If they were able to get in and then back out quickly, they might be able to spring him before anyone was wiser.

The rumors of the dragon plains were true. The ground was barren and rocky, and in the faint moonlight, it seemed as if it were all a gray or black rock. The haze seemed to drift up from the ground, steam rising from rock that still was heated by the dragon flames.

"I can't believe a flower could grow here."

"That's why it's so unique. The flower should not be able to grow, and somehow it is. That's why we need to find it. If we can find the flower, and we can reach the dragon heart, we can..."

There was a sound off to the west, and Alison trailed off, looking into the night.

Fes's gaze followed the same direction, but he could see nothing other than the haze of the strange fog that drifted up. He fought the horse, keeping it from moving and stamping its feet. Any sound they made would only draw attention to them.

"I think we have to leave the horses," Fes said.

Alison glanced over, her eyes wide. "If we go by foot…"

"What choice do we have? Listen to the horses as we move. If I can hear it, then others can. We need to go by foot where we can sneak more quietly."

"What do you propose that we do with them? They can't be left in the dragon fields. There's nothing for them to graze on, and it's possible we won't be able to return this way."

Fes glanced back at the direction from which they had come. "There's only one thing we can do with them. We need to send them back."

Alison was shaking her head. "That's a terrible idea, Fes. The moment we do, we commit ourselves to staying here."

"I thought we were already committed to rescuing Talmund."

"How do you intend for us to break free if we don't have any way to escape quickly?"

"I didn't say that we wouldn't go on horseback, only that we wouldn't go on the horses we came in with."

"Think about what you're saying, Fes."

"I don't think that we have many options. If you want this to succeed…"

Alison stared at him for a long moment before climbing from her saddle. Fes joined her, and when his boots thudded on the ground, he stiffened, afraid of how much noise they were making.

He leaned toward the horse's ear. "You need to go back to the others," he said, patting the creature on the side. The horse huffed softly but tipped his head toward him. He patted it another moment and shook his head. "You need to go. What we're going to do isn't going to be safe for you."

When he patted the horse on the side again, the creature took off, heading back the way they had come, and moving quickly and surprisingly quietly. It was almost as if the horse understood what he wanted of it.

Alison was having a harder time. Her horse seemed to be fighting, shaking his head as she was trying to whisper something to it.

Fes looked at her with an urgency in his eyes. He hadn't heard the same sound again, but he worried that he would, and he didn't like the idea of staying here, especially with something as noticeable as a horse outlined against the night. At least by themselves, they could crouch down behind the rocks and hopefully disappear.

Finally, she patted the horse on the side, and the mare took off, heading after the other.

"That took you long enough," he said.

"I can't help that she cared about me."

"Or maybe she simply knew that you had the food."

Alison frowned.

"And mine listened better…"

The sound came again, this time a little more distant than before, but just as distinct.

Fes frowned. He glanced over at Alison, and she nodded. "I heard it."

They started across the rock. It was uneven, and Fes paused at one point to pick up one of the stones, examining it. He hadn't seen anything like it before. Some of them were light, almost porous, while others were smooth and slick, reminding him of his dagger.

They paused every so often, attempting to listen, but there was no other sound. Fes surveyed the land around him. It was incredibly bleak, nothing more than the broken rock, with no sign of life. They were it. He began to understand what Alison and the commander had said about the possibility of a flower growing here. If flowers could grow, then what else could be here?

As they walked, Fes unsheathed his daggers. Alison looked over, but he only shrugged. He felt foolish, but he would have felt much more foolish not having them in hand if they were jumped. With the haze that rose up from the ground, the steam or fog or whatever it was, it made it difficult to see well enough whether anyone would be approaching. He wasn't about to be surprised here. Fes would not have his last days be in this place.

Gradually, the ground began to rise, though the slope was gentle. Every so often, there would be a gust of cool air, and it was a welcome reprieve from the heat around them. It was strange that they should feel so warm here, especially as they had felt nothing but cold air over the last few days.

"Do you know where we're heading?" Fes asked.

Alison pointed. "They were heading north, and this is the safest path for that."

"How do you have any sense of where you're going?"

"How do you not?" she asked.

"With the fog around us, I can't see a thing."

"We both know that it's not fog."

"Fine. With whatever steam this is, I can't see a thing."

Alison pointed to the sky. "Every so often, I catch glimpses of the moonlight. With that, I can see through it clearly enough that I can get a sense of which way we're heading."

Fes wasn't sure that was the best way to navigate, but he wasn't going to argue with Alison, not on this. They continued to make their way across the dragon fields, and night continued to grow deeper around them. There was a strange stillness to the air, and at first, Fes thought it was his imagination, but the longer they walked, the more he began to be aware of it. It was almost a physical presence, one that reminded him of the heat that had radiated from the fire mage. As he went, he thought about what Carter had said about needing a fire mage to cross the plains. How was it that they were able to do it without one?

After walking like that for nearly an hour, the heat continuing to bother him, Fes grabbed Alison's arm. She frowned at him. "Do you feel that?" he asked.

"Feel what?"

"The heat. Does it feel familiar to you?"

Alison looked away from him and scanned the ground. "I don't feel anything different."

"There is something different." Fes was certain of it, even if he couldn't put a finger on what it was or why he would be feeling it.

They continued on, and though they managed to walk softly, with muted feet, every so often the rock would tremble beneath his feet, and he would slip, almost enough to give them away. It made him extra cautious with each step, almost unpleasantly so.

The longer they went, the more and more certain Fes was that there was something more that he detected. How could Alison not be aware of it? The heat was building, rising around him, and it was so similar to what he'd experienced in the place beneath the dragon base. Did that mean the fire mage was here?

They weren't ready for her, if so. He'd gotten lucky the last time. He doubted it would happen again.

Fes swiped at the air with his daggers. The heat dissipated, just as it had when they'd been attacked by Reina.

That wasn't his imagination.

"I think we will need to move more carefully," he said.

"What is it?"

"I'm not certain, but I think the fire mage is nearby." He turned to Alison. "We know Carter has a fire mage." Fes still didn't know if the fire mage employed Carter—and if that were the case, it meant there was something else taking place that Azithan hadn't known about—or whether she'd hired them. "We know a fire mage destroyed the caravan. And we came across Reina beneath the dragon base. She got away from us, which means she's probably with Carter."

And for him to feel the effects of her spell meant they were close.

And now he might have revealed himself.

Alison pressed up against him, her body not nearly as warm as the air around him had been. It was better now, but it was still hot, the wind pushing out, making him uncomfortable. "You don't know that."

"Alison, I know what I was feeling. It was the same

thing as what I felt beneath the dragon base. And just like there, there was a relief when I cut through the air with my daggers."

"I trust you. If you say that we need to be careful, then we will be careful."

They continued forward, and as they did, Fes paid attention to the shifting currents in the air. All he needed to detect was the presence of the heat. If he could pick up on that, it might be enough to know whether the fire mage was active again, or whether there was something else taking place. Maybe it had been only his imagination. Perhaps it was nothing more than the strangeness of this place getting to him.

Fes didn't think that was the case. He had been in strange places before, and he had done things that made him uncomfortable, but this was different. He wasn't sure how to explain it any differently than that, other than that it was so similar to the heat that he had experienced when in the tunnels.

It didn't come again.

That made him uncomfortable. It should be a relief that the heat didn't continue to rise and the presence of the painful burning didn't return, but the fact that it had not returned left him worried that perhaps the fire priest was aware that they were here. Fes had been lucky the last time to escape her and didn't like the odds that he might be forced to encounter her again. And now that she might know that he was coming?

Deshazl.

He could practically hear her call him that, the strange way that she had spoken seared into his mind.

Alison looked over at him. "What is it?"

"Nothing but my imagination."

They took another step, and he heard rocks tumbling nearby.

He grabbed for Alison and pulled her to the ground. "There is someone here."

Alison reached for her sword and unsheathed it quietly. Fes still gripped both daggers, and he crawled forward, leading Alison now. He made his way toward the sound. He would rather find whoever might be out there before they reached him.

It was possible that they didn't know where to find him, not yet, and if they moved quickly enough—and silently enough—they might not ever realize where he was.

A soft gust of wind picked up. It carried a little of the haze away and cleared the night for a moment.

A shadow stood outlined.

Fes nodded toward it, but Alison shook her head. "I don't see it," she mouthed.

Fes crawled forward, and when he was near where he had seen the shadowed figure, he launched and slammed into the person. He found a tunic and grabbed it, sliding his dagger up into the flesh of whoever was standing guard. The man let out a strangled cry, too loud in the silence of the night, and then fell to the ground. He landed with a soft thud.

When he was down, Fes was able to examine the man. He wore the crimson colors of the empire, and that left Fes nervous for a moment, but nothing else struck him as a soldier. He carried a crossbow but surprisingly didn't have a bolt readied.

Had it been Fes standing guard out in this place, he would have been ready with not only a crossbow bolt but he would have had a sword in hand. There was just something about this place that made him incredibly uncomfortable, and he would not have been willing to stand so helplessly, especially not when he was forced to stare out into the darkness, unable to see anything.

Alison reached him. "How did you see him?"

"How did you not?"

"I heard the rock, but I couldn't see anything through the haze."

"The wind picked up, clearing it."

Alison frowned. "There hasn't been any wind since we've come to the dragon fields."

"There's been an occasional gust of cold northern air that's cleared some of the haze."

Alison stared at him. "If you say so. I haven't detected

it. But I can't argue with the fact that you saw this man and managed to get to him before he got to us."

"If there's one guard, there will likely be others," Fes said. "We need to be careful and keep our eyes open."

"I think that you need to be the one to search through here. Maybe there's something to your Settler heritage."

And, she didn't need to say, the possibility that he *was* Deshazl.

Fes took a deep breath and crawled away from the fallen man. He made his way along the rock, and when they were far enough away, he stood. At least now they knew they were heading in the right direction. If Carter was here—and had sentries stationed—then they had to be getting close.

The hardest part of all of this would be getting into wherever she was camped and dragging the priest out without anyone noticing. Then again, it was possible that with the haze hanging over everything, they wouldn't have as difficult a time sneaking in and out as he had thought. Maybe the haze could be used to their advantage.

When he moved forward another dozen steps, he began to feel the same strange heat building once again.

This time, he knew it wasn't his imagination. This had to be the fire mage. And yet, he wasn't willing to use his daggers to cut through it, ending whatever spell she was creating. Doing that would undoubtedly reveal their presence, if she didn't already know how close they were.

Fes paused every so often, listening to the air. There were no other sounds, nothing that would reveal whether there were other sentries. The last time had been a fluke, nothing more than chance, and he didn't count on the same chance occurring again. Somehow, they would have to find a way to reach the other sentries—or slip past them.

"Have you heard anything?" he whispered.

Alison leaned in, pressing her mouth up to his ear. "Nothing other than you."

"I'm moving quietly."

"As quietly as you can."

"And what does that mean?"

"It means that you are a man. You move quietly, but you're quite a bit heavier than me, so there's only so quiet that you can be."

She spoke directly into his ear, her voice barely more than a breath, and it left him shivering, thinking of the times long before when they had shared different whispers.

"I haven't heard anything, and I heard the rock tumbling the last time."

"Like I said, you're moving as quietly as you can." She smiled and stepped away.

Fes continued forward, and the wind shifted again,

gusting slightly out of the east. When it did, he saw a slight clearing in the haze. With it, he caught sight of a strange glow.

Hopefully only a campfire, but with what he'd detected from the fire mage, he couldn't know if it wasn't her magic.

He nodded in the direction that he'd seen the light. "Did you see that?"

"I didn't," she said.

"It's either a campfire or something worse."

"Like what?"

"Like a fire mage."

Her breath caught. "I don't see anything but darkness."

"Maybe that's your eyesight. You blamed me for being too heavy, but maybe my heaviness is offset by my much better eyesight."

She pinched her mouth in a frown but didn't say anything. She pushed on his back, sending him forward. Fes started after the firelight that he'd seen, and the longer he went, the more clearly he saw it. It began as little more than a hint of glow against the night, and the closer they came, the more obvious it was. Fes paused, not wanting to approach too quickly and waiting to see whether Alison would detect the same thing. It wasn't until they were nearly upon it that she finally caught his arm.

"Now you see it?" he whispered in her ear.

She nodded. "How is it that you were able to see it so far away?"

Fes shook his head. "Like I told you—"

Stone shifted nearby.

Fes had grown accustomed to the sound, having come to recognize when his feet were shifting in just such a way that the rock beneath his boots began to slip. It was the same sound.

And it was near Alison.

Fes pulled her behind him and spun, twisting toward a dark shadow that appeared through the haze.

His dagger met resistance, and he cut up, intending to slice through whoever might be here. He held his hand in place, afraid to withdraw, and the person that he had attacked hung from the end of his dagger.

Fes darted toward the person and grabbed them, lowering them to the ground.

It was another mercenary, dressed much the same as the other, though this one carried a sword unsheathed.

At least they were ready for whatever they might face.

Alison crouched next to him. "I don't know how you're seeing through this haze."

"I don't know either."

He continued toward the firelight. As they did, he stayed low, creeping on hands and knees, not wanting to be too exposed. Anyone who would be looking out into the darkness would be looking at head height, searching for anyone coming toward them, and would be much less likely to be looking down at the ground. And down at the ground, it was easier to remain hidden. The haze drifted up, masking them even more.

The heat continued to build against him, but it wasn't the same as what he had felt in the tunnels. It wasn't a barrier that seemed to push against him so much as it wasn't an unpleasant sort of heat. Maybe the fire mage was using some kind of magical spell to increase the haze of the dragon fields. If that were the case, why would she want to make it more difficult for the mercenaries to remain concealed?

After another four steps, Fes saw the fire.

It was difficult to see through the haze, almost as if what rose up from the rocks drifted around the fire itself, swirling toward the night. Muted voices drifted up toward the night, barely more than a murmuring. How many would be camped here?

Fes remained in place, listening. Alison held onto his arm, and he glanced over at her. Neither of them spoke. Fes was afraid to say anything, and he was thankful that Alison didn't attempt to whisper in his ear. It seemed as if doing so would put them in danger.

After listening for another moment, he started forward again. As he did, the heat began to build. It was a barrier, a resistance, and it prevented him from getting too close to the campfire. The barrier was too much like what he'd detected when facing the fire mage to be anything different.

She was powerful. He'd known that from facing her, but he could *feel* it, like a strange sensation that washed through him.

He crawled back to where he and Alison had first waited. "I don't think we can get through this barrier," he whispered.

"What barrier?"

"The same barrier that we experienced in the tunnels."

"Didn't you say that you cut through it?"

Fes nodded. "I think that I can, but the moment that I do, I think we will expose our presence. We have to be ready, which means that we need to know exactly where Talmund is kept."

"We could search our way around the campsite."

It was a reasonable idea. So far, they had come across only two sentries, so even if they came across a few more, Fes thought that he could bring them down, allowing them a chance to stake out where the priest was held.

As they made their way around the camp, the haze became no easier to see through. Fes continued to keep his daggers squeezed tightly in hand, afraid to release them and afraid to use them, not wanting to slice at the air and reveal themselves.

Alison stayed close, crouching next to him, and she did move more silently than he could. It was evident in the way that she controlled her breathing much better than Fes. He was breathing heavily, though not necessarily panting. It was a steady breathing, and he strained to keep it under control but didn't think that he managed as well as he wanted.

The haze surrounded the entire encampment. It was more than just the haze that surrounded everything, it was the sense of the power—and the flame—that built around them. Fes half expected to see the fire mage but saw no evidence of her. Wherever she was, she remained hidden and hidden enough that he could not see her.

They had made a nearly complete circle of the encampment when they came across another sentry. This time, Fes wasn't quick enough.

The man hollered out. Fes noted his position and jumped at him, stabbing him in the chest with one of his daggers as he reached for the sentry's mouth, clamping a hand across it.

Fes grabbed Alison, and they scrambled back, moving around the circle and away from the sentry. If they were lucky, the mercenaries would track this man back to the others, and maybe leave the camp altogether, but Fes doubted that they would be lucky.

When they had circled what seemed to be halfway around the encampment, coming at it from the other angle, they waited.

The men in the camp were talking quietly to each

other. Or maybe it only seemed that way. It could be that the men were talking excitedly, but he couldn't hear them with the muted sound of their voices.

"We have to do it now. They know we're here and any longer..." Fes took a deep breath. He readied himself and looked at where he knew the campfire would be. "Are you ready?"

Alison nodded. "Let's see what we can find."

CHAPTER TWENTY-ONE

F es slashed at the air, cutting at it with his daggers, no longer sure whether it made a difference or not, but he had a sense that doing so would help him get free from the haze and the barrier that prevented him from reaching the campsite. As he slashed through it, a sizzling sort of energy dissipated.

That was a first. When he had faced the fire mage before, he'd not felt anything other than the heat from her magic. What did it mean that he was able to detect her magic as it dissipated?

He scrambled forward, and the campfire came into view.

They reached a clearing and, once inside it, the haze faded. It was still there but almost as if pushed back by the campfire. Fes raced forward and looked around the campsite. He reached the fire, but there was no one there. He could smell roasting meat and ale from whatever keg the mercenaries had managed to bring with them.

"You think all of them left?"

"I don't know how all of them would have. They would've left—"

The sense of movement nearby startled him, and Fes spun, lashing out with his daggers as he did. They cut into a man's belly, slicing him open as he appeared out of the haze that still surrounded the camp.

Alison's eyes widened, and she kept her sword unsheathed, moving in a stance that put her at the ready.

Fes scanned the encampment. It was little more than a row of small tents, not enough to hide someone. Where would they have been keeping the priest? There had to be a place for him, but it would have to be somewhere that he could remain secured, and that wouldn't necessarily be by the fire.

Fes started away from the campfire, moving into the darkness and making his way quickly. They wouldn't have much time. If Carter was with the mercenaries here —and Fes suspected that she was—then Carter would recognize the dagger wounds.

It meant that he needed to move even more quickly.

He and Alison spiraled out from the campfire. The haze around everything made it difficult for them to see clearly and they hurried, wanting nothing more than to figure out what else might be in this encampment.

They encountered another soldier, and Fes barely had time to block with his daggers. Alison slipped around, slicing through him with her sword. Fes had a moment to marvel at her speed and grace before another attack came, the man sliding toward them with the same speed the first had shown. Both men were dressed the same, crimson colors that made it seem as if they served the emperor, and both were armed with swords.

A troubling thought came to him. Could they actually *be* the emperor's men?

With a fire mage involved, it was possible.

Could he have made a mistake?

"I don't think that we have much time," Alison said.

Fes shook his head. "I don't think we do either."

They still hadn't seen any evidence of the fire mage. Wherever she was, however she was making this haze that hung over everything, he had not discovered the key to it. If she was nearby, somehow hiding from him, he needed to find her, if only because he suspected the priest would be with her—if he were to be found anywhere in this encampment.

They continued their spiral outward, and Fes realized that they had reached the part of the camp from which they had started.

He nearly stumbled over the fallen sentry.

Fes glanced at the fire. The campfire, the haze that he saw, was no different, but there was nothing else that would explain how many men might have been here. There were far too many sentries for the number of men he'd heard disappearing into the night.

Unless...

Fes grabbed Alison and pulled her back.

"What is it?"

"I think we made a mistake," he said.

"Why?"

"Because I think that they are—"

A dozen men approached from the far side of the camp. They moved quickly, swords blazing, catching the reflected firelight. Fes slipped the first attack but barely missed the second. The sword that swung past him whistled through the air, nearly taking off his head. He dropped to his knees and rolled, sweeping up with his daggers, driving them at the nearest attacker.

Where was Alison?

He rolled over and saw one of the men swinging his sword behind her.

Fes lunged, unable to suppress the scream of anger that surged through him. He swiped out with the daggers, sweeping one down, and he stabbed the man in the back, jerking the dagger free as he kicked at one of the next men who approached.

Alison glanced over her shoulder and realized that he

was there. She nodded to him, and Fes jumped, driving his shoulder into an attacker, dropping him to the ground. He swung out with his blades, sweeping them across the next man and managing to cut him down.

How many were left?

"There's too many of them," Fes said, backing up to Alison.

"We need to find Talmund," she said, hacking with her sword, sweeping around as she cut down another.

"If we're dead, we won't be able to find anything."

Alison jabbed with her sword, and the man who was attempting to cut into her was forced back, ducking under the sweep of her blade.

Fes hurried forward, getting in front of her and sweeping out with his daggers. Each time that he did, he managed to somehow diminish the haze.

There had to be something here. Regardless of what they had seen, the presence of the fire mage and her magic was enough to tell him they had something they needed to protect, even if he couldn't see it.

Only, what was it?

"Where will we go?" Alison said, backing into him.

Fes didn't know. They thought to hide on the dragon plains, but how well would they be able to remain concealed? After leaving the horses, could they return to the rebels?

Fes hesitated.

It was only a moment, but it was enough. One of the swordsmen got close—almost close enough to strike him —and he turned at the last moment, bringing his daggers around and catching the sword blade between them. Fes twisted them, and the blade snapped. He stabbed the man in the chest, taking a moment to look around.

These men wouldn't be here alone, which meant that this was only a distraction. This was part of Carter's plan. This camp hadn't been the only camp. It couldn't be. If it was, where was Carter? Where was the fire mage?

Carter was testing the rebellion. That had to be what it was.

And she had Talmund. Maybe Theole.

The idea of that angered Fes in a way that he hadn't felt before.

Rage boiled within him, and he struck.

He jumped, twisting around, cutting with his daggers, sweeping from side to side, carving through the mercenaries. Each time he swept around, he diminished the haze and was increasingly able to see more clearly.

And then all of the mercenaries were down. There was no one else to fight.

He paused, looking around before wiping his daggers on one of the fallen men. He took a few deep breaths, steadying his breathing as he looked over at Alison.

"Is that it?" he asked.

"So far," she said.

"Good, because I think this was only the first wave."

"What you mean?"

"Only that I think this was designed to draw us in. Where are the horses? Where are the other men? Where is the fire mage, and Talmund?"

Alison's eyes widened slightly. "You don't think that she would do that."

Fes looked around. "You mean sacrifice her men in this way? Carter is clever. This is exactly the kind of thing that she would do, especially if she intended to use this camp as a way of determining when the rebels might attack."

"Why?"

"For starters, I doubt she thought there would be much of a challenge. I suspect whatever the fire mage is doing is enough that it obscures the possibility of an attack. She probably thought they weren't in any danger and that there wasn't a chance that anyone would be able to get in and challenge them."

And instead, it had only taken the two of them. Once again, Fes had allowed himself to be wrapped up in the anger, letting it consume him. Each time he had allowed himself to embrace that rage within him, he had helped them survive something that they would not have otherwise.

What did that mean?

Was that what it was to be Deshazl?

It was more reason to find the priest—and return to Azithan.

"Where do you think they are?"

Fes shook his head. It would have to be nearby, wouldn't it? If the fire mage were causing this, she would need to be close enough in proximity to be able to create that effect.

But where?

"I don't think we can remain here," Fes said. "She'll know I cut through her spells."

Alison looked around the clearing. "Maybe we should," she said.

"You want to draw the fire mage to us?"

"I don't really want to, but think about it. We don't know where she is. We don't know where the rest of the mercenaries are. But if she knows that you were here, don't you think that they would be sending others?"

"What happens when they come in even more numbers?"

"With your ability to see through this," she said, looking up at him with an intrigued expression, "we might be able to see what else they are planning."

Fes didn't like her plan, but mostly because it meant that he had to rely upon abilities he didn't know how to control. And they had to be abilities, didn't they?

Alison watched him, and he nodded. They made their way to the edge of the soldiers' camp, the edge of the haze, and though it wasn't nearly as present now as it had been before, there still was enough that drifted up out of the ground, as if the dragon fields were everything that rumors had claimed them to be. They crouched behind a few small rocks and waited.

Fes wondered how long they would have to wait. Neither he nor Alison said anything, almost as if both of them had an unspoken agreement to remain silent, worried about whether breaking that silence would betray their presence.

He didn't have to wait too long.

At first, Fes noted only a strange shimmering of the haze, almost as if shadows tried to push through it. It came slowly, but eventually, it parted the haziness, and he counted the soldiers as they appeared. Ten, then twenty, then thirty soldiers appeared. All were heavily armed.

If they turned their attention to him and Alison, if they somehow discovered them, then they would be trapped. Likely, they would be killed.

Alison leaned in and mouthed a question in his ear. "Did you see which direction they came from?"

Fes pointed but wasn't sure that where he pointed was right. That was where the shadows seemed to come around the haze, but was that where he had actually seen them appear? It could have been anywhere. For that matter, they could have been circling around them, waiting to see whether anyone else would appear. Maybe they had approached the same way in which Fes and Alison had.

Either way, Fes stayed in place, barely willing to move. They watched as the soldiers continued to make a circle of the clearing, coming within a few paces of Fes and Alison. Somehow, they overlooked them. When they were done, they started back out.

They were mostly silent, but every so often, they would make enough noise that he could hear them. Alison sat stiffly next to him, trying not to move, and trying not to even breathe. He could feel the way that she resisted the urge to take a breath, unwilling to do anything that might make the men aware of their presence.

And then they were gone.

Fes got up and hurried out into the darkness as he followed them. He moved as quietly as he could, and even then, he still didn't know whether he was completely quiet, not as he wanted to be. Alison did a much better job and managed to conceal the way her feet slid across the stone much better than he did. For his part, he would occasionally slip, and each time that he did, he was aware of the sound that his feet made. Thankfully, there didn't seem to be anyone noticing him.

Through the haze, and with the help of the faint moonlight, Fes managed to keep pace with the men as they departed the clearing. They climbed along the rock, moving with less concern about noise than Fes and Alison did. They went nearly a quarter of a mile before they finally came to a stop.

Fes noticed the light from a dozen different fires.

Now, *this* was the mercenary camp.

How had he believed the other camp could have been the mercenaries? With only one fire, it wouldn't have been likely, even if Carter hadn't been there. But this one contained enough different campfires, and the sound of activity within it, that left Fes thinking that they had finally found it.

They found a place to hide, and he pulled Alison down. "I don't know how we intend to sneak into that," he whispered.

"We have to figure out where they're keeping him."

"And when we do, what do you expect the two of us to be able to do?"

"The two of us need only to be able to sneak in and then back out. We don't have to do anything more than that."

Fes breathed out. That was all they had to do, but somehow that seemed almost impossible. How could they manage to get into the campsite and back out without having any idea where they were heading once they were there?

Alison looked at him. There was desperation in her eyes.

How could Fes do anything other than what he'd agreed?

Only, he doubted they would be able to get in safely.

The haze still hovered off the ground, creating a fog, and remained just as prominent here as it had been before. "Something about this troubles me," Fes said.

Alison stared at him for a moment. "After everything on this trip, *this* troubles you?"

"This fire mage. I can't get past the fact that she has to be working with Carter, but I don't really understand why."

"What is there to know why?"

He stared through the haze toward the campsite. "There is the issue of trying to understand who she is and what she knows." He turned back to Alison. "You weren't there, and you didn't see just how powerful she was. Why isn't she working on behalf of the empire?"

"What if she is?" Alison whispered.

Fes shook his head, thinking through it. "She doesn't serve the emperor. She can't. They destroyed a caravan—"

"You think the empire wouldn't do something like that?"

He stared at her. The emperor wouldn't. Not harming defenseless people like that. It just didn't fit. Only... as he watched Alison, he could tell she didn't—and maybe couldn't—believe him.

Now wasn't the time.

"Let's just get this over with," he said.

"I will go along with whatever you think that we need to do," she said.

"Talmund knows where the dragon heart can be found. He'll be valuable. Which means he'll be in the center of the camp."

For their attack to work, they would have to somehow draw off others, splitting up to distract the mercenaries so that one of them could sneak in, but how would they decide who would do it?

"I'll be the distraction," Alison said, watching him.

"That's not—"

Alison smiled. "That's exactly what you were thinking. I can see it on your face. I will serve as the distraction. One of us has to. I think that if I do it, I can hide in the darkness for long enough for you to get in and do whatever it is that you need to do. We can meet around to the south."

"If you let me be the distraction, I can give you enough time," he said.

"I can move more quietly."

"Which is why you should be the one to go after Talmund."

"I think you have a better chance of surviving if we come face-to-face with the fire mage."

Fes opened his mouth to argue before clamping it

shut again. There was no point in arguing. He *had* survived when facing a fire mage. "Circle around to the west and see if you can draw them in that direction," Fes said.

"And what will you do?" Alison asked.

"I'm going to do what I promised. I'm going to help get him. Then we're going after that dragon heart to finish this job."

She studied him for a moment before nodding. Alison leaned close, and he thought that she might whisper something in his ear, but she kissed him gently on the cheek. Her lips were warm, and he remembered the gentle touch that she had when she kissed him, and Fes had to resist the urge to pull her in and kiss her more deeply.

Now wasn't the time, and even if they could return to what they had, Fes wasn't sure that he wanted to. There had been too much between them.

Alison started off, circling around to the west. He waited, wondering what sort of distraction she might use. It came as a crackling of rock, the sound of footsteps that clattered, almost as if someone had unintentionally made too much noise.

Fes watched the campsite, and many of the mercenaries burst into activity. At first, it was only a few, but as one of them must've neared Alison and she had stabbed him and shouted, others hurried out into the darkness.

Fes waited, knowing that he needed to utilize this time but needing to ensure that as many people as possible would depart the campsite.

Maybe the fact that he and Alison had managed to bring down that entire sentry camp would be beneficial. It was possible that the mercenaries would think that there were more people here than there actually were.

When he was content that there weren't any more people leaving, he kept low and crept into the camp.

He didn't see anyone at first and scurried toward the largest fire, the one that was at the center of the camp. He didn't know whether it would mean anything but suspected that wherever they were holding the priest would be near the center. Maybe there would be others he would have to rescue, but it was the priest he was most interested in.

Him and Theole.

Maybe he could fulfill two promises this night.

When he reached the center of camp, he saw no evidence of the fire mage, not as he had expected to. Fes was convinced the fire mage was here, but where was she?

Movement startled him, and he turned. Three soldiers approached.

Three wasn't too much for him, not with the way he'd been fighting lately, and he jumped toward them before they had a chance to yell out. He slipped out with his daggers, catching both of the men on either side in the stomach, and kicked the central man. He fell backward, and Fes lunged toward him, landing on his stomach and driving his daggers into his gut.

Fes quickly wiped the daggers clean and hurried off, heading again toward the center of the campsite. It was larger than he had expected, and despite the haze and the heat radiating from the dragon fields, only a few tents. Most of the tents were quite large, and he hurried to the nearest one, slashing through the fabric to peek inside. Two men sat at a table, whispering. When Fes appeared, they lunged their feet, but he was faster and darted toward them, cutting the first one down with a sweep of his dagger to the throat, and spun around to catch the other man in his chest.

Fes slipped back out the tent the way he had entered. He moved on to the next and decided to make only a small slit in the fabric, small enough that he could look inside but not so large that he needed to fight were it not necessary. He didn't know how many times he could get lucky. One of these times, he feared he would come across someone who was waiting for him. If he did, it would take more than a knife to the belly to bring him down.

This tent was empty.

Fes moved on. At the next one, he found three people.

None of them were Carter, but none were the priest or the fire mage.

Fes neared a massive fire, and the tent near it seemed to radiate heat.

Fes approached this tent more carefully. When he made a small slit in the fabric, he found her inside. She was dressed in a crimson robe, and she was bent in front of a chalice, running her fingers along the inside. Every so often, she would bring her finger to her lips before placing her fingers back into the chalice.

He surveyed the inside of the tent and was not surprised to see Talmund chained to one of the posts. He had a bruise on one cheek, and dried blood was worked along the corner of his mouth, but he seemed otherwise unharmed. There was another prisoner, though his back was to Fes and he couldn't see him clearly. He was too large to be Theole, but who was he?

Somehow, Fes would have to draw the fire mage out of the tent to rescue Talmund.

Fes glanced over her shoulder, not wanting to step inside the tent, not quite yet. What he needed was a way of drawing the fire mage out, but he wasn't entirely certain how to do that. If she hadn't been drawn out by Alison's action, then there might not be anything that he could do.

The other option involved confronting her head on, but Fes didn't think that was all that good an idea. He'd barely survived the last time. He had no misconception about the fact that he would be unlikely to survive another confrontation, especially one where she would be more prepared for what he might be able to do.

A distraction. That was what he needed.

What kind of distraction would work against a fire mage?

As he looked around the campsite, taking stock of the campfire burning brightly, an idea came to him.

Could he draw her out through fire? Could he somehow use the flames to appeal to her?

It was worth a shot.

Fes hurried over to the campfire. With Alison's distraction, no one tended to it. The main part of the camp appeared deserted, leaving everything untouched.

He grabbed a branch out of the fire and ran with it over to the tent. He took it and use the flame flickering along the branch to ignite the canvas. When it was burning brightly, he tossed the rest of the branch into the tent.

Then Fes waited.

He wasn't entirely sure what to expect. He didn't know whether the fire mage would extinguish the flames before it had a chance to consume the rest of the tent or not. He wasn't entirely sure what power she had over flames.

The fire began to lick along the canvas, crawling toward the top of it.

Fes crept around the other side of the tent, staying as close to it as he could and trying to remain concealed, and slit the fabric, poking his head inside. The fire mage had moved to the back of the tent. She was doing something with her hands, circling them in a strange manner that caused the fire to ripple. Fes wanted to watch, but a more urgent need pressed on him.

He ran into the tent.

Talmund's eyes widened when Fes approached. Fes kept his gaze looking over the priest's shoulder, looking at the fire mage, worried that he couldn't act quickly enough. She continued to run her hands along the canvas. How much longer would he have?

Chains bound the priest to the pole.

There would be no way for him to unlock the chains, not without the fire mage knowing what he was doing.

He looked around, quickly surveying the inside of the tent, but didn't see anything that would help him.

"Your daggers," the priest whispered, the sound barely above the rising crackle of the flame threatening to consume the tent.

Fes shook his head. "I can't cut through the metal."

"You don't have to." His gaze flicked to the pole.

Fes had cut through a significant number of things with his daggers, but he'd never attempted to cut through wood. He frowned at the priest, and his attention flicked back to the fire mage and saw that she had nearly tamped the flames on the canvas down thoroughly. Whatever way she had of controlling the fire was almost complete.

Fes took a deep breath and crossed his daggers in front of him. He swept out, striking the pole.

He half expected them to sink partly into the wood before stopping, or maybe bounce off, unable to cut through anything, but they slipped through the wood as if it gave no more resistance the tent canvas. Everything began to sag.

Fes took a step back, and the priest stood, freeing his chains from around the pole.

The other man—the much larger man who was confined to another pole in the tent—watched Fes. If the fire mage was willing to capture this man, maybe he could be of help. He was large enough that he looked to be a fighter, and Fes suspected that having someone able to fight their way out of the encampment might be beneficial.

Fes started toward him, and as he did, the fire mage finished whatever she was doing. He swept with his daggers, cutting through the pole.

The tent began to collapse.

The fire mage pressed out, and a streak of flame shot toward him.

Talmund stepped in front of it and, with a wave of his hand, the flames dissipated. "Go," he said.

"I came for you. I'm not leaving without you."

"You don't have to. Just keep going." Talmund pushed on Fes, sending him staggering forward. He glanced over his shoulder to see the priest lunge at the chalice. He spilled it, sending a splatter of what had to be blood along the canvas. He grabbed something from atop the table and pointed it at the mage. As he did, flames burst from his hands and power exploded away from him, sending the fire mage flying backward.

Talmund turned and raced with Fes out of the tent and into the night. Once out of the tent, the priest turned back and pointed dragon bone at the tent. It exploded again, flames leaping out of it.

"There's another they captured. A Toulen merchant—"

Fes didn't have a chance to finish. Three men converged on him.

One of them slashed at him with a long sword, and Fes turned the blade with his dagger, twisting it, and jabbed forward, sliding his dagger into the man's chest. As he withdrew the dagger, he prepared to turn, ready to face the other two men, but found that he didn't need to.

The large man that he had freed had wrapped the chains that had confined him to the pole around one of the men's necks and twisted, snapping it. The remaining man was already down on the ground, his chest caved in from what appeared to be a vicious kick.

"Which way do we go?" the priest asked.

"Alison was going to make a diversion to the west of the encampment before heading south," Fes said.

"It's just the two of you?"

Fes nodded.

"Not the others?"

Fes shook his head. It did no good to explain to the priest that he had been deemed a necessary sacrifice. Fes could tell from the hurt look on his face that he recognized that fact. Talmund wasn't with the rebellion. Not really. He had been a means to an end. Did he see that?

They headed toward the west side of the camp, but as they did, there was quite a bit of movement, so Fes didn't want to continue in that direction. He motioned for them to follow him to the north side of the camp, a path that led them through a series of tents. Near one, there was some motion, but Fes managed to get a jump on the man on the inside. Near another, the massive man with him managed to prevent them from attacking.

And then they reached the edge of the camp. Once there, Fes glanced back. The haze that covered everything seemed to obscure the camp even more. As he watched, there came a sudden thunderous explosion. Fes glanced back to see smoke rising above the haze, filling the air. The priest's eyes widened.

"Reina."

"You knew her?" Fes asked.

"Knew of her. She is a dangerous fire mage that we haven't fully understood. Our insight at the fire temple hasn't been able to help us know her, almost as if she never trained there."

As they spoke, the large man glanced from Fes to the priest and then raced off into the darkness. When he was gone, Fes motioned for them to continue making their way toward the west. They needed to find Alison, and when they did, they could return to the rebellion campsite.

"Who was he?" Fes asked.

"A man she had picked up along the way. I'm not certain what she wanted of him."

"There's another I'm looking for. Someone Reina—or Carter—might have grabbed. A merchant by the name of Theole."

"It was only the two of us," the priest said.

Fes looked back the way the man had gone, disappearing into the night. Where would he have gone? "You didn't know anything about him?"

He turned back to the priest, who was shaking his head. "We aren't the only ones she was interested in," he said.

Fes sighed as they hurried through the darkness, trying to find any evidence of Alison. The longer they went, the less likely Fes thought that it was that they would find her. Not only was the haze challenging to see through, but the darkness was nearly complete. Little moonlight shone overhead, making it difficult to see anything.

"Neither of you should have come."

"I agreed to this job even if I wasn't told everything."

Talmund watched him a moment. "That's not all this is to you."

Fes squeezed his eyes shut. "Maybe not. That doesn't matter. What matters is getting away. Do you know how to navigate through here?"

The priest stared at the darkness and Fes tried to look around, trying to see if there was anything that would help, but he came up with nothing. Whatever was out there was too difficult for him to see through.

"I can get us through here, but where do you want to go?"

There was a sense of movement near them, and Fes hesitated. What was it?

As he listened, staring into the darkness, he couldn't tell what it was. At first, it sounded as if there were traces of debris falling, and then he realized that it was the sound of feet along the strange rock of the dragon field.

He glanced over at the priest. "Wherever you think we can make a stand."

The priest stared into the darkness, squinting as if he

could somehow penetrate the night in that way. And maybe he could. Maybe he was so well connected to the dragon lands that he could.

"Talmund?" Fes asked.

The priest turned toward him and then nodded. "I will guide you out of here."

"Which way?"

"North. We need to go north."

CHAPTER TWENTY-TWO

When dawn came, Fes had grown so tired that he wasn't confident he could keep his feet. They had been walking most of the night, having run at times, the priest managing to move more silently than Fes, and by the time the sun was creeping over the horizon, he wanted nothing more than to sleep. Unfortunately, there was no time for that, not when Carter's men were still behind them.

And he still hadn't seen her. Had she been at the camp? If she had, why hadn't she attacked? If not, where would she have been?

Every time they attempted to turn south again, trying to veer back toward the rebels, they encountered evidence of more of the mercenaries. Most of the time, they heard them, but there was one time when Fes had damn near run into one of their sentries and nearly collided with the man. It had taken a quick attack, slipping a dagger into his belly before he could cry out, to keep from ending up on the wrong end of things.

It was almost as if they were herded to the north.

"I'm going to need to rest," Fes said.

"We can take a break if you need it," Talmund said.

Had someone told Fes that he would be the one needing a break before the priest, he wouldn't have believed it. Somehow, it was almost as if the priest was energized, revitalized the longer they trudged into the dragon lands.

Talmund guided him to a larger rocky section. In the growing daylight, Fes was better able to make out the different types of rock in the dragon fields and still marveled at how bleak everything looked. The particular section that he sat on was slick and smooth and reminded him of his daggers. The rock was warm, though not unpleasantly so. Surprisingly, the longer that they traveled, the more Fes seem to be adjusting to the strange warmth.

"Who is she?" Fes asked the priest.

Talmund stared at him for a moment. "Reina?" When Fes nodded, the priest shook his head. "She's a fire mage who has managed to acquire significant power. It has made her dangerous."

"Does she serve the empire?"

Talmund watched him a moment. "Would that matter?"

He'd never seen Azithan act the way Reina had, but that didn't mean he couldn't be cruel like that. Could all fire mages?

"It matters," he finally said.

"I don't know," Talmund answered.

"And by power, you mean dragon relics."

He nodded. "Dragon relics. She is a fire mage, after all."

"And what are you?" Fes smiled at Talmund. "I saw the way that you stopped whatever it was that she did while in the campsite. I saw the way you extinguished the flames she threw at me. That tells me that you're either some sort of fire priest as well, or that there's something more to you than is easily explainable."

"We are not so different, her and I."

"And why is that?"

"Both of us can manipulate the power stored in the dragon relics. The difference is the intent we have behind it."

"I don't know anything about intent. All I know is that you and her both seem to have the same abilities."

"It's difficult to explain. What I do, and what others like me do, is a way of harnessing the power trapped within the relics. We don't destroy it; we simply redirect it. Fire mages extract power from within dragon relics and use it for their own purpose. Sometimes, it's something as simple as creating flames such as what you saw today. That is often the path of least resistance, and when they are incredibly skilled, they can use the natural state of power from within the dragon bones and force it out into the world."

"And that natural state is fire," Fes said.

He nodded. "That natural state is fire. It takes much less power to transfer fire from a relic like that, though there is still the need for talent. Not all have the talent."

"Nothing you've said tells me how you and her are all that different."

The priest looked at him and smiled. "To some, we wouldn't be that different. We use the same source of power. The priests seek to preserve the power within the relics while the mages do not care."

Fes stared at him. As the sun began to rise, it seemed as if light reflected off Talmund strangely, leaving him with an almost hazy glow around him. That was his imagination, Fes was sure of it, but it lent the priest a certain supernatural quality.

"Why?" Fes leaned forward, trying to ignore the fatigue that was starting to overcome him. "Why would you serve the dragons? They have been gone for a thousand years. Everything I've seen about them tells me they shouldn't return."

"Because I don't believe that." Talmund took a seat on

the rock next to him and looked over. "What do you think that people living a thousand years ago would have said had we told them that the dragons would be destroyed? What do you think they would have said were we to tell them that the empire has existed ever since the destruction of those dragons? What do you think that those people would have said were we to tell them that the magic of the dragons seeped out into the land and was stolen by those who defeated them?" The priest smiled sadly.

"What will bringing that magic back accomplish?" Fes asked.

"I think that it will bring about change," Talmund said.

"And are you certain that's the kind of change we need? Are you certain it's the kind of change we want to experience?"

"Those of us who have lived outside of the city have a very different experience with the empire than those of you who have lived in the city."

"The empire is the empire," Fes said.

"The empire is not only the empire. You have seen Anuhr, but you haven't seen anything else. You haven't seen the way that they treat those who live outside of the city. You haven't seen anything."

"I've seen enough to know the empire provides order." The empire—or Azithan, at least—had rescued him.

"As I said, you haven't seen much outside Anuhr. And

if you were to understand who you are—who you *really* are—you wouldn't question. That which allowed you to cross the dragon plains is a power that fills you. It grants you the strength of the dragons. You might not know it yet, but that power burns within you." Talmund studied him a moment. "Are you rested?"

Fes didn't have anything to say. There *was* a power that burned within him. If that was Deshazl, then so be it. If it was something else... "I'm as rested as it seems I get to be," Fes said.

Talmund guided them, leading them across the dragon plains, their path taking them ever closer to the mountains. They were something that Fes had not expected to come quite so close to. "Will it work?" Fes asked while they were walking. The idea that they could resurrect one of the dragons seemed impossible, though Talmund believed.

"That's just it. We don't know. There have been reports of dragon hearts before, but none that are reliable. For all we know, this will be the first one we've ever found."

"Anything that's in the dragon plains belongs to the empire."

"That's what they would have you believe."

"And you'll steal it."

The priest turned to him. "I seem to recall how you stole from me the very first time that I met you."

Fes looked at him, unblinking. "As far as I know, you had stolen that from the empire."

The priest met his glare for a moment before smiling. "You're right. I did."

Fes cocked his head to the side. "You did?"

"I did. Certain items should not be in the possession of the empire, and that is one of them."

"Because it's a bone?"

"Because it's a bone that we need."

Fes shook his head. "That's right. For your dragon reconstruction."

"You don't have to believe in it. That doesn't mean it is any less true."

"Your belief in it doesn't make it true, either."

They fell into a silence, and every so often, Fes swore that he heard the sound of footsteps along the stone, and he would turn but found nothing there. Through the haze of the dragon fields, he wasn't sure that he would see anything.

"There was a time when all of these lands were covered in bones," the priest said. "No one knew then what we do now. No one understood the power stored in the bones, and if they did, I imagine that much would have been different."

"What happened then?"

"After the dragons were slaughtered, the empire was

still young. They sent their servants through here, and they collected bones, and they scattered them."

"The empire did that?"

"The empire tried, but they found that they weren't able to do so very easily. Only those who are descended from these lands, people whose blood came from these rocks, were able to enter the dragon fields and move the relics. They were known as dragonwalkers, a term that many speak with derision now, but at that time they were looked upon with something bordering on awe. To be a dragonwalker was something incredible. It meant that you were connected to those dragons, and that you could handle the artifacts, and that you could provide a glimpse into a world that others could not."

"Your people must've been dragonwalkers."

The priest looked over. "My people were never dragonwalkers. They had a different purpose."

"And what purpose was that?"

"They were asked to preserve the relics." He stared at Fes for a long moment. "The longer that we went from the time of the war, the more it became clear that the empire was using that power in unfortunate ways. They twisted it, taking what the dragons had protected, and forced it on the world, destroying everything that they came into contact with. You wonder why we oppose the empire, but that is the reason. We oppose because it is necessary. We oppose because it is the right thing to do. We oppose because we have no choice but to do so."

"What are the Deshazl?" Fes asked.

He wasn't certain that the priest would answer. When he had asked that of the rebellion commander, he hadn't gotten a straight answer.

"The Deshazl are the dragonwalkers," the priest said. "I assume you asked because you heard it from Reina?"

Fes nodded. "She said I was Deshazl."

"As I suspect you are. That *is* the reason I wanted you on this journey."

"Why?"

The priest looked over at him. "Tell me what do you feel when you are in the dragon plains?"

Fes shrugged. "I don't know. It's hot, and the steam rising everywhere makes it difficult for us to see anything, but other than that..." He shrugged again.

"You have traveled across the dragon plains for longer than many who dared to risk it," Talmund said.

"Because we came for you."

"You did, though I am certain that Alison chose you for a particular reason."

"And what is that?"

"Most people who come to the dragon plains feel the heat from the fields. Most are unable to tolerate it for more than a few hours. Some don't even tolerate it that long. But you have been out here for a day at least. Maybe longer. And you seem to show no ill effects other than fatigue that one would expect from spending so much time walking."

"Alison came with me. Alison didn't have any difficulty."

"Alison shares the same heritage I do. She would be able to tolerate it, but not more than that."

"What about those who came with the mercenaries?"

"You've already seen the way they managed to survive the crossing."

"Reina?"

"Reina borrows the power from the dragons as a fire mage. She's able to push back the effects and temporarily grant others passage. Without her—or someone like her —the mercenaries, as you call them, would not have been able to survive."

"But the rebellion intends to cross."

"Have you not wondered why that is?"

"Are you trying to tell me that all of those in the rebellion are Deshazl?"

"Not Deshazl. Many within the rebellion are Settlers. They have a natural resistance, but the power of this place does not live within their blood, not the way that it does for the Deshazl." Talmund glanced over at him. "You don't have to believe, Fezarn. All you need to do is allow yourself to keep an open mind. Let the rest of us believe."

Fes chuckled. "All I want to do is see this task completed."

"And yet you continue to do more than is necessary to complete it."

"I told Alison that I would help. She asked, and..."

"You have a connection. I appreciate that she had the insight to recognize that you might be the only person who would be able to successfully get me free."

"At least, without sacrificing all of the rebellion," Fes said.

The priest studied him for a moment. "You asked about the dragon heart. I suspect that you wonder whether it is real, or whether it is what you heard described."

"I heard there was a flower growing in these lands," Fes said.

"That's what the Bayars tell us. It can't be left anywhere that the empire can reach it. If the empire gains the dragon heart, they will gain something incredibly powerful."

"And what is that?"

"A source of power that will forever change what we can do. If the empire resurrects the dragons, they will try to control them, breed them, and have an endless supply of power for the fire mages. They can't be allowed to do that."

CHAPTER TWENTY-THREE

Night had fallen, and Fes needed to sleep. He was tired and hungry and thirsty, a combination that left him irritable, but more than that, it left his mind feeling hazy, the same sort of haze that hung over everything here in the dragon fields. How much longer would he be able to keep this up? How much longer would he be able to hold this pace? He doubted that he would be able to keep at it for much longer, and the moment that he began to let up would be the moment that Carter and her mercenaries would get to him.

The longer that they traveled, the more that Fes was determined to stay ahead of Carter. But could he?

He wasn't even sure, not anymore. As much as he wanted to stay ahead of her, and as much as he wanted only to find this dragon heart, he no longer knew whether there was anything that he could do to get it before Carter and the mercenaries did. The longer they wandered, the more he began to wonder if perhaps he should even try to stop them. If Reina served the empire...

"How much longer is it before we reach the dragon heart?"

"I'm not bringing you to the dragon heart."

Fes shot the priest a hard look. "What have we been doing if not heading toward the dragon heart?"

"I'm leading you away from the dragon heart. And you are leading the mercenaries away from it."

"I'm not leading anyone," Fes said.

"And yet they have been following us for the last day," Talmund said.

Was he using him again? Was it all because they believed him to be Deshazl?

"What is your plan?"

"I plan to bring the mercenaries far enough away that the rebellion can get around them."

"You didn't think this was necessary to share with me?"

Talmund paused. Fes waited, but as the silence went on for more than a beat, his attention was caught, again, by the land around them. The ground had not changed from what they had been crossing over for the last day. All around was the barren rock, and it was amazing to think that at one point, this had been something else. It was amazing to believe that life had once lived here, and amazing enough that Fes wasn't sure that he could even believe that it had. Maybe it had never been anything more than what it was, this unending bleakness, leading up to the mountains.

"I thought you would have recognized I could not lead you so close to the dragon heart, especially with Reina after us."

"Is it your intent to lead to a confrontation?"

"Not if we can avoid it, but if we cannot, then we will do what must be done."

Fes stared at him. "You haven't said anything about Alison. Aren't you concerned about what happened to her?"

"Alison is much more talented than you give her credit for."

"I give her plenty of credit for her talent," Fes said. "But against as many men as were in that camp?"

"It was as you said. She drew them away. If everything went as she would have planned, I imagine that she reached the rest of the rebellion, and they are in pursuit."

Fes tried to think about what they had done. If she believed that he was Deshazl, she would have thought that he could cross the dragon field without difficulty.

"Where would you have this attack take place?"

Talmund paused. Every so often, the wind would

pick up and carry away some of the haze hanging over the field. When it did, the heat dissipated, leaving a strange chill washing over everything. It wasn't unpleasant, but then, Fes didn't really find the heat terribly unpleasant, either. It was surprisingly comforting.

"I intend for us reach the pass. From there, there won't be any way for the mercenaries to put up much of a defense."

"The Draconis Pass," he said. Talmund nodded. The commander had mentioned it, but Fes hadn't expected them to travel so far. It was beyond the central part of the dragon plains and beyond where their journey was supposed to take them.

It was a place where nearly a dozen dragons were said to have died, all heading to one spot, almost as if drawn there. According to rumors, it was a narrow section of land, hidden in valleys and near the base of the mountain. It created the northernmost separation to the dragon fields. Beyond the Draconis Pass, the mountains began to rise, and life began to return.

"There's another reason for heading for the pass. What do you think can be accomplished there?"

The priest stared at him for a moment. "Nothing other than a chance for us to get ahead of our attackers. Isn't that enough?"

"How do you intend to handle Reina?"

"Reina isn't nearly as difficult as she would like us to believe that she is."

"She managed to capture you."

"She didn't capture me. The mercenaries did. With enough men, anyone can be captured, even you."

"Why do you say it like that?"

"Only because I've seen what you are capable of doing," he said. "There have been several times when you were outnumbered, and you managed to survive."

Fes looked around him. With the steam still rising from the field, he couldn't imagine engaging in any sort of battle out here. Anything they might do would put them in danger and expose all of the rebellion to violence. How many would be lost?

Would anything come of Indra?

He felt that she was his responsibility, somehow. Until he managed to find her father, he owed it to her to keep her safe.

"How do you propose we stop her?"

"Reina can be defeated, the same as any fire mage can be defeated. The key is removing their power."

"You mean the dragon relics."

Talmund nodded. "Someone like Reina has acquired many artifacts over the years, and it makes her incredibly powerful. She probably draws upon all of those constantly, keeping her radiating power."

"Does it weaken her to use any power to allow the others to cross the dragon field?"

"By necessity, it would take more and more strength from her to maintain the ability to resist the effects of the dragon plains."

"And because the Draconis Pass is a place of great power?"

"It should weaken her even more."

"Has this always been your plan?"

"Not until I learned of Reina's involvement."

"And you're not worried about her?" The easy way he'd dismissed her as a threat surprised Fes.

"She's not the fire mage I fear."

"And who is that?"

"The Emperor. With his hoard of artifacts, he has become incredibly powerful. Why else do you think he's called *the dragon*?"

"And if the rebellion intends to overthrow the emperor, how do they think they can manage against such a powerful fire mage?"

"It will take a dragon to unseat a dragon."

Fes stared at him and realized that the priest still wasn't joking. "That is why you want to resurrect the dragons? You need them to face the emperor?"

"It's about much more than that, but as far as you are concerned, that is all that matters. If we can resurrect the dragons, we can combat the emperor, and we can finally restore the order that has been disrupted for over a thousand years."

They fell into a silence. The priest continued to lead them, heading with a steady gait across the rock. Surprisingly, the priest managed to keep a firm footing, even when Fes slipped from time to time.

"How much longer do we have until we reach the pass?"

"Not much longer," the priest said.

"And when we do? Are you prepared for fighting?"

"I won't be the one doing any fighting."

"What if I refuse to fight?"

"In that, I'm afraid, you might not have much choice."

"Why is that?"

"Can't you feel it?"

"Feel what?"

"She's coming."

Fes focused on the surrounding air, thinking back to the way it had felt when he had been aware of her power before. There was a heat to it, and it seemed to sear his throat, burning his skin. Could he feel that now?

What he detected was faint, subtle, and nothing more than what he had already detected from the dragon plains. "I don't detect anything."

"You will."

They continued walking, and as they did, Fes began to have the same unpleasant sensation as he had before. At first, it was little more than an irritation. A steady increase in warmth, a heat that nagged at him, gnawing at the back of his throat. It began to intensify, growing stronger. As it did, he wasn't sure whether it was real or imagined until it became impossible to ignore.

Reina.

Fes could feel her presence. He slashed at the air with his daggers and felt a moment of reprieve. The priest glanced over, watching him for a moment.

"Why did you do that?" he asked.

"It seems to make it easier," Fes said.

"It makes what easier?"

"The pressure from her magic," Fes said.

The priest waved his hands in the air, performing a strange pattern. When he was done, he regarded Fes with a bright interest. "How is it that you discovered that you could do this?"

"I didn't have much choice. When I first encountered Reina, she was attempting to kill some of the people with us. I wasn't given a whole lot of choice in what I did. I thought that if nothing else, I would throw one of my daggers at her."

"I doubt that would be effective," the priest said.

"I don't know that it would be, either," Fes said. "All I know is that it seems to help me ease the heat I feel from her magic."

"And yet you still question whether you are Deshazl."

"I thought it was the daggers."

"It is you and not the daggers. The daggers are an extension, but nothing else. I imagine that with enough understanding of yourself, you would be able to deflect her power even without the daggers."

"The same way that you did," Fes asked.

"What I did was different, and it came from my connection to the Settlers. I suspect the way I use that connection is quite a bit different than what you use when you use your daggers. How is it that you accomplish it?"

Fes shrugged. "I don't have a good explanation. I simply swipe at the heat in the air. Nothing else."

"You simply swipe at the air and you managed to cut through a fire mage's spell?"

"It's not as if I knew what I was doing."

"Obviously. Otherwise, you wouldn't have thought that it would work."

Fes chuckled. That was the kind of logic he could get behind. "How will you know when we reach the pass?"

"The pass is unmistakable."

They continued making their way, and as they did, the haze around them began to thicken. At first, Fes wondered whether it was real or whether it had to do with Reina and her magic. The longer he experienced it, the more he realized that it wasn't Reina or anything that she did. It came from everywhere, pushing up from the ground, as if the dragon plains had intensified. Attempts to swipe at the air, trying to cleave away the magic, did nothing.

"Even you can't do anything here." The priest clasped his hands together as he walked, making his way across the ground, and he took deep breaths. A sheen of sweat coated his brow, and Fes realized that he didn't suffer from the heat the same way as the priest.

"Is this the pass?"

"We begin to near it," Talmund said.

Fes fell into a silence. If they were nearing the pass, they would slow and have to look for signs of the mercenaries. He would have to stay vigilant, knowing that it would be difficult to see anything through the haze. Anyone could spring upon them before he had a chance to react, but they needed to draw them into the pass.

"How do you intend to fight through this?"

"I'm hopeful that we won't have to," the priest said.

"Why is that?"

"For the mercenaries to see anything, it will require Reina to expend a great amount of energy. I'm hopeful that she will decide that it is simply not worth it and will turn away."

"And if she doesn't?"

"Then, unfortunately, we will have to fight."

The longer they walked, the more the heat began to build around them. It was more than unpleasant, and he swiped at the air, despite Talmund telling him that it would make no difference, feeling as if he had no choice but to attempt it. Each time he did, he had a brief respite from the heat, barely enough to make a difference.

"She's close," Fes said.

"I feel it," Talmund said.

"And if she's here?"

"Then we will have to fight," the priest said.

They walked deeper into the haze, the fog surrounding them, and it seemed as if despite the haziness all around them, the priest knew precisely where he was going. Somehow, he was able to either see through it, or he managed to navigate without seeing where he was going.

And then he stopped.

"What are you doing?" Fes asked. He could barely see the priest in front of him. He could scarcely see more than his hand in front of him.

"Now we wait."

"Wait for what?"

"For her to make the first move."

Fes looked around. As he did, he felt the heat continuing to build. He understood what the priest was getting at and knew that whatever was going to happen would be soon. Reina was working her magic, and it would have to be something to allow the mercenaries the ability to see through the haze of the dragon plains. In order to do that, she would have to do something, but what?

Fes made a small circle, walking around the priest, looking for anything that would provide him any answers, but the priest remained silent. He merely stood in place, his hands clasped together.

The air began to sizzle.

Fes sliced at it, slashing his daggers through the air, and the dragonglass practically crackled.

Why should it do that?

Bluish light sizzled along the edge of the dragonglass. He had never seen that before. Could Reina's magic be enough that it would overwhelm anything that he—or the priest—could do to counter her?

If she had enough dragon relics, it was possible—and probable—that she could. With enough relics, she would be unstoppable.

He looked over at Talmund. Fes hoped that his plan would work. He hoped that Talmund knew what he was doing when it came to Reina, but what if he didn't? What if she was more powerful than he knew?

He had opened his mouth to ask when the air exploded with power.

CHAPTER TWENTY-FOUR

F es's ears rang. The sizzling energy in the air had disappeared and the haze lifted, practically sucked into the sky. It was almost as if a wind pulled upward, drawing with it the heat and the fog that had obscured everything. The land around him was just as bleak as it had been, but the rock was different here, smooth, and there were strange spikes that jutted out of the ground that reminded him of…

No.

Could there be dragon bones here?

All of them had been picked over. The stories all said that. But what else could they be?

"Be ready," Talmund said.

"For what?"

He didn't need to answer. Movement caught Fes's

attention, and he spun around, unsheathing his daggers to see a line of mercenaries streaming toward them.

There had to be at least a hundred. Too many for him and Talmund to withstand.

Fes debated lowering his hands and accepting his fate. It was possible that the mercenaries would capture him, nothing more, but there was also the possibility that they would kill him and retake the priest.

Fes wouldn't go down without a fight. He crossed his daggers, preparing for battle. As he did, he summoned every angry thought that he could come up with, anything that he could bring to the forefront of his mind that would allow him to call upon the rage boiling within him. If this was the Deshazl part of him, he needed to embrace it.

He thought of his parents, and he thought of the slaughtered merchants, and he thought of Indra, looking so helpless when he had come across her. Surprisingly, that affected him almost as much as anything else.

Anger burned within him, and Fes practically snarled as he jumped forward, meeting the first of the mercenaries.

He didn't see the man fall, and barely felt his daggers slice through them. He spun, slashing from man to man, spinning as quickly as he could. Heat began to steam up around him, obscuring the landscape, yet Fes could see the mercenaries. These were the men who had killed the merchants. These were the men who would have tormented Indra. This kind of man had been responsible for what happened to his parents.

He continued to carve through them, and then... he was caught in the middle.

There had to be ten mercenaries surrounding him.

Fes ducked down, slicing with his dagger, but one of the men blocked it with his sword. He rolled, flipping, and stabbed, but wasn't fast enough. He didn't know if he could be fast enough.

He heard the twang of a crossbow firing at the same time as something struck him in the shoulder. He screamed but continued to squeeze his daggers, refusing to let them go. Pain surged through him, agony searing in his bones.

One of the men tried to stab him with his sword, but Fes leaped away, swinging his bad arm around to jab the man in the eye. He fell back with a spray of blood.

Two men came in, but Fes swiped with his dagger, still managing to keep his arms up, but how much longer? How much longer would he be able to maintain his posture?

It didn't matter. He would hold out for as long as he could.

Screams echoed toward him.

They were muted, and there was something strange about them.

The attack hesitated.

Fes used that hesitation to streak toward them, stabbing two men before they could react.

The scream came again. There was something odd about it.

This time, even Fes hesitated.

He took a moment, but he registered the source.

The rebellion.

If they were here, it meant Alison had brought them. Which meant he wouldn't have to fight all these mercenaries alone.

The air exploded, and the haze that had grown around him began to lift again, sucked out with a strange wind that drew it upward.

A dozen men littered the ground around him. The rage boiling within him called for more, a bloodlust that he appreciated given what he would have to face.

The mercenaries crashed into the rebellion.

Fes stumbled back, away from the attackers.

He felt someone moving near him and spun around, coming face to face with Talmund.

The man grabbed at the crossbow bolt in Fes's shoulder and gently pried it free. He pressed his hand on Fes's shoulder and warmth flooded through him. When it was done, the pain had disappeared, leaving Fes with the ability to use his arm again.

"You planned this," Fes said.

"If only I had. The rebellion would have known about the pass. I'm only glad they came. We must still deal with Reina. She is the most dangerous one here."

"I'm dangerous."

Talmund tipped his head to the side. "Yes. You are, Fezarn."

Fes stared at the battle. Men were crashing against other men, fighting unlike anything that he'd seen before.

The air began to sizzle again, and he looked around, searching for signs of Reina. "We have to stop her. Otherwise, the mercenaries are going to succeed."

"I need to have her expend the remaining energy she has, and then we can defeat her."

"And if that doesn't work?" Fes turned his attention to the dragon bones. "What if she uses one of those other artifacts?"

The priest turned where Fes was looking. His eyes widened. "Oh."

"You didn't know those were here, did you?"

"The pass has been obscured. We haven't been able to see anything. Most have assumed the dragonwalkers picked it over."

The haze began to build again. It covered the dragon bones, but if Fes could see them, he suspected that Reina could see them, too. And if she could see them, she would be able to reach them and access the power stored within them. "Not so picked over after all," Fes said.

"We have to find her," the priest said.

Fes tested his shoulder. When he was confident that he had enough movement in it, he started back into the battle.

Talmund followed him, and Fes glanced back, surprised to see the priest keeping pace with him. In each hand, he held a short knife that was similar to Fes's daggers.

"Dragonglass?"

The priest nodded. "Mine aren't quite as impressive as yours, but they will do if needed."

"Why aren't they as impressive?"

"That is for another time. Let's survive this first."

"Any suggestions on how to reach Reina?"

"She will be well protected."

"I'm not surprised by that, but do you have any other suggestions?"

"I have none," the priest said. "Only that we must not allow her to reach any additional relics. If she succeeds in that, she will have incredible power, and we might not be able to counter what she can do."

The dragon bones he'd seen were too large for him to move, and with that size of bone, Reina might have limitless power. Fes looked along the line of mercenaries. Most of them had their attention focused on the rebels fighting them, and he suspected that the moment he attacked, they would turn toward him.

There had to be a different way of searching for Reina.

Could he pick up on the change in heat?

It seemed unlikely, but maybe he could use the steady buildup of energy that caused the dissipation of the haze rising off the dragon plains to help.

"She won't be there," Talmund said.

"Where will she be?"

"Near the relics. When the haze lifted, I bet she saw them the same as we did. If so, she'll get close to them and draw on them."

It made sense, but it meant leaving the rebellion and people who might need his help. Fes made his way toward the dragon relics. The haze still obscured them, making it difficult for him to see, but he remembered where they were, and as he approached, there was a shifting to the heat around him. The power building up from what Reina did changed, replaced by the steady energy that seemed to come from the dragon bones.

"How can I detect this heat?"

Talmund shook his head. "One of the Deshazl would be sensitive to them. It was this sensitivity that once made the dragonwalkers so effective. They were the only ones who could enter the dragon plains and successfully find relics."

"There are others with that ability, though."

"Not with the same ability. Once enough relics were

obtained, the fire mages managed to find ways of withdrawing the haze around the dragon plains, at least enough for them to see where to find other relics. It required a significant expenditure of energy, and often they burned out everything that they brought with them to do so. After a while, it became too risky for them to continue to do it. What was the point, especially when everything had been picked over?"

"Did they ever look in the Draconis Pass?"

"It has been too difficult for anyone other than a significantly powered fire mage to come here."

"You are here."

"I am with you, Deshazl."

Fes glanced over at the priest. "I thought you said you were able to come through the dragon plains?"

"I can come to the dragon plains, but I've never been to the pass. It is too difficult, even for me. This is a place where only the Deshazl would have managed to come." Talmund smiled at him. "Do you still doubt what you are?"

Fes looked around. It was this ability that Azithan had hired him for, wasn't it? It was the connection to the relics that made Fes valuable. "I stopped doubting a while ago."

"I can help you understand, especially with everything that you've done for us."

Fes shook his head. He wasn't sure that he wanted the

priest to help him understand. Wasn't sure that he wanted anything other than what he had always wanted. Wasn't that enough?

Energy began to sizzle around him, and Fes looked up. Reina was working at her magic again. Much longer, and it would explode away from her, and then the dragon bones all around Fes would be exposed. How many times before she discovered how extensive the collection of bones was?

When the explosion came, sucking the haze back up into the sky, drawing the heat away, if only momentarily, Fes looked around and saw the bones near him. One of them was enormous, curving out of the ground, looking like a finger pointing at the sky.

A robed figure moved toward them.

Reina.

"There she is," Fes said.

He started toward her. If she reached the relic, she would be able to draw on the power that remained in this place, and then she would become unstoppable.

"She will have just used up much of her power," the priest said. "Now is as good a time as any to attempt this."

Fes took a deep breath and stalked toward Reina.

As he approached, the heat barrier began to shimmer around him, the same barrier that he had detected when he first encountered Reina. With it came doubt.

What was he doing? What was he thinking coming

here, and assuming that he could somehow confront a fire mage? Who was he other than a collector for the empire?

Did it matter who he was?

All that mattered was that he needed to stop her. Once he did, then he could reach the dragon heart.

That had to be the focus of his plan. Stop Reina. Reach the dragon heart. Figure out the rest later.

The haze built quickly, making it difficult for him to see anything.

Surprisingly, he could *feel* Reina. Heat radiated from her. Fes slashed at it, using his daggers to part her magic as he approached.

It worked, but only barely. The heat built again and he tried to ignore it but found it difficult to do. It seemed to push him away, a physical presence, as if Reina used the energy drawn from the dragon relics to throw him back.

Fes considered his options. As she approached, the haze of heat building off her seemed to shimmer, reminding him of the haze hanging over the entire dragon fields. Each time he attempted to swipe through it, slashing with his daggers, he failed to make any sort of change to it.

"Is there anything that you can do?" Fes asked Talmund.

"I will have the same restrictions as her," the priest said.

"And by that, you mean that you can only use the dragon artifacts?"

"I can use the dragon relics, but she will have much more power than anything I can generate."

"See what you can do to slow her," Fes said.

They needed to have her continue to draw off the haze coming from the dragon fields. If they could do that, it might weaken her enough that he could get close. If he managed to do that, he thought he might be able to sink a dagger into her chest.

Would that even be enough?

Would her magic let her survive a stabbing like that?

The barrier exploded out from her.

Fes was thrown back, away from the dragon bones.

She had targeted him and not Talmund.

Fes stumbled to his feet, staggering toward her, slashing at the air with his daggers. Energy sizzled along the blades, and he couldn't take his eyes off it. There was power there, but something else, too.

Could the daggers somehow be storing the energy she expended?

It was a possibility that he hadn't considered. If that were the case, then Fes had to believe that he had a chance of using them against her.

If only he could get close enough.

It was possible he would not be able to. If she continued creating the same barrier, if she continued to attack him with it, then she could prevent him from reaching her.

Fes continued to swipe at the air, cutting over and over again, and each time he did, he managed to get only a step closer. None of it was enough.

The air exploded, and Fes readied to be thrown back again.

It wasn't targeted at him.

He glanced over at Talmund and saw him holding a length of dragon bone. The bone glowed, the striations within it radiating colors. He aimed it at Reina, almost as if it were a crossbow or a sword.

Reina swept her hand toward the priest and flame exploded. The priest lowered the bone and made a swirl with his free hand and the flame dissipated.

She turned her attention back to Talmund, focusing more intensely on him.

"You are more than a simple dragon priest," she said. She held both of her palms up, angled together. A ball of fire formed between them.

Even from where he stood, Fes could feel the heat rising from whatever it was that she was doing. If it exploded from her, would the priest be strong enough to withstand it?

"You will not claim these relics," Talmund said.

"The dragons are gone. It is time that you and your ragged band recognize that. And this empire will fall.

Now that we know—"

Talmund didn't let her finish. "They're not gone. They live within us."

The priest reached into his pocket and pulled out a small object. He held it open in his palm. It was a sphere, hints of blue color glittering against the gray sky.

A dragon pearl.

Fes was sure that was what it was, though it was small and certainly didn't seem to be large enough to withstand a fireball the size of that which Reina intended to throw at the priest.

Talmund angled his hand toward Reina. The pearl began to glow, taking on the bluish color that Fes saw coming off it.

She released the fireball held between her hands, forcing it toward the priest.

Fes cried out.

The dragon pearl exploded outward, and the blue flame met the red of Reina's fireball.

When it did, the air exploded with heat and energy and the blue from the dragon pearl pressed through the red fireball, destroying it as it continued to make its way toward Reina.

She reached into her pocket and withdrew an object and pointed it at the blue flame. It hovered in the air for a moment before streaking up into the sky.

"A challenger. I had not expected to meet one in these lands."

"I am no challenger."

She smiled. "No? Then perhaps you will simply die." She pointed the object that she had in her pocket at Talmund. When she did, Fes could see that it was a dragon pearl, and it was more significant than what the priest had used.

The priest's eyes widened. He scrambled into his pocket, trying to reach for something, but as the pearl the fire mage held began to glow, Fes could tell that he wouldn't be fast enough.

He launched himself forward, cutting at the air with the daggers, not wanting Talmund to die. He screamed.

The air hung with a strange energy and his body practically burned with it. He streaked like an arrow at the fire mage.

She turned to him and pressed out with the dragon pearl.

A glowing ball of red flame shot toward him.

Fes could do nothing. His momentum carried him forward, and he couldn't change direction. He led with his daggers, holding them in front of him, pointed together like a tip of a spear or an arrow. Energy sizzled along the blades.

The fireball would envelop him.

There was nothing that Fes could do that would prevent that. Not now.

When it reached him, the heat was tremendous. He gritted his teeth, preparing to be burned, but the flame parted around his daggers and sizzled out.

The fire mage's eyes widened slightly, and then Fes reached her.

She waved her hands quickly, and a barrier sprung into place. The haze began to lift, rising from the ground, practically obscuring everything so that it was only Fes and the fire mage. He slashed at the barrier, sweeping his daggers across the magic, trying to part it, but she continued to move her hands, blocking him.

"Who are you? How are you here?"

He ignored her question, sweeping the blades toward her. The barrier began to part, separating, and she continued to weave her hands around. Each time she made a movement, the barrier reformed, pushing Fes back. He didn't know enough about how to use the daggers to separate it, and if she had enough time, he suspected that she would be able to push him back completely.

An explosion struck her from the back.

Reina turned and pressed her hands together quickly, sending flames shooting out.

At that moment, Fes slashed at the air, separating the magic, and stabbed one of his daggers into her back.

Reina fell forward, and the dagger slipped free. She rolled, facing him on the ground. She tried to bring her hands together, but Fes leaped on top of her, jabbing into each shoulder with the daggers. He pressed down, holding them in place.

"Perhaps you are more than Deshazl," she said.

He jerked on the daggers, and they carved through her flesh. Blood poured from her wounds. Heat rose up from her, washing over his hands much like the warmth of her blood. Fes held her in place, afraid to move, afraid to withdraw the daggers, and afraid that she would get back up. If she did, if she somehow managed to reach for her magic again, he didn't know whether he would be able to stop her.

Someone grabbed his shoulder, and he glanced up.

"It's done," the priest said.

"What is?"

"All of this. Her," he said, motioning to Reina. "Your mission."

Fes looked down at Reina. Her eyes were glazed, and her skin had gone pale, much paler than it had when she was alive. Her curly raven-colored hair had lost its luster and age wrinkled her face in ways that had not been there before.

"That wasn't the mission."

"Not at first, but now it was."

Fes removed his daggers and wiped them on Reina.

He reached into her pockets, searching for other dragon relics, and found another dragon pearl. He held it in his hand, feeling the warmth and noting the reddish striations along it. There were a few other dragon relics, and he pulled them from her pockets, lining them up on the ground next to her. When he was done, he turned to the priest and held out the dragon pearl.

The priest shook his head. "That is not meant for me."

"Why not?"

"It's difficult to explain."

Fes pocketed the dragon pearl. There was no question that this one was authentic; he could tell in a way he hadn't been able to with the others. When he stepped away from Reina, Talmund removed another dragon pearl from his pocket and set it on her body. He pressed his hand down on top of it and flames began to envelop her, quickly burning her body to nothingness. The flames continued, catching through the rock and exploding with small pops.

"What was that about?"

"She cannot defile this place," the priest said.

The haze had nearly completely returned. Fes realized that he no longer heard the sounds of battle, not as he had.

"What now?"

"And now you return."

"Just like that?"

Talmund nodded. "Your mission is complete."

It wasn't, but maybe that didn't matter. "What of Carter and the rest of the mercenaries?"

"The mercenaries will find it much more difficult to traverse these lands without Reina."

Fes chuckled. "You still might find it difficult to overpower Carter."

"If she's smart, she'll run from here as quickly as possible." He turned his gaze to the north and the mountains that were now obscured by the haze of the Draconis Pass. "And she will find it much more difficult to return."

"What of the dragon heart?"

"The dragon heart will be harvested, and it will be protected."

"And my payment?"

The priest regarded him for a long moment. "Is that what it's all about for you?"

Was it? That was why he'd taken the job, but now he had different questions. Was there anything he could learn from Talmund? Would there be any reason to remain with the rebellion? "What else should it be about? I took this job with the incentive of getting paid."

The priest stared at him for a moment before reaching into his pocket and withdrawing a small satchel. He handed it over.

Fes took it and found the satchel heavier than he

expected. When he opened it, he saw it filled with gold coins.

He glanced up. "This is more than what Horus agreed."

"It is, but you've done more than you agreed as well."

Fes looked around. "What about you?"

The priest turned in place, surveying everything around him. "I will be well enough to get out of here. I know how to get free."

"And these dragon relics?" Fes asked.

"They will remain. This place should not be disturbed."

Fes debated whether he should stay with the priest before merely shaking his head. There was no point in remaining. He had his gold. He had completed his task. And now it was time for him to return.

"What about you?" he asked.

"Now I will find the dragon heart."

"To raise a dragon."

The priest smiled. "After everything that you've seen lately, is that so hard for you to believe?"

Fes thought about the dragon plains and what he had seen. It *wasn't* hard for him to believe. If anything, he could almost imagine dragons returning, especially if there were others as powerful as Reina. Fes had never seen how powerful Azithan could be, but he suspected that he was more potent than that. Would *he* be able to raise the dragons again?

"I guess it's not." He looked at the rebellion, who had gathered, post-battle. Alison was there, and a part of him wanted the chance to reconnect with her, but the time for them had passed. He had seen that during their travels. She had moved on, joining the rebellion, and he had Azithan. Regardless of what Alison believed, Azithan had treated him well.

But maybe there was something he could still do for her.

He regarded the priest. "Do you have everything you need to raise the dragon again?"

"Ah, for that we don't. In time, we should be able to. Then a dragon will confront the dragon. And the reign of the empire's violence will end."

"What happens if a new violence takes its place?"

"The dragons deserve to be a part of this world, Fezarn. If you would stay with me, I could help you understand. You of all people deserve that opportunity."

It was tempting. A chance to better understand who he was and where he came from. But if he did, it meant working against the empire, and that wasn't something he was willing to do. Besides, he suspected Azithan had answers for him. That had to be the reason he'd sent Fes in the first place. And if he did, Fes might be better served returning to Anuhr than by staying with the priest.

"Good luck," Fes said.

"Luck?"

He nodded. "Finding the dragon heart. Good luck."

"For that, we don't need luck."

"You don't?"

The priest smiled. "I already know how to find it. As I said, you could accompany me. I will help you understand what it means to be Deshazl and you could—"

"I don't intend to join the rebellion. And there's still something that I need to do."

"What is that?"

"Keep a promise."

CHAPTER TWENTY-FIVE

F es crept along the rock, moving slowly as he trailed alongside the rebellion caravan. Every so often, the wind would shift, and he would catch sight of them, and when he did, he looked for signs of Alison, but he didn't see her again. She was there. He was certain of it. He had stayed close enough to the rebellion caravan to ensure that she was.

As he followed the rebellion, he began to overhear sounds that made him think that they passed the reminders of the mercenaries. He veered off, making his way through the haze, and came across the expected remnants.

Fes moved closely, keeping track of them, watching for signs of Carter. She would be there, he was sure of it, and while he wasn't concerned about chasing her, not anymore, he didn't want to deal with a confrontation any sooner than he needed to.

He waited until late at night, long after they had camped, and he used the fog to sneak into their camp. When he reached the first guard, he wrapped his arms around his throat, knocking him out rather than cutting him down. He didn't have much reason to be kind to him, but he had no interest in slaughtering these men.

With that guard down, he hurried forward and reached a tent that had two other men on either side of it. Fes lunged forward, slamming his fist into the side of one man's head and sweeping his leg around, knocking the other down to the ground and punching him in the chest, knocking the wind out of him before he could react.

He used his daggers to cut through the tent and then he stepped inside.

A part of him expected there to be guards inside, and after everything that they had been through, he worried that there would be another fire mage. A part of him feared that perhaps he hadn't removed the threat of Reina quite as effectively as he had believed, but he had seen her die, and there was no way she was coming back from the wounds she had sustained.

The tent wasn't empty. There were two men within it.

Fes hurried toward Theole, cutting free the bindings around his wrist. Theole looked up at him. "What are you doing here?"

"Fulfilling a promise," Fes said.

"Is she…"

Fes nodded. "She's with the caravan not far from here. I can bring you to her. She's safe."

The old man breathed out heavily. "After the attack, and after I was abducted, I thought that I wouldn't see her again. How were you able to save her?"

"I came across the place where they were holding her. When I found her, I ensured that she was safe."

"You didn't have to come after me."

"I'm not sure that Indra would've allowed me to do anything else," Fes said with a smile. He pulled out one of the figurines that she had carved, and Theole's eyes widened as he looked at it.

"You still have it."

"I still have it."

"Thank you," he said.

Fes turned to the other man bound to a post. He was broad and heavily muscled and dressed in a black jacket and pants. "What about you?"

The man nodded.

Fes sliced through his bindings, and he hesitated only a moment before darting out of the tent and disappearing into the night.

Fes guided Theole free, and they snuck off through the haze, leaving the mercenary camp behind. It didn't take long for them to see nothing more than the softly glowing lights of the mercenary caravan, and eventually, even those disappeared.

"You intend to leave them there?"

"I'm not going to cut through all of them."

"Even after everything that they did?"

"Most of them were hired for a job. The only one that is really responsible is gone."

"She wasn't the only one responsible."

Fes took a deep breath, glancing back toward the direction of the mercenary camp. Eventually, he knew that he would have to come to terms with Carter. She had warned him that he didn't want to make an enemy out of her, and now it was too late. He *had* made an enemy out of her. Azithan could offer a little protection once he returned to the city, but if he were to stay in Anuhr, he would have to deal with Carter eventually.

And there was what Reina had said. If she had been Carter's employer, then Fes had additional questions. Hopefully, Azithan had answers. What had she meant about not expecting to meet a challenger in these lands? It had almost sounded as if she hadn't been from Anuhr.

"She will be dealt with," Fes said.

Theole watched him for a moment. "You are everything that she thought. Indra has a way of seeing people."

"And what did she see of me?" Theole pointed toward Fes's pocket.

He reached into it and pulled out the totems. "These?"

"They suit you. Perhaps in time, you will come to understand."

"It would be easier if you were to simply tell me."

"If I were to simply tell you, you would miss out on the journey."

"I think I've journeyed enough. And now it's time for you to end your journey." He pointed toward the distant rebellion caravan. They hadn't needed to travel that far to reach it; it was much closer than Fes would have preferred, but the rebellion had the numbers, and there was no reason to fear the mercenaries now. "Will you return home?" Fes asked.

"We will. We're near enough to the mountains that it should not be difficult any longer."

"Travel safe," Fes said.

With that, Theole clasped him on the shoulder and looked into Fes's eyes. "You are more than you allow yourself to be. Eventually, you will see what Indra sees. Eventually, you may be that person."

"What person?"

Theole flashed a smile. "The person who might disrupt everything."

He nodded and turned toward the rebels and made his way toward them, cutting through the haze as if he had no difficulty seeing through it. Fes frowned, wondering how he could, but suspected that perhaps it had something to do with his totems.

When he reached the rebels, Fes heard a soft shout, but then, a few moments later, a cry of relief. He allowed himself a moment to smile.

The next day, the caravan continued to travel through the dragon plains. After a while, a few of them branched off, and Fes stayed with the smaller group. He wasn't surprised to see the priest and Alison among them. Fes stayed far enough away that he didn't think they were aware of him. He trailed, managing to keep them in sight, and near nighttime, he saw something strange along the ground.

It was different from the rock that he had become accustomed to seeing.

Fes hurried over to it.

A strange growth erupted from the ground. Had he not known how others described it, Fes wasn't sure that he would have called it a flower, but seeing it, noticing the black stalk that rose from the rock along with the deeply tinted petals that seemed all a different hue, with striations that matched what he often saw in dragon pearls and the bones, Fes recognized it as the flower marking the dragon heart. It had a bitter and surprisingly hot fragrance.

He looked up. The priest and Alison, along with the commander, were approaching, but they weren't quite to him, not yet.

If what they said was true, he had time.

He began digging, probing the rock with his daggers, pulling the rock away around the dragon heart. The rock came apart easily, almost as if it wanted him to dig through it, and he reached the dragon heart. When he pulled it apart, he saw the heart.

It was enormous. Shaped like a sphere—much like the dragon pearls that he had seen—the striations along it were of many different colors. There were blues and reds and oranges and greens, and shades of other colors. Each one faint and shimmering, but there was no doubting that they were there.

Fes ran his hands along the dragon heart, feeling the striations and the warmth that radiated from it. There would be power to this. There would be no question that this was what Reina had been after. There was no question that this was what the emperor would want.

Fes looked up as he heard the muted sounds of Alison and the priest. He had time. All he had to do was dig out the rest of the dragon heart, and he could disappear into the haze.

He smiled to himself and set to work.

The journey to Anuhr took a while, especially with a detour to find a specific artisan once he reached the city. By then, his pack was heavy, and he was exhausted from all the days on the road. He had managed to procure a horse in a village along the way and had made much better time after that, but he still worried Carter would reach the city before him.

He met with little resistance passing through the city and by the time he reached the palace, Fes was ready to be done with this entirely. If it worked out the way he hoped, he might not need to take another job like this.

He made his way through the back entrance to the palace, and into Azithan's rooms. Then he waited. He didn't have to wait long for Azithan to appear.

Fes lounged in one of the chairs, a leg draped over the edge of it, and smiled when Azithan entered.

"Fezarn. I will admit that I am a little surprised to see you."

"You didn't think that I'd return?"

Azithan made his way past him and smiled. "Not quite so soon."

"I finished the job."

Azithan frowned. "And what, exactly, was the job Horus wanted of you?"

He shook his head. "Did you know Reina would be there?"

Azithan sat forward. "Reina? She should not have. She was in the temple..."

The fire mage temple, the place where all the fire mages trained. "Why?"

"Rehabilitation."

"I don't think it worked." He told Azithan about Reina and shared with him how she'd been defeated, explaining it only as Talmund defeating her. "Is she from the empire?" That had plagued him in the last few days.

"There are many questions about Reina. We had hoped to understand but never had the chance. Perhaps we never will."

"She hired Carter."

Azithan nodded. "Then it's good that you went. Did you learn anything useful?"

"More than I expected."

Azithan studied him a long moment. "And what did you find?"

Heat radiated from him as Azithan used a spell. Fes made a show of shifting and reached for one of his daggers, fingering the hilt of it. He wiggled the dagger in its sheath, wanting to slice through any magic that Azithan might use on him.

"You made a promise."

"And it's one I intend to fulfill." Azithan watched him. A hint of a smile played across his face. "You found the heart, didn't you?" Azithan stood excitedly, and his hand moved slightly in place.

Fes was aware of a slight shifting of energy, almost as if the heat he sensed radiating from Azithan pressed toward him. It was similar to what he had felt with Reina but far subtler. Fes shifted the dagger in his hilt and stared at Azithan, unblinking.

"For the right price."

"Fezarn..."

"You know that's how this works. I take jobs for you, and you pay."

"Even for something like this?"

Fes pulled the dragon heart out of the bag he'd brought with him. "If you don't want to pay, then maybe I need to see if there's another interested in this." He slipped it back into the bag, concealing it.

"You really did get it, didn't you?"

Fes shrugged again.

"Interesting." Azithan turned away from Fes and made his way to the table at the back of the room. When he returned, he handed Fes a pouch. It was heavy, and he pulled it open to glance at the gold coins inside. It was a prize unlike any he had ever imagined. "I would have expected the priest to have put up more resistance to you taking it."

"They didn't know."

Azithan took the offered bag. He sat down near the hearth before pulling the dragon heart out and staring at it as he traced his fingers over it.

"Is it real?" Fes asked.

Azithan traced his fingers along the striations of the dragon heart. He kept his hand above it. "I cannot tell. A dragon heart is rare enough that I don't know how to test its authenticity. If it *is* real, it's something the empire has not seen in quite some time."

Fes watched Azithan, but he seemed to pay Fes no mind, more interested in staring at the dragon heart, continuing to trace his fingers along the surface. Fes looked at the dragon heart. Even from where he stood, the striations were visible. There was no flash of color, but why would there be in a replica?

Fes pocketed the pouch of coins and headed out of the palace.

Grab book 2 of The Dragonwalker: Dragon Blessed.

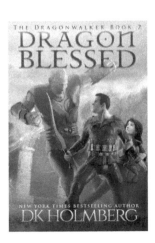

The magic of the ancient dragons cannot be ignored.

Learning he's descended from the ancient Deshazl, those once known as the Dragonwalkers, has changed nothing for Fes. He continues to serve Azithan and the empire, even after deceiving them. The ancient Deshazl magic lives within him, but Fes doesn't know how to control it or even if he should try.

An old nemesis approaches him with a job he can't refuse, and he's forced to head toward Toulen. When betrayal separates him from from a friend in need, Fes must begin to understand how to use his Deshazl magic. If he can't, not only will he lose his friend, but innocent people will suffer.

With a growing magic within him, Fes questions not only the nature of his power, he's forced to make a choice between these new connections and the empire.

ALSO BY D.K. HOLMBERG

The Dragonwalker

Dragon Bones

Dragon Blessed

Dragon Rise

Dragon Bond

Dragon Storm

Dragon Rider

The Teralin Sword

Soldier Son

Soldier Sword

Soldier Sworn

Soldier Saved

Soldier Scarred

The Lost Prophecy

The Threat of Madness

The Warrior Mage

Tower of the Gods

Twist of the Fibers

The Lost City

The Last Conclave

The Gift of Madness

The Great Betrayal

The Cloud Warrior Saga

Chased by Fire

Bound by Fire

Changed by Fire

Fortress of Fire

Forged in Fire

Serpent of Fire

Servant of Fire

Born of Fire

Broken of Fire

Light of Fire

Cycle of Fire

The Endless War

Journey of Fire and Night

Darkness Rising

Endless Night

Summoner's Bond

Seal of Light

The Book of Maladies

Wasting

Broken

Poisoned

Tormina

Comatose

Amnesia

Exsanguinated

The Shadow Accords

Shadow Blessed

Shadow Cursed

Shadow Born

Shadow Lost

Shadow Cross

Shadow Found

The Collector Chronicles

Shadow Hunted

Shadow Games

Shadow Trapped

The Dark Ability

The Dark Ability

The Heartstone Blade

The Tower of Venass

Blood of the Watcher

The Shadowsteel Forge

The Guild Secret

Rise of the Elder

The Sighted Assassin

The Binders Game

The Forgotten

Assassin's End